T0329252

DANGEROUS GAMES

"Before we shake hands and call it a night, gentlemen, you're going to want to see what's on this. Can I use your desktop, Ed?"

"Go ahead. What've you got, Danny?"

Danny described what Greg had found, then swiveled Ed's desktop monitor around so the men in the conference area could view it.

"So you think that's a schematic for an assassination attempt?" Hooper asked.

"It ain't a Disney movie," Ed said.

"That's my guess," Danny said, ignoring Ed's commentary. "An assassination attempt followed by what looks like a very bloody escape plan."

"It's not the most sophisticated setup," Hooper pointed out. "But if people are willing to sacrifice themselves to make it work, it'd be hard to stop."

"Except that now we know about it," Ed said. "Which means we know what to watch out for."

"One thing bothers me about that, Ed," Danny said. "It's so crude, so bold, that it almost seems like they must know something we don't. They have somebody on the inside, or there's some other element we haven't put together yet."

"Well, we may not know if it's a real plan or not, but we know that it's at the very least a potential threat," Ed said. "And here at the Montecito we take potential threats seriously."

"That's right," Danny agreed.

"Which means," Ed continued, with a meaningful glance at Danny, "that Danny here will work up a new plan to counter this new threat, and present it first thing in the morning. And one more thing. Time's getting short here. Whatever Danny comes up with will be the best plan he can put together in the time we have, utilizing the combined resources of our team and both of yours. But there's not going to be a lot of time for bickering and jockeying for position. We all have to put that nonsense behind us and just do the damn job."

Charles Hooper interlocked his fingers behind his head and stretched in his seat. "Why beat around the bush, Ed? Just tell us how you really feel."

LAS VEGAS™

SLEIGHT OF HAND

JEFF MARIOTTE
BASED ON THE HIT NBC SERIES CREATED BY
GARY SCOTT THOMPSON

POCKET **STAR** BOOKS
New York   London   Toronto   Sydney

An *Original* Publication of POCKET BOOKS

A Pocket Star Book published by
POCKET BOOKS, a division of Simon & Schuster, Inc.
1230 Avenue of the Americas, New York, NY 10020

ISBN-13: 978-1-4516-4434-0

This Pocket Star Books paperback edition May 2007

10 9 8 7 6 5 4 3 2 1

POCKET STAR BOOKS and colophon are registered trademarks of Simon & Schuster, Inc.

Cover photograph of lights by Greg Adams/Getty Images

Manufactured in the United States of America

For information regarding special discounts for bulk purchases, please contact Simon & Schuster Special Sales at 1-800-456-6798 or business@simonandschuster.com.

TO THE PEOPLE OF LAS VEGAS,
AND THE PEOPLE OF *LAS VEGAS*.

ACKNOWLEDGMENTS

Great thanks to the cast and crew of *Las Vegas* for the hard work behind one of TV's most entertaining shows, and to Gary Scott Thompson for putting it all together in the first place.

In Las Vegas, my Vegas-size appreciation goes out to Donald Kaye, Greg and Sharon, and Johnny Crow. In New York, to Jen, Howard, and Katie. Elsewhere, to the two Cindys, and Maryelizabeth, Holly, and David.

LAS VEGAS™

SLEIGHT OF HAND

I

"Have you seen any cute cowboys?" Delinda Deline asked. She and Mary Connell threaded their way through the packed aisles of the Montecito Hotel and Casino's gaming floor. Sounds of laughter and whoops of joy filled the air, people celebrating big wins on slots or rolls of the dice or spins of the roulette wheel. Mary knew that Delinda enjoyed being on the casino floor and felt at home there even though she rarely gambled. Delinda preferred the sure thing to the long shot, and somehow she had the power to make things materialize when she wanted them badly enough.

"Dozens," Mary said, smiling at a couple of particular memories. Another memory in the making pushed through the throng just ahead of them, a good-natured grin affixed to his handsome face. He wore snug-fitting jeans, with a green-and-white-striped snap-button shirt. A white hat and boots with two-inch heels added to his already considerable height. "Maybe hundreds. I like the Stampede," she added, turning to watch him pass. The jeans fit just as well from this angle. "We should do it more often."

"There can only be one centennial of Las Vegas's first cattle drive," Delinda pointed out. Her dangling earrings were shaped like horseshoes with ten-gallon hats hanging from them, sculpted from twenty-four-karat gold. Like most of the Montecito's staff and guests this weekend, Delinda was wearing a western-style shirt; hers was in a silky gold fabric with pearl snaps and contrasting indigo piping on the yoke and cuffs, and she wore it like the supermodel she could have been, had she chosen that path in life. As it was, with her flaxen hair and glowing skin, she looked like the goddess of gaming, if goddesses wore two-hundred-dollar jeans. "There might be another one in another hundred years, I guess, if you're willing to wait."

Mary shrugged. The National Rodeo Finals came to Las Vegas every year, so if Mary really ached for cowboys, she could find them there. But she wasn't on the prowl. Window shopping could be fun, but she had never found a boyfriend by looking for one. Somehow men always seemed to find her when she was least prepared for them. Why that happened she had never been able to figure out. Then again, she hadn't devoted a lot of effort to trying. *If it ain't broke . . .*

"There's just something about a cowboy," Delinda said, apparently unwilling to drop the subject.

"There is indeed," Mary agreed, watching another pair of tight jeans sidling toward the Sports Book. Then she glanced away and spotted a familiar face, shaded by a very unfamiliar hat. "Then again," she said, "some guys just don't pull off the look all that well."

Looking in the direction Mary indicated, Delinda laughed. "Oh my God," she said. "That is just something Danny should not do."

Danny McCoy, director of surveillance and security for the Montecito, worked his way through the crowd toward them. Tall and handsome in a dark blue Armani suit, he had a dusty black cowboy hat with a tall crown and a wide brim pulled low over his eyes, gunfighter-style. The effect of the hat paired with his contemporary power suit was simply comical. Danny had been Mary's best friend in childhood, then her first real boyfriend (Delinda's boyfriend too, for that matter, although not her first), and Mary knew that no matter where her life led, she would always love him.

But that didn't mean she couldn't burst out laughing when he looked ridiculous.

Danny tossed Mary and Delinda a bashful glance, reminding Mary of the two-year-old boy he had been when they'd met. He obviously had some idea of how goofy the big hat looked on him. Maybe if he had pulled an entire western outfit together, he could have carried off the hat—but not with that suit. "Hey, ladies," Danny said. "Place is rowdy today."

"Must be all the beer and beef we're selling," Delinda said. *"Tex."*

Danny touched the hat's brim. "That's funny," he said, not meaning it in the least. "I did a guy a favor, okay? He was losing big-time at blackjack. He swore it was his unlucky hat's fault, so he took it off and stuck it on my head. Next hand, the dealer busted. The guy told me to take the hat away and never let him have it again, no matter how much he begs."

"That thing looks like he's been wearing it for the entire hundred years since that first cattle drive,"

Delinda said. "You sure his head won't come apart without it?"

"I think as long as the cards fall his way, he doesn't care," Danny said.

"Did you check it for livestock, Danny?" Mary asked. "Lice, maybe? Fleas?"

Danny lowered his voice, cocked his head closer to Mary's. "Look, I don't like the hat either. But the guy is one of Sam's whales, and she was standing right there when he put it on me. She told me that if I took it off, she'd reach down inside me, grab me by the ribs, and turn me inside out."

"That sounds like Sam," Mary said. "Anything for a big spender, even disembowelment."

"Especially disembowelment," Delinda said. "For a girl who hates guns, she has a definite vicious streak."

"So I'm stuck with it," Danny continued. "Make all the cracks you like, the hat stays on. At least for tonight."

"It could have been worse, Danny," Delinda said. "What if he'd had unlucky spurs, too?"

"It's really fine, Danny," Mary said. "If anything, it makes you easier to spot in the crowd." She let a few moments pass for effect. "Unless the crowd is full of guys in cowboy hats, of course."

"Ha-ha," Danny said, without humor. "Sorry, ladies, but the hat stays."

"What the hell are you doing in that stupid hat?" Ed Deline's voice was a low, intimidating growl, and Danny spun around when he heard it, his eyes widening in surprise. As president of operations, Big Ed ran the Montecito, and everyone on the staff— even Delinda, his only daughter—treated him with respect. That respect was often tempered by the slightest trace of fear—especially among people who didn't know him well enough to realize that Ed only truly exploded at those who had earned his wrath. Mary knew he could be a pussycat when he wanted to be, but she'd seen him in tiger mode too, and facing the tiger side of Ed was never fun.

"Sam said . . ." Danny sputtered.

"I don't give a damn what Sam said, you're an executive of this hotel and casino and you look like a clown. If you want to go all out on the western duds for the duration of the Stampede, then go for it. But the half-assed look doesn't cut it. You look like you're making fun of our guests."

"It's really just—"

"Take the damn thing off," Ed growled. He turned to Mary and Delinda, gracing them with a charming smile. "You ladies, on the other hand, look delightful. Please excuse me and Hopalong Cassidy, here."

"He's all yours, Daddy," Delinda said.

"See you later, Danny," Mary said. "Don't take any wooden Indians."

Ed led Danny away, toward the stairs that led up to the executive offices. "Did Ed seem angry to you?" Mary asked, watching them go.

"Oh, no," Delinda replied. She knew her father better than almost anyone on Earth, and Mary often looked to her to explain his moods. "Maybe a little stressed out. There were some rodeo clowns on the floor earlier, and you know how he is about clowns."

Mary had heard about the clowns, playing craps in full makeup and tattered outfits, although she hadn't seen it for herself. She got the picture, though, and nodded. "Perfectly understandable, then." *I wouldn't want to be Danny right now,* she thought.

Danny took the hat off and deposited it, as he passed by, on the head of a white-haired woman playing two slots at once. He couldn't tell if she even noticed. If Sam saw him without the dusty old thing, she would be pissed, but that was an abstract concern. Ed was right here, right now, and already unhappy. "What's up, Ed?" he asked as Ed led him toward the front staircase.

"What's up is that you're on the floor talking to Mary and Delinda and wearing a stupid hat when you're supposed to be focused on coordinating security with the Secret Service and Klaus Aickmann's people. Aickmann arrives tomorrow, and he's going to be a much bigger security nightmare than all these good old boys put together."

"I know, Ed," Danny assured him. He had, in fact, been taking a short break from his almost nonstop effort to mesh the needs and requirements of the United States Secret Service and the German magnate's private security force, without compromising the Montecito's own systems and procedures. The long struggle and tenterhook diplomacy had resulted in an increasing ache beneath his temples, as if his head were being drilled into from both sides at once, and he had made a circuit of the casino floor in an attempt to shake it. That was when he ran into Sam and her unlucky whale, then Mary and Delinda. And finally Ed, who assumed he wasn't working because—well, because at that precise moment, he was not, in fact, working. "I'm on it," Danny continued. "It's tough, though, getting them to even talk to each other, much less agree on anything."

"And that's why you get the big bucks, right?"

They had almost reached the staircase that would take them up to the second-floor overlook, where they could talk without being disturbed by the racket from the casino floor. Before they made it to safety, however, Dieter Klasse, the Aickmann team's second in command, broke from the crowd and walked toward them. Klasse's back was ramrod straight, his arms and legs scissoring precisely as he approached, looking like a man with something on his mind. He kept his white hair chopped very short, with pink scalp showing through, his face clean-shaven, his suit pants pressed to knife-edge creases. "He wants something," Danny muttered. "I swear the man thinks I'm his personal wish fairy."

Ed gave Danny a sidelong look, head cocked, as if trying to read the younger man's mind. "Wish fairy," he muttered, shaking his head sadly.

Dieter Klasse joined them at the foot of the stairs a moment later, coming to an abrupt military stop. "Mr. Deline, Mr. McCoy," he said. His words carried the warm, conversational tone of a whip crack.

"Something we can do for you, Mr. Klasse?" Ed asked. He sounded remarkably composed, Danny thought, considering he had assigned Danny to deal with this situation because he wanted to keep his own involvement to the barest minimum. Before being promoted to president of operations, Ed had run surveillance and security; his CIA background and years of experience meant that no one in the hospitality business had been better at the job. Danny had almost dreaded taking over the gig precisely because he didn't want to follow Ed's act. Ed had left awfully big footprints to fill, and part of filling them was keeping problems like this away from Ed when he didn't want to be bothered.

The whole situation would have been easier if this had been a "normal" week at the Montecito, but Danny had worked there long enough to know that normal didn't exist. With the Stampede in full swing, the place was crowded with cowboys, cowgirls, and western wannabes, all intent on enjoying a rowdy good time, Vegas-style. The huge exhibit hall in the resort's convention center was jammed with western and ranch merchandise, from the smallest gift items to giant tractors and stock trucks. Some of the Montecito's sprawling grounds had been turned into a makeshift rodeo arena where exhibition bull riding, barrel racing, and other events took place from noon to midnight. Livestock had been fenced into a section of the vast parking lot, filling the air outside with sounds and aromas that had not been experienced in Las Vegas for the last century. Animals had even been put on display inside the hall, creating a feast for the senses that even the Montecito's state-of-the-art ventilation system had to work overtime to control. All in all, it was another atypical week in a place where nothing ever stayed the same.

"I'll handle this, Ed," Danny said. "Why don't you go on up and I'll meet you in your office."

Ed didn't budge, as if, having been buttonholed by Klasse, he was determined to see it through.

"We have a request," Klasse said. His thick German accent made his *w*s sound like *v*s and his *v*s sound like *f*s. "We would like feeds from all the Montecito's cameras routed to our control van."

Danny saw Ed's mouth start to move, and he quickly held up a hand to stall whatever rude comment Ed might make. "You understand, Mr. Klasse, that we have five thousand and three cameras on the premises." He had already gone through the Montecito's statistics with the people in charge of both groups, including Heinrich Hartung, Klasse's boss, who headed up Aickmann's private security team, and Charles Hooper of the Secret Service.

"Yes, I am aware of that," Klasse said.

"You can't possibly have enough monitors in that van to keep track of five thousand cameras," Danny said. The van was similar to those that local TV stations sent out for remote broadcasts. They'd need a moving truck to hold that many monitors and the associated equipment to run them and to record the feeds.

"This is our problem, no?"

Danny started to respond, but Ed cut him off, his impatience bubbling to the surface. "No, this is *our* problem," Ed said. "We want very much for Mr. Aickmann to have a good trip to Las Vegas, to make his speech and to enjoy his stay. But we will not sacrifice the integrity of our surveillance system, and that means nobody—nobody, am I making this clear?—gets full access to our internal security systems. Not you, not the Treasury Department, not the president of the United States, and not Klaus Aickmann."

Danny's head swiveled between the two men. "Ed, I've got this. Mr. Klasse . . . what Ed said. I'm afraid we can't do that."

"Afraid?" Ed repeated, shooting Danny an anguished frown. "He's not afraid. It's an absurd request!"

"I can only relay what Herr Aickmann asks for," Klasse said.

"Let Herr Aickmann know that we absolutely intend to guarantee his security," Danny said before Ed could speak again. "But that we have to dictate the terms of that security. We're happy to take input, but we don't take orders." He glanced at Ed, who gave him a nearly imperceptible nod. "Are we understood?"

Klasse clamped his lips together in a thin, unhappy line and held that pose for a moment before speaking, as if to demonstrate his dissatisfaction with Danny's response. "Yes, Mr. McCoy. I understand."

Swiveling on his glossy wingtips, Dieter Klasse departed as stiffly as he had arrived. For a fraction of a second, Danny thought Ed had a smile on his face, but it faded so fast he couldn't be sure it had ever been there. "Danny?"

"Yes, Ed?"

"Just . . . deal with this, okay? Make it so I don't have to think about it."

"If that's how you want to handle it," Danny said.

"That's how I want to handle it." Ed started up the stairs without another look back. The stained-glass wall behind him cast a multicolored glow on his ascending form.

Danny knew that his boss meant what he said. Aickmann's trip would be the biggest security and logistical nightmare Danny had encountered thus far at the Montecito. If he screwed it up . . . well, he could *not* afford to screw up. Multibillionaire Klaus Aickmann had connections at the very top of Germany's government. He served as an advisor and confidant to politicians throughout Europe, and in the United States. His speech, scheduled for the next evening, would be broadcast live on cable news stations and was meant to relay to the world Germany's international intentions for the next several years. Aickmann couldn't officially speak for the German government, but everyone knew that he would air their views unofficially, and because he was a private citizen, he could be more direct than government officials allowed themselves to be. Any problems that arose during his visit would reflect badly not just on the Montecito, but also on the city of Las Vegas and even on Washington. To call it an international incident would border on the cliché, but that's what it would be.

Which meant it had to run as smoothly as any other event at the Montecito, in spite of the increased complexity and the potential for catastrophe. And Danny was prepared to do whatever it took to ensure just that.

2

When her cell phone chimed, Sam was in the middle of a difficult negotiation. Not an unpleasant one—she stood in a semicircle with four tall, handsome cowboys, trying to convince them to teach a client of hers the art of bull riding. The sticking point was her client, Burl Bradenton. Forty-two, Burl was an advertising executive whose primary exercise came from racquetball and tennis. He came across as reasonably fit, but hardly an athlete. Although Burl was happy to waive any claims that might arise from injuries he received during the lessons, the cowboys weren't certain they wanted to accept responsibility for him. She couldn't really blame them, but when one of her whales wanted something, Sam went out of her way to make it happen.

"Excuse me one second," she said, glancing at the phone.

The name BYRON showed in the window.

She let out a small sigh.

During her career as a casino host, catering to the high rollers who thought of Las Vegas as their own personal playground, Samantha Jane Marquez had dealt with every kind of whale imaginable (except for the aquatic variety). Her client list had included inveterate gamblers, those who came for the shows or the gourmet meals or the easy availability of beautiful women and had to be tempted to the tables, profligate spenders, and others whose every dollar had to be pried from their wallets with a crowbar.

She had started out downtown, on Fremont Street, where the casinos were older and considerably less luxurious, the definition of "whale" less restrictive, and the competition as likely to come at her with a knife as with a cutting remark. By honing her skills, learning how to anticipate a client's needs, and building the network of contacts required to satisfy those needs, she had worked her way up to the Strip's more glamorous resorts. Once she had "arrived," professionally speaking, she had shifted from a freelance gig to the Montecito's most important on-staff casino host. She knew that her position was crucial to the casino's success—that she, as much as any ad campaign or promotional effort, drew in the millionaires and billionaires who could afford the major play. Sam understood that through sheer volume, the tourists, the mom-and-pop visitors, even those who never gambled but spent money at shops and restaurants, had become as vital to the company's bottom line as the high rollers. But those people would never come in if not for the big players, the celebrities and the wealthy whose spending levels, suites, and perks the rest aspired to.

So she suffered all her clients with a smile, no matter how pushy, rude, obnoxious, or upsetting they were—and to be fair, plenty were just the opposite, gracious and genuinely appreciative of her efforts. Nice or nasty, their gambling provided her with a very good living. Sam loved her job.

There was, however, one type of whale that bothered her above all others. Byron Hammer—a prime example of this type—had spent the last few days climbing all over her last nerve, walking it like a tightrope, and she feared it would snap if she couldn't get him under control.

He was what she called (privately of course) an ADD whale. She had met loads of people with short attention spans, but Byron Hammer made most of them look like paragons of patience. She had seen him get bored by the spinning wheels of a dollar slot machine between the moment he punched the button and the time the wheels stopped spinning. The clanging of a jackpot could usually refresh his interest, but never for very long.

Ordinarily, Sam wouldn't care how brief someone's attention span was, but when that someone was one of her clients—and he looked to her for constant stimulation—it got really tiresome, really quickly. Not because Sam ever ran out of ways to entertain her whales, but because when one of them couldn't seem to think for himself and had her private cell phone number, it tied up her line and her time, making her less available to her other clients. Any casino host who only took care of just one whale at a time was a casino host who would soon be looking for a new steady job.

Like maybe something in shoe retail.

"Look, I'm sorry about this," she told the cowboys. "I have to take this call, and it might be a while. You think about what I said and I'll get back to you, okay?" She flipped the phone open as the men shuffled off. "Hi, Byron," she said, the epitome of cheerfulness. "How's the poker going?"

"Boring," Byron Hammer said. "I guess I'm up twenty or thirty."

Thousand, Sam knew. Not the direction the casino preferred, but it could be a lot worse. She didn't mind when her whales won—her bonus was based on how much they played, not whether they won or lost, and as a rule winners came back to town more often than losers. And they tipped better. "Are you ready for something new?"

"You bet, Sam."

"How about baccarat? High stakes, steady action, classy environment."

"That's a little slow-paced, isn't it?"

"Only to spectators," Sam assured him. "Not when it's your money on the line, believe me."

Byron hesitated. She could hear his breathing, his slow inhalations and exhalations. *Thinking,* she knew. He did a lot of that.

It nearly always meant trouble.

"I think I'm tired of gambling for now," he said. Words a casino host did not want to hear, especially from someone like Byron Hammer.

"What do you think you'd like to do, Byron?" she asked. "It's a little early for a show."

"Let's see . . ." Another long pause. *More of that damn thinking.* "Maybe a massage. And a manicure."

"Done and done."

"And what about an hour by the pool?"

"Regular pool or topless?"

"Regular is fine, thanks," he replied. "Let my wife

and daughter know they can join me if they'd like."

"I'll do that." She had already started walking toward the poker room, ready to escort him to wherever he decided he would rather be. Leaving him to his own devices wouldn't do, since he would most likely get distracted by something else altogether and end up who knows where. She had little enough control over Byron as it was, and she didn't want to risk that by losing track of him. On the way over, she phoned Marcella, Byron's wife, and told her about Byron's pool plans.

"That sounds fine, Sam," Marcella said. Sam found her as eminently reasonable as Byron was wearying. She didn't know how Marcella put up not only with Byron but with Kaylie, their six-year-old daughter, whose attention span mimicked her father's. "We'll join him at the pool in about an hour, then, after his manicure and massage."

"I'll meet you at the pool entrance," Sam offered, "and take you to his cabana."

"Wonderful," Marcella said. "We'll see you then."

Sam ended the call, made another quick one to Polly at the spa to schedule Byron's M&M, then, folding the phone, she made a sharp turn past a dollar slot bank, toward the poker room. Halfway through the turn, she collided with Mike Cannon.

The impact with the considerably taller Mike nearly bowled petite Sam off her feet, but she held her ground. Mike, a handsome black man with a lean physique and a smooth head, caught her hands just in case. "It's funny," he said, with a friendly smile. "There are literally more than five miles of walking space within the Montecito's walls, and yet you ran smack into me."

"Me? I ran into you? I don't think so."

"Oh yes," Mike insisted. "Physics indicates that given your trajectory and approximate rate of speed—"

"Save it, Einstein." Mike had a master's degree in engineering from MIT and took every opportunity to put his knowledge to use, or to show it off. *Even*, Sam thought, *when it's boring*. "I'm in a hurry."

Mike waved around himself, indicating a clear path. "Never let it be said that the Cannon slowed the tide of commerce."

"And watch where you're going next time," Sam said. "And stop calling yourself the Cannon. It's weird." She gave him a three-fingered wave and followed the course he indicated, hoping Byron hadn't already decided to wander away from the poker table.

Mike watched Sam disappear into the crowd. Her shapely behind made for a pleasant diversion, but his real problems wouldn't be pushed aside for more than a couple of minutes. Since being promoted out of his position as head valet, Mike worked for Danny McCoy in surveillance and security. He had enjoyed the valet gig—the tips were great and Mike enjoyed meeting people, being outside, and driving brilliantly engineered machines. But his skills served him better upstairs than on the pavement, and Danny put his technical expertise to the test on an almost daily basis. This week, though, Mike had found especially challenging. The Montecito's security technology, ranging from cameras to infrared and X-ray imaging, to facial recognition, EVI and video IQ software, laser-induced breakdown spectroscopy, and much more, had been designed to keep tabs on people inside the building, and on people and vehicles in the parking lots and garage areas.

Cows and horses had definitely *not* been part of the original plan.

But cows and horses were what he had to contend with this week. Prize animals, with an aggregate value of millions of dollars, had been brought to the Montecito for display and auction during the Stampede. Danny and Ed had impressed upon Mike that their security was every bit as important as that of the paying guests. Their odd sizes and shapes, however, played havoc with the resort's automated systems.

Before running into Sam, Mike had been on his way to the exhibit hall to reconfigure some of the on-site hardware, in hopes that it would be more responsive to the unusual conditions it had to deal with. He was sure the system could cope, given a few precise tweaks.

The tricky part was figuring out just what to tweak, and where, and how much. He didn't want to spend a lot of time messing with the wrong equipment, or fiddling with hardware when what he really needed were software fixes.

The safety of millions of dollars on the hoof had been put in Mike's hands, and he didn't plan on leaving the livestock in limbo.

After watching Ed drag Danny away—not quite by the ear, except maybe in spirit—Mary and Delinda spent a few more minutes scoping out the denim-clad crowd. Finally, Mary glanced at a passerby's watch, clocks being a rarity inside casinos. "Lordy, Delinda, time's a-wastin'," she said in an exaggerated corn-pone accent. "I gots to git to the chuck wagon!"

"That's right, I forgot about that," Delinda replied. She refused to play the accent game. "I guess I still don't understand what's the big deal about cooking up a few pots of beans."

"It's more than just beans," Mary said. "Ezra, the chuck wagon chef, is preparing full meals. Steaks, burgers, beans, biscuits, cowboy coffee, and various other side dishes." She smiled and shook her head briskly, sending her long red hair flying in every direction. She wore a tight red satin western shirt, un-snapped just far enough in the front to display impressive cleavage, and faded jeans that could have been painted on over boots of wine-colored leather. "But yeah, there will be a lot of beans."

Delinda suppressed a shudder. Not that she didn't like barbecue as much as the next girl, but still. What was the point of living in the twenty-first century if you ate like it was the nineteenth? "Well, you just make sure the people who are going to be eating all those beans stay outside. I've got to make sure the inside people have *real* food to eat." Delinda was responsible for running the Mon-tecito's food and beverage services, which meant overseeing all its bars and restaurants. She refused to include chuck wagons in that job description, leaving Mary, as hotel manager, to take charge of that one.

Mary shot her a grin. "Delinda Deline, keeping the world safe for haute cuisine."

"You know what they say. It's a dirty job—well, not as dirty as cooking outside in pits dug in the ground. Are they really cooking in pits?"

Mary hesitated, which Delinda took as confirmation. "Among other places . . ."

"Like where?" Delinda asked. She shook her head. "Never mind, don't tell me. I don't want to know."

3

Ed Deline liked his new office. Some executives would have *loved* it, but Ed wasn't a guy who used such superlatives to describe his feelings about a place to work. He had, over the years, worked out of shabby hotel rooms and the backs of vans, shadowed alleys in European capitals, teahouses in Asian mountain villages, and thatch huts in Latin American jungles. Once, he had spent two weeks sleeping outdoors, with no tent or fire, in an Eastern European forest, watching an ancient castle that was rumored to be the site of a transaction involving Soviet-era processed weapons-grade plutonium. He'd had to fend off wolves, bats, bugs, and birds, and in the end had determined that the only people visiting the place were local villagers who used it for extramarital trysts. On another occasion, he had spent four days and nights inside a tiny Fiat, high in the Swiss Alps, wondering where the manufacturer expected to find a customer base of people with fourteen-inch legs and truncated torsos.

His current office was, in comparison, comfortable and functional, which Ed liked. The predominant material was wood, polished to a glowing sheen, but between the office and the entry where his receptionist sat stood a thick, textured glass wall that allowed light from his windows to flood her work area. Huge windows afforded a Strip view, while flat-screen monitors allowed him to keep track of the action inside the casino. A plush conference area occupied one end of the big room. Behind his desk Ed had left the carved ivory tusks that had belonged to Monica Mancuso, the office's previous occupant, who had briefly owned the Montecito until a stiff wind blew her off the roof.

It beat the hell out of some of the other places he had worked, but he couldn't get emotional about it, because it was still just a place. Walls, a floor, a ceiling, panes of glass, and furniture—comfortable furniture, but still. Who could get worked up about furniture? His real job involved people—the good ones on his staff, the bad ones who tried to take advantage of the system, and all the people who spent their hard-earned dollars at the Montecito and who were Ed's responsibility. Ed's focus had to be, of necessity, splintered in several directions. He managed what were called in the trade the "back of house" activities, which included all the behind-the-scenes workings the customers never saw, and made sure that they ran smoothly. Then there was the front line, those aspects the customers did see, from the reception counter to the guest room attendants to the meals they ate to their interactions with dealers and casino personnel. Ed's primary concern was the front line, but keeping a handle on the back of house was what kept the front line humming.

He liked to avoid trouble by anticipating what might go wrong and making sure it didn't. He had taught Danny McCoy the same strategy, and Danny, thanks to his marines training and his natural sense of responsibility, had caught on immediately. Now they worked almost in sync, as if they'd been allies for decades, not just a couple of years. Every now and then Danny still surprised him with a stupid decision or a move that hadn't been thought through all the way, but not nearly as often as he had done even a short time before.

At the moment, Danny sat in a visitor's chair across from Ed's desk. The stupid cowboy hat a thing of the past, Danny now looked crisp and professional in his navy suit, white shirt, and red-and-black-striped tie. His hair was dark brown, neatly cut, and framed a face handsome enough to get him into all sorts of trouble. For a time Danny had been on Ed's bad side because Ed had caught him in bed with Delinda, but that relationship hadn't lasted long, and Ed figured both Danny and Delinda were old enough to form their own attachments. Ed had been more bothered by the fact that he hadn't known Delinda was in town—and that Danny clearly had known and hadn't bothered to tell him. He had moved on, forgiving the younger man, and all in all he was glad he hadn't given in to his initial impulse and hurled Danny out the hotel room window. "What's the situation?" Ed asked him. "Are Aickmann's people going to be reasonable?"

"I don't know if I'd say reasonable, Ed. That might be a little too much to ask of either party."

"The Treasury Department has always been that way," Ed said, speaking from bitter past experience. "Bunch of stiffs in cheap suits. They should really spend more time chasing tax cheats and let another agency handle Secret Service matters."

"Like maybe the CIA?"

Danny's grin was mocking, but with good humor. "They could make a worse choice," Ed said.

"I'm sure."

"Are you going to get to the point sometime today?" Ed asked. "Where do we stand?"

Danny straightened in his chair, all business now. "Where we stand is that Aickmann's people have dropped their demand for full access to the camera feeds."

"Because it was a stupid demand and we'd never let 'em have it."

"That's right," Danny said. "But they do want to see all guest registration records. The Secret Service heard about that and decided they want to run complete background checks on all guest registrations. They want us to contact all the guests with reservations and ask them for their Social Security numbers."

Ed resisted the impulse to call Charles Hooper, head of the Secret Service contingent, and laugh in his face. "That's not gonna happen."

"That's what I told them. So then they said they wanted to have access to all our facial recognition records, for everyone who walks in the door from twenty-four hours before Aickmann shows up until he leaves."

"And you told them . . . ?"

"Not gonna happen."

"That's my boy." Ed rubbed his goatee, satisfied so far with Danny's performance. "What else?"

"Aickmann's group heard about that and wanted the same, plus the ability to listen in on our radio traffic."

Ed laughed. "Have these people ever been involved in a real security operation? I know they do things differently in Germany, but this is freakin' nuts."

"I know, believe me. I've been tearing my hair out with these people, trying to get them to listen to reason. They keep wanting to one-up the other group, and none of them seem to care that we're trying to run a casino here."

"Aickmann will care," Ed said. "That's why he wanted to give the speech in Las Vegas, after all. He likes the action. Anyway, it's not like we're the United Nations."

"We're better," Danny said with a laugh. "Most countries secretly hate the UN, but everyone loves Vegas."

Ed fiddled with the remote on his desk, flipping through the signals from different surveillance cameras on the flat-screen plasma monitors built into his wall. He paused when he found an image of Dieter Klasse, sitting in the Opus lounge with a couple of members of the German security team. They had a plan of the hotel spread out on a table in front of them, and Dieter was pointing out different spots on it. "There are the Germans," Ed said, continuing to flip to new images. He paused again on their mobile control van outside. "And the rest of them are in there, it seems."

"That's where I left them," Danny explained. "Heinrich Hartung, the head of Aickmann's team, is

in the van with them. I told him what we could supply and showed his people how to get it set up."

"Good." Ed kept changing the screens, feeling like
a kid who can't decide what TV show to watch. He
stopped again on a picture of a tall, lean man in a
brown suit, standing at the edge of the Sports Book.
The man had dark hair, almost black, cut military-
short, and pale eyes that never stopped roving. A
white wire coiled from under his jacket into his ear.
"There's a dead giveaway," Ed said. "That's no iPod."

"That's Charles Hooper," Danny said, studying the
monitor.

"He's the joker running the Secret Service team,
right?"

"That's right."

"I met him at a party in D.C. once," Ed said, not
giving away the fact that he had known Hooper years
before that. "He has a lot of years under his belt, but
he's kind of a dork."

"That's him," Danny agreed. "He's okay, I guess—
seems like he knows his stuff, and he can lie back
when he needs to. But he expects everyone to jump
when he says so. Even if they don't work for him."

"I can jump," Ed said. "But the orders have to
come from a lot higher up than Hooper. Is he getting
along with Hartung and his people?"

"Except when they try to outdo each other,"
Danny said.

As they watched, Hooper's gaze flickered toward
the eye in the sky, the camera broadcasting his image
into Ed's office. "Think he knows we're on him?"
Danny asked.

"It gets to be a sixth sense in the business," Ed said. "You know when someone's watching you, even if they're doing it from a mile away."

Another man strode briskly into the picture, a heavyset man with a round, bald head, like a white-washed cannonball with eyes. He tugged at his suit as he walked, as if he could make it fit better by pulling it around his girth. "There's Hartung," Danny said. "He doesn't look happy."

"Is he ever?" Heinrich Hartung ran the private security company—owned by billionaire Klaus Aick-mann—that provided Aickmann's personal protection services. Ed had run across him a few times too, at various flashpoints around the world. Hartung was in his sixties at least, maybe older—if not old enough to be an ex-Nazi, Ed had often thought, old enough to have learned his ideas about discipline from them. He had put in time for at least a half dozen different intelligence agencies over the years, but he always seemed able to walk away from them—uncommon in a world where old spies were rarely allowed to retire peacefully.

But I did, Ed thought. *I guess it all comes down to which skeletons you know about, and in whose closets.*

On-screen, Hartung leaned into Hooper and spoke rapidly, jabbing a meaty finger at Hooper's chest. Charles Hooper looked as if he was trying to keep his cool, but the more that finger wagged at him, the more the blood rushed to his narrow face, turning it red, then a kind of eggplant color.

"I wish we could hear them," Danny said.

Ed felt the same way. "They want to hear our

transmissions, we ought to bug them just out of general principle."

They watched a few moments longer. Hooper's right hand balled into a fist, and the camera picked up a vein on his temple that throbbed like a pulsating blue worm. "Maybe we should have someone go in and break this up," Ed said. "I don't think Aickmann will be thrilled if his head guy gets his clock cleaned in our casino."

"Hang on," Danny said as a third figure entered the frame. This one was taller than either Hartung or Hooper, with an athletic build and a tanned face that would have looked at home hanging ten off the California coast. His hair, bleached by the sun, was short but shaggier than Hooper's, and in his blue eyes burned a determination that Ed could see from here. He planted himself between Hartung and Hooper, and Ed could tell from his body language that he was defusing the conflict before it escalated.

"That's Garrick Flynn," Danny explained. "He was a ranger in Iraq. I'm surprised he works for Hartung instead of the Secret Service. He's pretty cool. I really wish he was in charge of the whole op. Be a lot more spit and polish and a lot less FUBAR."

"It's not FUBAR yet, Danny. Your job is to make sure it doesn't get there."

"I'll do my best."

"You know what your best is, Danny?"

Danny considered for only a second. "Not good enough unless it gets the job done?"

"That's exactly right." *I trained the kid well*, Ed thought, settling back into his comfortable desk chair.

4

Sweat ran down Will Streeter's sides like the flow of Fish Creek when the snows were melting in the Tetons. Best case, he was half a day late—setup had begun the afternoon before, and he had no doubt that some of the vendors, those with more elaborate booths, finished before the sun had gone down. Others, with fewer goods and less complex displays, could well have set up before the noon opening of the exhibit hall.

But Will hauled his goods in an ancient horse trailer, left over from his rodeo days. On Interstate 15, with desert off to his right and the peaks of the Pahvant Range cutting sky on the left, a wheel had come off the trailer. Will had managed to brake his old pickup carefully, but the rear left corner of the trailer had skidded across the pavement, kicking up a geyser of sparks, until he muscled the vehicle off the highway and onto the shoulder.

When he got out of the truck and looked inside the trailer, he saw that much of his merchandise, so carefully stowed, had shifted when the wheel went haywire. He'd have to repack and secure some of it. But first he'd have to unload enough to lighten the truck, so he could jack it up and replace the wheel.

By the time he got back on the road, aching and

sweat-soaked, night had fallen. Instead of pushing on to Las Vegas as he had intended, he stopped at a motel in Beaver. As he ate dinner of tough, stringy steak in a nearby café, he did some real soul-searching to determine whether or not he wanted to continue. At first, the Stampede convention at the Montecito had seemed like a great idea—he tried to make all the Western-themed events he could, partly because he enjoyed the company, and partly because selling in person generally proved more lucrative than the online auction houses where he did most of his business. Those online auctions had been slow lately, and he hoped that was because the serious collectors had been saving up for the Montecito show.

The way his luck had been going lately, he wondered if the wheel incident had been a sign that he should just stay home in Wyoming and lay off the travel for a while. One of the reasons he had turned his back (what was left of it, anyway) on rodeo in his late twenties was that the constant travel proved so damaging to any attempts to form lasting relationships with women. In the half dozen years since, however, his success at finding someone for the long term hadn't changed significantly. Carlotta, his most recent girlfriend, had announced a week ago not only that she did not want to see him anymore, but that during his absences over the past several months, she had taken up with another man, who she intended to marry before the year was out.

That, in the end, was what had convinced him to go ahead and head for Vegas—that, and the fact that at this late date he couldn't get his booth rental deposit back. Sticking around Wind River would only remind him of Carlotta. He would have to pass by restaurants they had dined in, shops they'd visited together, places they had walked. He didn't want to stay home listening to George Jones and Hank Junior, avoiding his favorite honky-tonk, but that was what he expected he would do if he didn't get out of Dodge. And there was the chance that he would run into her and her new friend, which he wasn't ready for.

In the morning, his mind made up, he hit the road again, driving through St. George and into Nevada. By the time he reached the Montecito and found the loading docks, load-in had officially ended. Will had to ask permission to load in late, and instead of using a big flatbed cart, he had to haul all his cabinets and merchandise on a two-wheel dolly, carting it through aisles already clogged with customers. The full heat of day had come on, and every time he wheeled the dolly back out to his horse trailer from the air-conditioned exhibit hall, he thought he was stepping into a giant oven. Perspiration pooled under the brim of his cowboy hat, spilling down his cheeks and stinging his eyes. His long-sleeved cotton shirt glued itself to his ribs. With all the walking back and forth, he was glad he was still wearing his Justin work boots and not the Lucchese vintage-style cowboy boots he planned to wear during the show.

Once Will had his goods moved into the booth space, he began organizing it all, shoving his display cabinets and racks into place and then filling them with cowboy memorabilia, most of which he had amassed during his years on the rodeo circuit. One of the occupants of the space next to his, a corner booth, leaned over a table and showed him a friendly smile. "We thought you was never gonna show up," the man said. He sported a bushy gray beard and was dressed in 1880s formal wear: white tab-collar shirt, long black coat, a ribbon tie, black pants, and boots. He looked like a traveling preacher or an undertaker, but the size of his grin would have seemed inappropriate on the latter. "Figured maybe we'd have to spread into your space just so's it didn't look like a ghost town around here."

"I had some trouble on the road," Will explained. He didn't want to go into detail, particularly not while still trying to get set up as potential customers passed by. "I made it, but not quite as early as I'd have liked." He glanced into the adjoining booth, where the man's female partner had dressed in late-nineteenth-century bordello finery. They sold cowboy music CDs—Will recognized the names of Dave Stamey, R. W. Hampton, Kip Calahan, Michael Martin Murphey, and many others, western fiction by such luminaries as Elmer Kelton, Will Henry, Louis L'Amour, Peter Brandvold, and more, and themed magazines like *True West*, *Wild West*, and *Cowboys & Indians*. Music by Gene Autry trickled from speakers set beneath one of their display tables. It looked like a booth where he could easily spend as much as he made over the two days of the show. "Guess I'll have some good tunes to listen to over the weekend," Will added. "Or what's left of it, anyway."

"We'll try to make sure you do," the man said.

"My name's Bob." He extended a hand, which Will grasped. "That's Shirlene."

Will introduced himself and shook Bob's hand, then waved to Shirlene, who was bent over a table helping a customer select a CD. Then again, the customer might simply have been enjoying the view of her décolletage.

Will exchanged similar neighborly pleasantries with the woman on the other side of the booth, who sold Indian-themed wood sculptures that looked as if they had been carved en masse by barely trained summer campers. Then he returned to the business at hand. In a glass-fronted case, he arranged items of particular value or fragility—his favorite old pinup calendar, a pair of beaded gloves worn by a participant in Buffalo Bill's Wild West Show, an old Paiute pot he had acquired from a Colorado trading post just before it went out of business, a quartet of autographed Roy Rogers Dell comic books, and other treasures. A selection of old lariats dangled from a wooden T-bar post. He draped a pair of red wooly chaps over a roping dummy. Worn, dusty hats went across the top of the glass-fronted cabinet, and heel-worn boots at its foot. Indian baskets held collections of spurs, brands, badges, buttons, and conchos. From a short wooden ladder, he hung saddle blankets he'd had signed by some of the great riders he had ridden with in his rodeo days.

When he felt the booth was sufficiently ready, he moved his chair out of the entryway and took a receipt book from his cash box, the equivalent, in this place, of hanging out the "open" sign. He'd had to turn away a couple of people who wanted to browse while he was setting up, and he hoped they would return, and plenty of others like them. The crowd seemed to buzz with energy, which he took as a good sign. Bob and Shirlene had moved CDs and books with regularity during Will's setup, and even the woman with the bad sculptures had found some takers.

Maybe, Will thought, *coming to Las Vegas will bring some good luck my way for a change. I sure could use a spell of it.*

"I'll be cornswaggled if'n I let anyone get away with this kind of . . . of hogwash!"

Mary Connell backed away from Ezra, the chuck wagon cook—"chef," she had decided, being too high-falutin' a word to describe him—so that she didn't inhale enough of his breath to get herself drunk. She figured him cooking around an open flame was a dangerous idea, although maybe if he literally exploded, it would provide scientific evidence of spontaneous human combustion. Mike Cannon had been complaining the evening before about that particular lack.

"What seems to be the problem, Ezra?" she asked, leading him away from the fire pits and toward the relative safety of the rear of the chuck wagon.

"What ain't a problem?" he replied. He spoke as if his mouth were full of rocks, some of which were bigger than his head. "It's like you folks ain't served a real meal in this city since I don't know when. The beans ain't had nearly long enough to soak. I got wood-burnin' ovens and fire pits that ought to be fueled with mesquite wood, but instead your people brung me bags of briquettes like this is some dadgum backyard barbecue. And them steaks—well, I ain't seen the beeves they come off of, but I ain't all that sure about 'em, let's leave it at that. 'Sides all that, I asked for ground beef to make burgers with, and I got *lean* ground beef. You can't make burgers with lean! They need the fat to stay juicy and tasty! This supposed to be a meal or a diet plate fer ladies who lunch?"

Not quite old enough to have been present at the original Las Vegas cattle drive, Ezra nonetheless cut a convincing picture of an old-time chuck wagon cook. Short and grizzled, he gnawed on the ends of his white mustache as he complained. While he worked, grease or some other unknown substance had spattered his beard, leaving brownish stains. His clothes— a torn bib-front shirt, canvas pants held up by suspenders laddered with holes, heel-worn boots, and a hat jammed onto his furry head as if it had grown there—looked as if he'd worn them on the trail for weeks without changing or bathing.

The chuck wagon itself fared a little better. Whatever his personal hygiene issues, Mary was glad to see that at least Ezra kept the wagon clean. Holes had been punched through its canvas cover, but the cook had mended them with a needle and thick hemp twine. Weather and wind had bleached the canvas and peeled the paint from the wagon's surface, giving it a realistically antique look. Ezra let the outside weather naturally, but inside, where food was stored and some preparation took place, he took great pains to make sure the dust and grime stayed at a minimum. The surfaces on which he actually prepared food, Mary noted with relief, were spotless, and he even kept modern sanitizers stocked inside the wagon, where the tourists couldn't see. Pots and pans hung from a center beam inside, and drawers and storage cubbyholes had been built into the interior. Outside, he had a work surface set up on a couple of sawhorses, in addition to the wood-burning ovens and the two-foot-diameter fire pits he had dug in the lawn and covered with steel grates.

For nineteenth-century cowboys on a long cattle drive or an extended stretch in a distant pasture, the chuck wagon had served as kitchen, pantry, social center, and camp headquarters for weeks or months on end. Ezra had explained that it had been the brainstorm of an early Texas cattleman named Charles Goodnight, and so his nickname, Chuck, had become inextricably linked to the concept. Ezra had learned his craft on cattle drives in the 1950s, and had done what he could to keep the historic American tradition alive.

Today, Ezra was working on all of his preparations, in anticipation of the big event. Tomorrow, he and a few assistants would feed hundreds, if not more, in the big closing event of the Stampede.

"Ezra," Mary said, hoping to avoid a meltdown, "those steaks came from the same suppliers we use for Mystique and Wolfgang's and all the other restaurants here at the Montecito. They're locally grass-fed, free-range cattle. Absolutely the best quality there is. But I'll try to get in some nonlean ground beef from the same ranches. I'll also take care of getting some mesquite wood in here, and I'll get those briquettes hauled away. As for the beans, you still have a full twenty-four hours before you have to serve them, so that should give them plenty of soaking time."

Ezra cocked his head and looked up at her from under the wide brim of his dust-caked brown hat. His wide-set, somehow sad-looking green eyes fixed on hers, which was unusual for her. Most men seemed not to notice she had eyes, or anything else above the neck. "I know you'll do your best, Miz Connell," he said, seemingly calmed for the moment. "I ain't worried about that."

"Good." She regarded him briefly, a man somehow yanked out of the time in which he should have lived and deposited into this alien, modern world. "Is there anything else I can do for you?"

He cast his gaze toward the ground. "Do you really think they'll like this chuck, Miz Connell? I know out on the range, or at guest ranches, my kinda cookin' is plenty popular. But here in Las Vegas—all these lights and cars and people and whatnot, I just don't know if they'll take to it here."

Mary gave him the warmest, most soothing smile she could manage. "They'll love it, Ezra. People come to Las Vegas for lots of different reasons—to gamble, to see shows, to play golf, to be pampered in the fine hotels and spas. The only thing that *everyone* who visits here does is eat. They do love that, whether it's fine international cuisine or burgers and fries. What it is doesn't matter so much as that there's plenty of it and it's available when they're ready for it. Don't you worry, these people will eat your grub like it's going out of style."

A ragged-toothed smile split Ezra's beard. "I'm right glad to hear that, Miz Connell. Don't you fret none, this'll be the best chuck ever spooned out in these parts, I guarantee that. If'n you get me what I need."

She leaned closer to him, lowering her voice. "That's great, Ezra. It might not hurt if you lay off the cooking sherry between now and then, if you get my drift."

Ezra's face—where hair didn't cover it—turned pink. "I don't use no sherry, Miz Connell. But you want me to cook without juicin' myself up a little, I reckon I could try that. Might be kinda fun. Different, anyhow."

"Let's try it," she said, patting his shoulder. "I think that would be a good idea."

5

Ed had not been entirely candid with Danny. He felt badly about it, but when a mission was classified he couldn't talk about it with anyone, even though he had long since left the agency and most of the people involved were either dead, in prison, or disappeared.

Most of the people. That was the thing.

Because one of the people he had met on this mission was Charles Hooper, and he was not only still alive, he was still working for the government, still in the trade to an extent, and here at the Montecito.

Ed had met him at a party in Washington. That much was true.

But the party had come years after the mission, their first meeting.

That had been in Honduras, in 1978. Nueva Ocotepeque, to be precise. Ed remembered the place all too well. The heat that summer had been stifling, and the humidity on that day made it feel as if he had put on his suit (lightweight linen, in eggshell white, he believed, although on second thought it could have been the pale tan one) straight from the washing machine.

What he had been sent for had nothing to do with Honduras, except that the troubles in El Salvador had sent thousands of refugees across the border into that neighboring country, and among those refugees was

Oscar Ramirez, a man the U.S. government felt deserved a place in the Salvadoran government. A high
place—not *presidente*, but in the palace. The fact that
Ramirez had been a college friend of the American
vice president's, and that his family and the vice president's had business interests in common dating back
to the late 1930s might have had something to do
with it, but Ed preferred not to dwell on those aspects
of the job. He did what he was told and left it to the
politicians and bureaucrats to figure out the whys
and wherefores.

Ed had gone to a sidewalk café in Nueva Ocotepeque, not far from the El Salvadoran border, to meet
with some of Ramirez's representatives. He intended to
outline his plan to get Ramirez back into the country.
The journey would coincide with a coup that would
eliminate General Carlos Humberto Rodriguez, and
Ramirez would accompany the force that moved into
the palace in San Salvador. Ed sat at the café, sipping
sweet local coffee, until two men strolled, too casually,
around the corner and between the tables. He met the
gaze of the first one, raising an eyebrow. The man nodded his head. He had a thick black beard and fierce eyebrows and wore a guayabera shirt with faded blue
jeans. Behind him came a slender man with short dark
hair wearing a gray suit with an obvious bulge near the
armpit. His white shirt was buttoned all the way up,
and a striped tie hung around his neck like a noose
waiting for the hangman to hoist it skyward. Ed knew
at a glance he was American.

Which meant that, once again, communication had
broken down somewhere. If Ramirez already had an

American spook on the inside, why did he need Ed to get him over the border and into San Salvador?

The two men sat down at the little wrought-iron table, which had been painted green a generation or two earlier. Now the paint flaked constantly and Ed had to keep brushing it off his light-colored pants. Ed signaled the waiter, and until he had returned with cups of strong coffee for the two newcomers, none of them spoke except to order.

"Is everything in readiness?" the Salvadoran asked then. No small talk. That worked for Ed.

"More or less," Ed replied. He nodded toward the third man. "Who's he?"

"Hooper," the American said.

"You're working with our friend?"

"We're all friends here," Hooper answered vaguely. "Let's leave it at that."

"Fine with me," Ed said.

"So you're ready to go?" Hooper asked. "Tonight?"

Ed shook his head. "Tomorrow night. Clouds should be blowing in tomorrow, and tomorrow night will be essentially moonless." He took a sip of coffee. "That's what the weatherman says, anyway."

"Good enough for me," Hooper said.

"Do we meet at the previously discussed place?" the Salvadoran asked. Ed knew he referred to a small cottage on the edge of town, its yard thick with banana trees. The road was paved to just past the cottage, and a streetlamp stood a couple of houses down, but the bulb had been shot out three nights before, and not yet replaced. From there it would be a simple matter to put Ramirez in a Jeep and drive him down the dirt road into jungle that, less than a mile away, felt as deep as the heart of the Amazon. A second road—really just a rutted, overgrown track—intersected this road, leading right across the border into El Salvador. In Metapan, on the other side, a guerrilla group would take over and Ed's job would be done.

Using coded phrases, Ed laid out the details for Hooper and the Salvadoran. By the time the three had finished their coffees, they had reached agreement on the basics of the plan.

The next day the sky was, as promised, full of clouds. They cut the heat if not the humidity, and although Ed had to scramble to get the Jeep equipped for the jungle trek, he was more comfortable than he had been for the past few days. When night fell, he was ready to roll. He had a light dinner at his hotel, then walked the four blocks to the garage where he'd parked the vehicle. Mosquitoes buzzed around him like fighter planes strafing King Kong on the Empire State Building.

Once he had the Jeep on the road, Ed felt the tingle of anticipation that always accompanied the beginning of action. Hyperalert, every light he saw seemed brighter than on other nights, every sound pregnant with meaning. People he drove past eyed him and he saw, in each one, the potential for trouble.

After driving around town for about twenty minutes, checking to be sure no one tailed him, he steered up the road that would take him to the cottage where Ramirez would be waiting. Slowly he drove past the cottage, onto the dirt road, and killed the engine a quarter mile away.

With the sudden absence of engine noise, the jungle seemed to erupt with sound. Chirps and trills and cries and caterwauling covered his footsteps as Ed walked back to the cottage. The rich, fecund smell of jungle filled the night.

When he arrived at the cottage, the noise stopped.

Ed drew his .38 automatic from a holster at the small of his back. Tonight he had worn a black T-shirt, jeans, and steel-toed combat boots. In the moonless night he blended with the shadows. He went into the jungle and approached the cottage from the rear.

No lights burned inside. That was as it should be; Ramirez was supposed to wait in the dark with whoever would accompany him across the line. When Ed came to the front yard and whistled twice, they would come out and walk together back to the Jeep.

So nothing looked wrong.

But the bugs and night birds stopping their otherwise ceaseless din, that was wrong.

From the cover of the trees, Ed saw a man standing beside the cottage, hugging the wall. At first all he could make out were eyeballs, white specks in a dark face. Then he realized that the man had applied camouflage blacking to his cheeks and forehead and neck. He wore a loose-fitting black shirt. In his hands he held a submachine gun.

Under the jungle odor, the never-ending cycle of organic growth, death, and decomposition, Ed smelled the tart, acidic tang of sweat, the kind they called flop sweat because it accompanied fear. The man was no professional.

With a gun like that, he didn't have to be.

If he hadn't spooked the birds, Ed might have walked right into the yard. Right into his sights.

It would have been his last walk.

Probably, he guessed, another man waited on the other side of the house. Maybe more inside. Ramirez had been killed, most likely, or taken prisoner. Perhaps he was on his way into El Salvador after all, but as a captive instead of a liberator.

Just walk away, Ed told himself.

The op is blown. Leave it.

But he couldn't. For his own curiosity if nothing else, he had to know. How many men had they set against him? And was Ramirez really gone, or was he inside, unaware of the trap?

Or part of the plan?

Ed whistled twice.

The man with the gun whirled toward him, raising his weapon. His mouth dropped open and now Ed could see his teeth, white as the headstones at a military cemetery. Ed aimed the .38 at a point about two inches above the top row and squeezed the trigger.

The gunshot boomed in the still night. Birds took flight from the trees with a roaring flutter of wings. The shot flew true, but as the man died he reflexively squeezed his trigger and a burst of automatic gunfire sprayed the jungle floor, slicing through vines and thudding into trees.

The cottage's front door swung open with a rusty squeal and three men charged out, weapons in their fists. Soviet ones, it appeared, AK-47s. Ed led the one in front for a couple of paces and dropped him with a single shot from the .38, then spun behind a tree.

Bullets tore the air around him, rapping against the tree trunk like an enraged woodpecker, but missed him. He stepped to his right, aimed, fired again, and threw himself down.

Another man fell. The third fired another burst into the trees, but the shots sailed over Ed. Leaves drifted down over him like snow.

From the ground (wet mud soaking through his T-shirt and jeans), Ed sighted beneath underbrush, pistol held in his right fist, left cradling it off the ground. The third and final man took a hesitant step toward the trees, not sure if he had hit Ed.

Ed answered the question for him with a double tap, chest and head.

That night, from the relative privacy of his hotel room, Ed made some phone calls to Washington and Langley.

An hour later, having learned where Hooper parked his boots at night, Ed let himself into Hooper's hotel room across town. A ceiling fan spun lazily over Hooper's bed. When the agent woke up, Ed was sitting on the foot of the bed holding a different .38, his last one having been wiped clean and tossed into the jungle between the cottage and the Jeep. Guns and coffee were easy to come by in this part of the world, even if not much else was.

"What the hell?" Hooper asked, blinking but instantly alert. He pawed the top of his nightstand for a weapon that Ed had already pocketed. "Deline? Shouldn't you be in El Salvador with Ramirez?"

His confusion sounded genuine, making Ed glad he hadn't simply plugged Hooper while he slept.

"Ramirez is dead," he explained, his voice soft. The hotel was quiet, and he hoped Hooper's waking outburst hadn't raised an alarm. "I found him inside the cottage with the El Salvadoran guy who came to the café with you the other day. Both their throats had been cut, and Ramirez's fingers had been lopped off and stuffed in his mouth. I took that to be a sign of some kind." He didn't mention the stink in the cottage, of blood and meat spoiling in the humid air.

"Jesus," Hooper said. Beads of sweat popped out on his forehead. Ed didn't think it was just from the heat of the night. "Someone got to him."

"Gee, you think?" Ed had fully expected Hooper to implicate himself in the first thirty seconds of conversation. He hadn't, though—on the contrary, everything he had said made it sound as if he was truly surprised by the night's events. "I thought you'd be at the cottage too."

"Alberto told me not to come," Hooper explained.

"That's the guy from the café?" He had never given Ed his name, and Ed hadn't asked.

"Right. He said one American on the trip was plenty, and two would raise too many eyebrows with the people in Metapan."

His answer made sense to Ed. As much sense as anything did in this crazy place. Ed still didn't entirely trust the guy, but he couldn't take him out based on a hunch and a bad feeling. More significant, the people he had talked to in D.C. had vouched for Hooper.

Ed threw a few more questions at him. When he provided satisfactory answers, Ed left the room. He hadn't seen Hooper again until the Washington party he had mentioned to Danny, and then this week at the Montecito.

The whole incident had always left him with a sour taste. Someone had betrayed Ramirez. No one, to Ed's knowledge, knew about the plan except Hooper and Alberto, if that was really the man's name, and presumably Ramirez himself. That left a narrow pool of suspects. Of course, any of them could have told any number of other people. Ed could have chased down the truth, but he had been ordered to Prague a few days later.

Now that Hooper was here at his hotel, Ed remembered just how much he distrusted the man. He would have to keep a close eye on Charles Hooper, and this was one aspect of the job he couldn't entrust to Danny. Danny had enough on his plate without trying to watch the guy he was supposed to be cooperating with. Especially since Ed couldn't tell Danny why he had a problem with Hooper in the first place.

No, Hooper would be Ed's problem. Just one among many, of course. But he couldn't afford to put this one on the back burner.

6

"Help! Security!"

Mike Cannon swiveled at the sound of anxious shouts. He had been on his way back up to the surveillance room to work on his software issues, but now he stopped, scanning the crowd until he saw the source of the desperate cries. They came from a solid man in his mid-fifties, Mike guessed, well over six feet tall and barrel-chested. Wearing a black Stetson hat and a western shirt resembling the lone-star Texas flag, the man ran out of the exhibit hall waving his arms in the air. "Security!" he shouted again.

Mike hurried to him, put a calming hand on his shoulder, and drew him off to one side of the floor. "I'm with surveillance and security, sir. What seems to be the problem?"

The man's lively blue eyes were wide with panic, and spittle flecked his lips. He clutched Mike's arm in a painful grip. "The problem is that someone's robbed my dang booth!"

Mike nodded toward the ceiling. "Sir, this casino is loaded with cameras. I'm sure we can get to the bottom of this in very short order. What was taken from you?" He smiled. "Somebody rustle your cows?"

"This isn't a humorous matter, mister," the guy said angrily. "My name is Leroy Snead. Of the Houston Sneads. And some low-down bastard out there is walking away with Cavanaugh's Virtue, while we stand here jawing."

"Whose virtue?"

"Apparently you don't follow the quarter horse circuit, son. Cavanaugh's Virtue is a champion race-horse many times over. He's sired half a dozen other champions. And now all that's left of him is gone!"

"I'm sorry," Mike said, not much more enlightened than he had been a minute ago. "Someone took a horse from your booth and you didn't notice?"

"Not the horse!" Leroy Snead looked at Mike as he might have at a slow child, slowing the pace of his speech accordingly. "A vial of his semen!"

Mike blinked a couple of times, trying to follow Snead's progression. "Someone stole a vial of horse semen from you. I'm sure that's a problem, but can't you always get more? Seems like the horse wouldn't mind."

"Cavanaugh's Virtue is dead, you nitwit!" Snead said. He had raised his voice again, so Mike lowered his, trying to keep a scene from developing.

"The horse is dead." Understanding began to dawn on Mike.

"That's right. The vial that was stolen is all I have left. It's supposed to go up for auction tomorrow."

"I see," Mike said. "And what do you think something like that would bring at auction?"

"The thing about an auction is you never know," Snead said, managing to compose himself a little now that he and Mike were finally on the same page. "But some of the top buyers and breeders in the country are in Las Vegas this week. All I can really say for sure is that the bidding would have started at one million dollars, but where it would have ended up is anybody's guess."

"A million bucks."

"That's right. That's the starting bid."

"For a bottle of horse goop."

Snead nodded. "That's not what we call it, son."

"The terminology isn't what's important right now, Mr. Snead. Let me get upstairs, start looking at the footage. I'll get right back to you." He handed Snead his business card, so the man could reach him if need be.

"You do that, son. I ain't ashamed to say, the day that horse passed, I cried like he was my own son. Wept real tears. An animal like that, it's smart, friendly, it creates a true emotional connection with you. Now I've lost all that I had left of him. I'd hate to have to hold the Montecito liable for my loss."

"You and me both, sir," Mike said. "You and me both."

"Mr. Fuzzkins wants to swim, Mommy! Can Mr. Fuzzkins swim?"

"We'll just have to see, Kaylie," Marcella Hammer answered. "Sam, can Mr. Fuzzkins go in the pool?"

"Who is Mr. Fuzzkins?" Sam asked distractedly. She had left Byron Hammer in a cabana while she fetched Marcella and Kaylie, but he had apparently moved to a different one. The one she had left him in had already been taken over by a family of seven, and Byron was nowhere to be seen. She tried to pretend that she knew where Byron was, not wanting to call him if she could help it. Calling would breach the aura of invincibility she liked to cultivate.

"My bunny, you stupid!" Kaylie shouted. Sam glanced down at the towheaded girl, her mouth a keyboard's worth of teeth and gaps, shaking an ancient brown stuffed rabbit that looked as if it had been dragged to Las Vegas behind the family car. Which in the Hammer family's case was probably a limousine.

"Now, Kaylie," Marcella said. She and her daughter both wore stylish, matching green one-piece suits covered by light wraps, with expensive sandals on their feet. "We don't say stupid. We say foolish."

"My bunny, you foolish!" Kaylie screeched.

That is so much better, Sam thought. "I really don't think the pool water would be good for Mr. Fuzzkins," she said. *And the diseases that thing might carry wouldn't be good for our guests.* "All that chlorine, you know."

"He's rough and tough! He's my big bunny!"

"I'm sure he is," Sam said, reminding herself to keep her cool. Snapping at clients' daughters did not build customer loyalty. She kept scanning the sunbathers for Byron Hammer. "But the pool at this hotel was designed for people, not bunnies."

"Mr. Fuzzkins can swim! He swims good!"

Sam bit the inside of her lip, trying to fashion a reply that didn't involve nudging little Kaylie into the drink. *We'll see just how well Mr. Fuzzkins can swim,* she thought. Marcella Hammer, tall, blond, vaguely glacial, smiled and said, "Sam said no, honey."

She's a paragon of patience, Sam thought. *Or else a Valium addict. Maybe both.*

Before Kaylie could belt out some other demand, Sam's mobile phone chirped. Byron's name flashed on the screen. "Byron," she said. "I'm here at the pool with Marcella and that adorable daughter of yours, Kaylie. Oh, and Mr. Fuzzkins too."

"That's why I'm calling, Sam," Byron said. "It's a little on the chilly side out there for me, so I went to get a haircut instead."

"I think Kaylie has her heart set on a swim."

"That's fine," Byron said. "She should go ahead. After my trim I'll probably hit the gym for a while, do some cardio, maybe some lifting. Then I'll head back to the casino after my shower."

"I'll let them know," Sam said. "Give me a shout when you're ready and I'll come and get you."

"Fine, Sam. Thanks." He ended the call. Sam folded her phone and caught Marcella's meaningful gaze.

"He's already moved on," Marcella said. She wasn't asking a question. She hadn't been with Byron for years without coming to know him.

"And then some. I don't see how you keep up with him."

Marcella smiled, her pretty face lighting up like a beacon and shattering the cold impression Sam had of her. "It can definitely be a challenge."

"I'm sure. If you two still want to swim, that's no problem at all. I can get you a nice cabana, something to drink . . ."

Marcella squatted down next to Kaylie. "What do you think, dear?"

"I want to do something Mr. Fuzzkins wants to do!" Kaylie shouted. She seemed incapable of speaking in normal tones.

Sam didn't bother reminding her that, two minutes ago, Mr. Fuzzkins had wanted nothing more than a refreshing dip in the pool. "Well, what does Mr. Fuzzkins enjoy?" she asked.

"He likes movies, and carrots, and playgrounds, and going for walks in the mall, and shopping, and he doesn't like people who are stupid. I mean foolish."

"You know what's a lot of fun for kids?" Sam said. "The shark exhibit at Mandalay Bay."

"Really?" Marcella asked.

"They just eat it up," Sam said. *And it really is impossible to feed your kid to them, as much as you might want to.*

Marcella shot Sam a sidelong glance, as if she could read Sam's thoughts.

Sam flashed her widest, most innocent smile.

Leroy Snead returned to his booth, fingering Mike Cannon's card and hoping the man's resources were everything he claimed. The faces he passed on the way melted into a blur. He thought he heard someone shout his name, but it didn't sink through his swirling miasma of thought and emotion until whoever it might have been had vanished into the crowd.

At the booth, Snead pushed past a middle-aged couple examining a simple braided leather bridle with the enthusiasm common to people who don't know horses or tack. The woman glared at him—he could feel her gaze on his neck like a sunburn—but he ignored her. No amount of tack she might buy, and he had a feeling she wouldn't buy any, would come close to making up for the losses he'd suffer if Cavanaugh's Virtue's semen didn't turn up.

He went inside the oversize luxury horse trailer he used as a booth office and sat down at a portable table, elbows on its surface, palms against his cheeks. He had a bottle of Jim Beam hidden in his filing cabinet, but to start hitting that right away would be admitting defeat.

Then again, he thought, *how much harm could a little nip do?*

He had the bottom drawer open and he was reaching behind the folders for the bottle when someone entered the trailer. Thinking it would be Linda Lou, who frowned on daytime drinking, he yanked his hand clear and slid the drawer closed. But it was Ryan Riddlehoover, a longtime employee who ran the booth when Snead had to be away and, back in Houston, operated the retail side of the business.

"Something wrong, Leroy?" Ryan asked. Although Ryan was as tall and thin as a telephone pole, he wore a tall crowned black hat, boots with three-inch heels, and a western shirt with wide teal and yellow vertical stripes. "You ran outta here in a big hurry."

"As wrong as it could possibly be, Ryan," Snead replied. He indicated the cabinet where the vial had been locked, its doors hanging open. "We've been robbed."

"The vial?" Ryan's face might have been made of rubber—his jaw dropped, which caused deep trenches to appear from his cheekbones to his lower mandible, while his eyebrows shot up, tipping the black hat backward.

"That's right. It's gone. I've alerted Montecito security, and they say they have cameras everywhere and will be able to find out who took it. But they don't have cameras inside here. You seen anyone sneaking around here?"

"No, boss," Ryan said quickly. "I've been in and out a few times, you know, writing orders or getting more paperwork and whatnot. Linda Lou's been in, and Sammy, and that's all I know of."

That was no help. Sammy had been with him for a dozen years, and Leroy had been married to Linda Lou for nineteen. None of them would have stolen the vial, because they all knew what its sale would mean for the business.

Or at least, they thought they did.

Leroy Snead did the company's books, though. Only he knew just how precarious the business was. Since Cavanaugh's Virtue had died, sales had been off across the board. The other animals in Snead's stable had qualities of their own—good breeding, fine musculature, and speed—but they were not proven champions. Their stud fees were lower than those Cavanaugh's Virtue had commanded, and they hadn't brought home any major purses to offset the difference. Since Cavanaugh's Virtue had been the cornerstone of the business, all the other areas had been affected by the horse's death as well.

Then there had been Snead's desperate attempt to offset his losses by investing in what had been offered to him as a sure thing but had turned out to be a sure loser, an oil company that had supposedly secured rights to drill in Guatemala. Turned out that the permits had been signed by a man whose tenure with the government had come to a sudden and unpleasant end, and from his prison cell he couldn't do anything to help Snead's new partners fulfill their end of the bargain.

He hadn't even told Linda Lou about that particular mess. He knew that he should have—should have consulted her before he even wrote the check, since according to the law and the documents of incorporation, she was a full partner in Snead Enterprises. Guilt had gnawed at him for the past month and a half. He had scrambled to find a way to cover the loss, but every avenue he had explored had fallen through.

The auction, however—that had always been the fail-safe plan. When the vial of Cavanaugh's Virtue's semen sold for the premium price it should bring, then he could absorb the loss on the oil deal.

Without that money, the time would come—soon, most likely—that he would have to explain the loss to Linda Lou. Not long after that, he might well have to explain to federal investigators why he had kept it off the books. What would be worse, he wondered? Jail or a messy divorce, with the details of his business failings spread through the Houston newspapers?

Of course, nothing guaranteed that he wouldn't experience both.

What a joy that would be.

7

Delinda wandered through the Montecito's largest exhibit hall, a little amazed at the sheer amount of western-themed merchandise the vendors had managed to squeeze into the big room. She could have filled a mansion with the furniture on display: rustic pine and smooth oak and wrought iron, accented with stars and horns and horseshoes and leather and fur and fringe. She saw what seemed like literally tons of antlers—tables, chairs, light fixtures, and hat racks made from antlers, and one booth selling nothing but loose antlers. *For the do-it-yourselfer,* she supposed. Every third booth seemed to offer leather goods, from jackets, coats, and boots to toothbrush holders, wall hangings, and other assorted housewares.

Enough western wear surrounded her to outfit a cowboy army. Delinda thumbed through brand-new, crisp blue jeans, some made as work clothes and some, torn and shot through by bullets or dragged across hot stones, selling for hundreds of dollars. Shirts ranged from casual cotton ones to thematic T-shirts to vintage 1940s and 1950s gabardine by Nudie's Rodeo Tailors, H Bar C, Rockmount, and other makers. Some booths sold cowboy music CDs, some western movie DVDs, some books and magazines focusing on the fictional west or the real one of ranchers, real estate development, drought, and other environmental issues, and of course the wide-open spaces, tall mountains, and beautiful landscapes that had drawn people there for more than two centuries.

The western theme didn't fit Delinda's personal style, but she could understand the appeal of it. Many of the items had beautiful textures and designs, made with fine craftsmanship and a reverence for history. Her tastes ran more toward the contemporary and to European and Asian antiques, mixing items from those exotic sources with today's sleek lines and high-tech materials.

Still, it was fun to browse the booths. And, not incidentally, to browse some of the cowboys running them.

She had entered a booth crammed with old cowboy and pop culture memorabilia—saddle blankets and leather cuffs, cartridge belts, boots, Roy Rogers and Gene Autry toys and games, movie posters, and the like—precisely because the cowboy behind the sales counter was outstanding. He had a swimmer's build, with broad shoulders and a deep chest, tapering to a narrow waist at which a huge silver and gold buckle rested. His straw hat was white and clean, his long-sleeved shirt form-fitting, and he looked back at her with obvious interest. "See anything you like, ma'am?" he asked when she had browsed for a moment.

"Oh yeah," Delinda said. "But you can drop the 'ma'am' stuff—it makes me feel like I'm your mother's age."

"Oh, I know you're not, ma'am," he said, grinning

at his own response. "It's just the way I was brought up is all."

"I'm sure your mother is proud of you."

"I like to think she is."

"You're not from around here, are you, cowboy?" Delinda asked.

"No, ma'am, I'm sure not. I'm from a little place called Wind River, Wyoming."

She picked up a pair of fringed leather gauntlets with intricate beadwork across the backs of the hands. When she saw the price tag had three zeroes on it, she set them back down carefully. "Is that where all your merchandise comes from?"

"No, ma'am," the cowboy said. "I used to rodeo some. Lot of the guys, well, they'd just blow into town, ride a bull or a bronc, dust themselves off, get drunk, and hit the road again. I was never much of a drinker, so I used to check out antique stores, thrift stores, anyplace I might pick up a little piece of cowboy history. Finally my place back home got to be too full." He touched the small of his back and winced. "And I got to be a little too tore up. So I gave up the broncos and put my energy into trying to unload some of what I'd collected. Turns out I like doing this, going to shows and meeting people, just about as much as I ever liked rodeo. And it's considerably less dangerous."

"You do have some great stuff here." Delinda peered through the glass windows of a display cabinet at a series of old TV cowboy comic books. Her gaze swept across something else on the shelf, and she stopped, staring at an oil-company calendar from

1962 with a painting of a leggy cowgirl on it. The girl wore short shorts and a skimpy blouse with a red and white checkerboard pattern and white fringe. "Hey, that's not so old!" she said.

"Nineteen sixty-two seems like a long time ago to me," the cowboy said. "Got to be before you were born, too."

"Not the calendar. I mean that picture. Can you take that out of the case?"

"Sure thing." The man bent down behind the case, slid open a door, and removed the calendar, holding it gingerly with both hands. He brought it out and handed it to Delinda.

"That's what I thought," Delinda said. The cowgirl's long red hair was parted in the middle and pulled to either side in loose pigtails, held by rawhide thongs. Her lips were full and red, her cheekbones prominent, her brown eyes smiling as if she kept a secret from the viewer. She sat on the top rail of a split log fence, twirling a revolver on the index finger of her right hand, although she did not look like a person who harbored violent impulses. Her checked shirt clung to voluptuous curves, which the dangling fringe accentuated still more. "That's Mary."

"That's who?"

"That's Mary Connell. She works here."

"What a beautiful woman," the cowboy said. "How old is she now?"

"She's that old. She looks just like that. I mean now, today."

He blinked at her, puzzled. "I don't understand what you're saying. This is an original piece, from

1962. That painting is more than forty years old. It might have been based on a photograph—probably was, given the photorealism—but there's no way that model would still look like this."

Delinda didn't know what to think. Looking at the woman in the painting, she could have sworn that Mary had sat for the artist just yesterday. "Do you know who the model is?"

"I wish," the cowboy said. "Tell you the truth, I've always kind of had a crush on her. I keep the calendar inside the case, priced way out of the market, just so nobody'll buy her."

Feeling like the floor might spin out from under her, Delinda handed the calendar back. She couldn't flirt with this guy anymore—not that he had stopped being a hunk, but the whole thing weirded her out too much.

Besides, this cowboy was just way too nice for her.

Mary, on the other hand, would like him.

A lot.

"Don't go anywhere, okay? I'll bring her over to meet you," Delinda said.

"I'm here until they close the show down," he said.

"I mean it," she warned. "I can track you down anyplace on the property if I need to."

"I'll be right here, ma'am," he said. "You can bank on that."

"Are they here on dates?" Mike asked, stepping into Danny's office. "Or looking for dates?"

Danny turned away from the monitor set into the wall behind his desk, which displayed two young women, a blonde and a redhead, both with showgirl figures well displayed by low-cut tops and microscopic skirts, sitting down before a pair of video poker machines.

"Or dating each other," Danny offered.

"You going to take a run at them?"

Danny clicked a remote and the screen shifted to another view of the casino floor. "Huh?" Danny smiled. "No, I'm just browsing, not buying. What about you?"

Mike tilted his head to the left, waggled his shoulders. "You know. Things could be better. I went out with a cocktail waitress from the Mandalay Bay the other day. I think I mentioned her. Glory?"

"Yeah, you did." Danny remembered what Mike had said about her. "Glory, glory, hallelujah."

"That's the one," Mike said. "Only it turns out that she's better-looking than she is interesting. She spent most of our date talking about her father, who's a sheriff up near Reno, and the people he's had to shoot."

"Nice," Danny said. "That really makes you want to get to know her, huh?"

"Tell me about it," Mike replied. "She didn't specify whether any of the victims were boyfriends, and I was afraid to ask."

"No, you just have to assume that they were. Does she think you're going out again?"

"I think I got the message across to her loud and clear," Mike said.

"So tell me again what was stolen from the exhibit hall," Danny said, abruptly changing the subject, Mike noted, before he could ask what Danny's action had been like lately.

"I'm pretty sure you heard me the first time, Danny. It's a vial of horsey love lotion." Mike dropped onto Danny's leather couch and clapped his hands to the sides of his head. "I cannot believe this is happening to Mama Cannon's little boy."

"Wait," Danny said. He put a hand over his mouth but Mike could see the amused grin behind it, could almost hear the stifled snicker. "You're saying someone actually stole horse semen?"

"Apparently it's a valuable commodity," Mike said. "Worth its weight in diamonds. Or something like that."

"Maybe you should check online. I've heard there are some websites where that kind of thing would go over big."

"This is not a joke, Danny. I know you think it's funny. But to Leroy Snead it's a million bucks or more, and he intends to hold the Montecito responsible if he doesn't get it back by auction time tomorrow night."

That mocking snicker came again. "Leroy Snead?"

"I'm telling you, man."

"Well, run through the footage, I guess."

"You think I didn't do that first?" After taking the report from Snead, Mike had gone directly to the surveillance room. He checked the plan of the exhibit hall, located Snead's booth, and asked Mitch to pull up all the footage from the two cameras with the best views of it. Then he had sat down in front of a monitor and run through it, first fast-forwarding to see if anything unusual jumped out at him, then in real time. Finally, he had slowed particular moments down to watch more carefully.

The hall had been busy, with a couple thousand people in the aisles at times. Snead's booth, backed by huge enlargements of some of Cavanaugh's Virtue's winning moments and featuring a variety of horse care products, drew plenty of traffic. Trouble was, the eyes in the sky could only do so much when ninety percent of the people in the room wore cowboy hats that shielded their faces.

Mike tried to catch everyone entering the private areas of the booth. Once he had isolated a few of those, he printed out stills of them and took them downstairs to Snead. The man identified one as his wife, Linda Lou, and the other two as valued and trusted employees. None of them would steal the semen, Snead explained, because they all stood to benefit too much from its sale at auction.

"Danny, I looked at footage until my eyes bled out of my head," Mike complained. "Then I stuck 'em back in and looked some more. I've seen every shape and color of cowboy hat you can imagine, including one made of what looks distressingly like real tiger skin. But I didn't see anyone who appeared to be stealing a jar of equine joy juice from Snead's booth."

"What did you say, Mike?"

Mike looked up to see Ed Deline standing in the doorway, his arms crossed over his deep chest. "Nothing, Mr. D," Mike said innocently.

"No, I distinctly heard you say something. Did you say 'equine joy juice'?"

Mike wanted to crawl under the couch. "I might have said that, yeah."

Ed leaned into the office as if he wanted to say

something, but then he just waved a hand at them. "Danny . . ."

"I know, Ed. Make it go away."

"Make it go away." Ed left the doorway, which Mike considered a blessing.

"Mike," Danny said. "You heard the man. Let's turn this over to Vegas Metro. This is a big-time theft, right? A million dollars. Robbery-Homicide will take it." Danny grinned. "Or maybe Vice?"

Danny had become Mike's best friend over the time he had worked at the Montecito. As best friends often did, Danny enjoyed sliding a sarcastic knife blade between Mike's ribs from time to time and giving it a twist. Mike had become accustomed to it and returned the favor whenever he could. But right now he just wasn't feeling it.

"Yeah, it's all a big joke when you're not the guy Snead's gonna hold responsible."

"Are you afraid of this guy, Mike?"

"Afraid? No, I'm not afraid. I just want to do my job, you know, get his stolen merchandise back to him before it . . . well, I don't know if it can go bad. But before the auction would be nice. And before the press gets wind of the theft. Can you imagine the headlines?"

"Mike, Ed wants it to go away," Danny said.

"And it will, as soon as we can figure out who took the stuff."

"You said you already reviewed all the footage."

"And I have. That's not the only way we catch bad guys, Danny."

"I don't want you to feel like I'm not taking this seriously, Mike. It's just that with Aickmann coming tomorrow and all the craziness around that, I don't have time to get into it with you."

"I'm a pro, Danny. I can work it solo," Mike said with bravado.

"I know you can."

"And I will. I'll handle it. I'll find the French dressing and make Leroy Snead a happy man."

"Go for it, Mike. But you're kind of on your own with this one, because most everyone else is on the Aickmann thing. I'll back you up when I can."

"That's all I ask, Danny. Just back my play."

"Done."

Mike rose, ready to go back to the surveillance room. Other angles he could play had already started to worm their way into his consciousness. And as much as he protested to Danny, he had to agree that he was vaguely amused by spending his day on the hunt for missing horse semen.

But at the same time, he knew that to Leroy Snead, the subject was dead serious.

8

Danny headed for Ed's office, still smiling to himself over Mike's predicament. No matter how absurd a situation might be, if it *could* happen, it would happen in a casino. Every now and then Danny started to think he'd seen it all, but that idea would be disabused almost immediately. He hoped his friend could track down the missing vial quickly, because nobody wanted to have someone named Leroy Snead gunning for you. Besides, the threat that Snead might sue the Montecito was all too real.

Every exhibitor had signed a waiver stating that the Montecito would take every reasonable precaution but could not be held responsible for the merchandise in their booths. For the hotel to assume that kind of responsibility, Danny's people would have to verify the contents of each booth at opening and closing, to make sure vendors didn't file false claims. He didn't have the staff to accomplish that, and with Aickmann on the way he wouldn't have wanted to try it.

Unfortunately, signing waivers didn't preclude people from filing lawsuits. A lawyer could always be found who would bring a suit on any grounds, or none whatsoever. In a case like this, the Montecito's own lawyers would probably suggest settling out of court just to make Snead go away. That settlement could cost the hotel millions. Danny hated to see people game the system like that, and even though they carried insurance just for such eventualities, he didn't want the Montecito to take a hit. His department worked to prevent just such events.

If he hadn't had the Aickmann business to worry about, he would have worked the case alongside Mike. They made a great team, bouncing ideas off each other along with the insults. Together they had solved bigger cases than this one, and while he had confidence in Mike's abilities, Danny believed that partnered up they might be able to bring it home more quickly.

Danny felt a great sense of pride when he thought about how much Ed trusted him to handle the day-to-day surveillance and security operations of the multibillion-dollar resort. It hadn't always been that way. At first, Ed's trust had to be earned, and the older man gave it grudgingly, only after Danny vividly demonstrated his abilities.

One of the things that had thrown Danny at first had been Ed's grasp of history, which had manifested itself in unexpected ways. Fortunately, Danny's dad had been a history buff who had tried hard to teach Danny his passion for learning what had happened in the past, and how those events related to the present. Danny had never been the greatest student, but he did seem to have a knack for remembering that kind of thing, which had served him well in OCS.

In his early days on the job, Ed tested him by tossing out dates—usually dates with attached military significance—and expecting Danny to not only recognize the date but to understand the connection that past military operation had to something going on at the moment.

Ed might, for instance, shout "June 9, 1863!" to Danny as the two of them were circling though the casino, closing in on a snatch-and-run who'd just grabbed a cup of chips from a player more focused on the next roll of the dice than on the whereabouts of his winnings. Danny would be expected to recognize the date as that of the Battle of Brandy Station, from the Civil War, and to know that Ed was reminding him that General David Gregg's division had arrived late for what should have been a classic pincer attack, almost consigning General John Buford's soldiers to a devastating defeat. From that, Danny could extrapolate that he should pay no attention to the two smoking-hot babes wearing next to nothing who stood forlornly beside a slot bank, looking for someone who could explain to them how the machines worked.

So, history. Knowing it had helped Danny's career, even though he still hadn't quite forgiven Ed for making him miss the chance to get to know those two women. According to Mike, they had eventually decided that gambling was too complicated and gone back to their previous occupation as topless car-wash attendants. On his next day off, Danny had driven his precious yellow Camaro through a muddy construction site, and then made the rounds of every car wash in town, but had never been able to find them. The Camaro had wound up sparkling clean, though.

In the hallway outside Ed's office, Danny's mobile phone buzzed. He fished it from his pocket. The call came from Greg, a longtime member of his floor security team. "Yeah, Greg."

"Danny," Greg said, his tone somber. "I have something here that you've gotta see."

"I'm about to walk into a meeting with Ed."

"You'll want to check this out before you see Ed. Can you meet me in the surveillance room?"

Danny suppressed a sigh. More bad news? That he could do without. "Sure, I'll see you in a minute."

On his way back to the surveillance room, he wondered what could be so important that it couldn't wait until after the meeting. Of course, with millions of dollars in cash and chips in play on the floor at any given moment, any number of problems might be major ones.

He found Greg sitting in front of a computer monitor. "Hey, Danny," Greg said, tapping the monitor's screen. "Have a look at this."

Danny leaned forward to see what Greg had on the screen. "What is it?"

"One of our floor guys found a CD tucked between two rows of slots. He said it looked like someone had stuck it there for somebody else to pick up. He brought it to me, and I put it in to find out what it was. And . . . well, see for yourself."

It took a few moments for Danny to make any sense of what Greg was showing him. On-screen, a crude computer animation ran—nothing at first but dots and lines. Greg reran it for him, and gradually Danny began to understand what he was seeing.

At first, one of the dots floated by itself at what might have been the front of a big room, an auditorium or meeting room of some kind, judging by some sketchy layout lines around it.

Other dots blinked into existence at some distance from the first one. Two, then four, and finally seven of the dots appeared, scattered at various points around the enclosed space. They shifted positions, then dotted lines emerged from two of them, intersecting at the original dot. Finally, sprays of dotted lines spread out from three of the others. When the sprays had faded away, all the dots shifted back to their original locations, then vanished. The first dot stayed where it was but gradually faded to black.

"What do you think this is, Greg?" Danny had already begun to form his own opinion, but he wanted to hear what Greg had come up with.

"Look at the layout of the space, Danny." Greg pointed to the lines that could have indicated walls and seating sections. "That's the ballroom where that German guy speaks tomorrow."

"It could be," Danny admitted.

"It's to almost perfect scale, Danny, like somebody had our blueprints to work from. Check it again." He restarted the animation, but Danny already knew that he and Greg were on the same wavelength.

"These dots, where they come in," Greg said, pointing at them as they appeared on-screen. "They're all at the different entrances to the ballroom."

"Right."

"And then these dotted lines." Danny watched the first two converge on the first dot.

"You're thinking that these dots are people, and they're shooting at Aickmann," Danny said.

Greg appeared genuinely worried. "Well, it could be they're just trying for a good view, but you tell me."

"What about these?" Danny asked as the sprays from the other dots washed across the seating area.

"Look how they cover these other dots as they're moving back toward the doors," Greg said. "I don't know if they're shooting gas, or machine guns, or what. But I don't like it."

"I don't either," Danny said. "And I think your interpretation is probably right. The next question is, is all this for real, or is it just somebody's overhyped imagination?"

"Making this disc would be a hell of a lot of work just for a gag, Danny."

"Right. But anyone who would consider pulling off something like this has to know we're going to be screening for weapons at the doors."

"That's true. On the other hand, even knowing that, they went ahead with this kind of preparation anyway. What does that tell you?"

"That they have some other angle—an inside connection, or something like that. Or else they're very, very determined."

Greg nodded, finally killing the animation on-screen and ejecting the disc. "That's all there is on the disc. I already had it dusted for prints, but no dice there. I was thinking I'd turn it over to Mike to see if he could determine anything about where the disc might have been burned, or how the animation was done, but—"

"Mike's busy."

"Yeah, that's what he said. Something about horse junk."

Danny took the disc from Greg's hands. "Still, you're right, it's worth investigating. I'll have Mitch work that angle later, but right now I have to get to that meeting, and I want to show this to Ed."

At Ed's office the receptionist greeted Danny and sent him right inside. Ed sat in the conference area, flanked by Charles Hooper on one side and Heinrich Hartung on the other. None of the men looked especially cheerful, and the pleasant mood Danny had enjoyed after talking to Mike had evaporated when Greg showed him what he'd found, so he fit right in. Outside Ed's window, the setting sun—not electric lighting—had turned the Las Vegas sky peach and rose colors. Once the sun had set completely, the city's lights would take over the skyline.

"We've been talking about tomorrow's speech," Ed said when Danny sat.

"I figured."

"We think we've got a pretty good handle on things. Mr. Hooper and Herr Hartung have had some disagreements about procedure, but I think we're all satisfied with the arrangements now."

"Ed here did some arm twisting," Hooper said. "The kind he's famous for in the community."

Danny knew he meant the intelligence community. He held up the disc. "He's good at that. But before we shake hands and call it a night, gentlemen, you're going to want to see what's on this. Can I use your desktop, Ed?"

"Go ahead. What've you got, Danny?"

Danny described what Greg had found, then swiveled Ed's desktop monitor around so the men in the conference area could view it. He played the animation a couple of times, and they sat silently through it until he stopped it after the second run.

"So you think that's a schematic for an assassination attempt?" Hooper asked.

"It ain't a Disney movie," Ed said.

"That's my guess," Danny said, ignoring Ed's commentary. "An assassination attempt followed by what looks like a very bloody escape plan."

"So it would appear," Hartung said. His bulk filled the big chair, and it groaned as he changed positions, crossing one leg over his knee. "Of course, it could be many other things as well."

"It could be," Danny agreed. "I can't think of any, but it's possible, of course. As Greg pointed out, though, the dimensions of the space in the video match pretty closely to the ballroom where Herr Aickmann will be speaking."

"It's not the most sophisticated setup I've ever seen," Hooper pointed out. "But if people are willing to sacrifice themselves to make it work, it'd be hard to stop."

"Except that now we know about it," Ed said. "Which means we know what to watch out for."

"One thing bothers me about that, Ed," Danny said. "It's so crude, so bold, that it almost seems like they must know something we don't. They have somebody on the inside, or there's some other element we haven't put together yet."

"I'm with McCoy," Hooper said. "Nobody could expect to get that many weapons so close to Klaus Aickmann unless they had an angle."

"Well, now we've seen the plan," Ed said. He ruled the meeting like a CEO, and the other two men, both important in their own rights, deferred to him. "We don't know if it's a real plan or not, but we know that it's at the very least a potential threat. And here at the Montecito we take potential threats seriously."

"That's right," Danny agreed.

"Which means," Ed continued, with a meaningful glance at Danny, "that Danny here will work up a new plan to counter this new threat, and present it first thing in the morning."

Danny looked away from Ed and out the window. The sky had gone from rose to the pale gray that it always took on over the city—reflected light from millions of bulbs and miles of neon that never allowed the city to reach full black. Since he knew that tomorrow would be a busy day, he had hoped for a relaxing dinner, followed by enjoying the night's MuzikMafia concert.

So much for that, he thought.

"Very well," Hartung said. "We will review Mr. McCoy's concept as soon as it is ready."

"One thing," Ed put in. "Time's getting short here. Whatever Danny comes up with will be the best plan he can put together in the time we have, utilizing the combined resources of our team and both of yours. But there's not going to be a lot of time for bickering and jockeying for position. We all have to put that nonsense behind us and just do the damn job."

Charles Hooper interlocked his fingers behind his head and stretched in his seat. "Why beat around the bush, Ed? Just tell us how you really feel."

9

Delinda rushed through Mystique to the restaurant's hostess desk. Her regular hostess was out sick. She had assigned Tyra, one of her best waitresses, to the hostess station, but then it turned out that she needed Tyra to fill in for Suzie, who had taken off early because of a family emergency. The upshot was that throughout the evening, Delinda and Tyra had been taking turns seating customers. As the dinner hour wore down, traffic at the hostess station had slowed. Tables turned over more slowly later in the evening, as those enjoying their meals tended to linger. Of course, Las Vegas was a twenty-four-hour city, so people got hungry and dined on their own schedules, and Delinda was happy to seat them until the kitchen had closed.

But without a steady stream of customers, she had allowed herself a few minutes to rest in the kitchen, until Kelly, stopping to grab an order, said, "Delinda, there's a party of three waiting to be seated."

Delinda despised making people wait for tables— unless it was because they were lined up to get in. Then she delighted in it, because everyone who passed by the line realized that they too should have dinner at Mystique. When tables stood empty and there were behinds waiting to fill them, however, she got upset. The fact that this time the wait had been her own fault didn't help one bit.

"I'm so sorry for your wait," she said when she reached the desk. "Three of you tonight?"

"No problem, darlin'," the man said. He was in his seventies, Delinda judged, with a head of thick white hair and a face as lined as the tread of a new radial tire. He had adopted the disco look sometime in the seventies and clung to it still. His open shirt—a poly-rayon blend, she guessed: Delinda could detect the stench of polyester a mile away—displayed an abundance of saggy chest, gold chains, and kinked white hairs, some of which interlaced with the links of the chains. The shirt was tucked into tight white pants, which he wore with platform shoes of a style Delinda hadn't seen in years outside of a sketch comedy show on TV.

Delinda's first response was repulsion, but obviously not everyone felt the same way—or maybe he had hidden charms that outweighed the generally horrible fashion sense. Since the outfit didn't leave much to her imagination, she guessed that any hidden charms were kept in his bank account. Two women accompanied him, both strippers, she guessed, or women who—from the looks of the manufactured, balloon-size breasts on prominent display—could have chosen that profession if they so desired. One was a bleached blonde, the other a dusky brunette, and the amount of fabric covering the two of them together might have made a complete dress for a more conservative person. But this was Las Vegas, after all, and Delinda tried not to judge other people based on how they looked or the company they kept, only on how much they were willing to spend at her restaurants.

"Thanks for understanding," she said as she grabbed up menus and started walking toward their table. She glanced over her shoulder as she did. "Are you all having a good night?"

"I'm up a little," the man said.

"But not as much as he's going to be," the blonde added. Her brunette friend found that hilarious. Delinda graced it with a smile but decided she didn't want any further detail. "Here's your table," she said. "And Tyra will be right with you. I hope you enjoy your meal."

"You can count on that, honey," the man called to Delinda's departing form.

She had just made it back to the hostess station when Mary passed through the front door, coming toward her with a pensive expression. "Oh, Mary," Delinda said. "I meant to find you earlier, but then I got too busy to track you down."

"Well, I'm here now," Mary said. "But I think I might need the teensiest favor?"

"Sure, name it."

"Remember Ezra, the chuck wagon cook I told you about? He's really the most adorable old guy."

"Not like the Hef wannabe I just seated?"

Mary looked toward the table Delinda indicated and shook her head. "No. Not at all like that. It's just that he's making some demands. A lot of demands, really. And I'm not so much the food service girl, you know? So I don't know if he's being reasonable or if he's just being cranky for the sake of upholding some chuck wagon crankiness tradition."

"I don't mean to rush you, Mary, but I'm a little short-handed tonight and there's a lot going on. What is it you want?"

"I was wondering if maybe Wolfgang could go out there with me in the morning," Mary said. Delinda could tell that she felt uncomfortable even making the request. "Just to kind of size up the situation and let me know what's okay and what's, I guess, overboard."

Delinda hesitated for just a second. Mary was her friend, and she didn't want to laugh in her face. "Mary, I can't even quite imagine Wolfgang's reaction if I asked him to do that. I mean, he's a great guy and all. But he's a serious chef, and with a new restaurant to get off the ground, he's crazy busy."

A hurt look flitted across Mary's face, but it vanished quickly. "What about Gunther? Will he be around in the morning?"

"I'll see what I can do, Mary. Maybe I can get Chef Lester from the buffet to help you out."

"Anything, Delinda. I'm begging here." She started to turn away, then stopped. "Are you going to be able to get away for the concert?"

"Oh yeah," Delinda said. "I'm there. Oh, and before I forget, in the morning—when you're not wrasslin' with Cookie out there—"

"Ezra."

"Whatever. Anyway, you have to come with me to the exhibit hall. There's a picture that I'm dying for you to see. And a hunky cowpoke you have to meet."

"A hunky cowpoke. Gotta like the sound of that," Mary said. "I'll see you at the concert!"

Watching Mary walk away, Delinda thought she would never meet a nicer woman as long as she lived.

She almost felt like someone had to watch over her. But then again, maybe somebody already did that.

Nobody that sweet could survive as long as Mary had without a little help.

Lost in thought as she was, Danny almost didn't recognize the hot brunette talking to Garrick Flynn as Samantha Marquez. He saw Flynn leaning on one of the columns near the elevators, looking like he was chatting up some willing woman in tight pants and a skimpy top. It wasn't until he had taken a few more steps and the angle changed that he realized the woman was Sam.

There was nothing necessarily wrong with it, and a number of possible explanations, Danny knew. Maybe Flynn knew Sam worked for the Montecito and was trying to get her impression of a guest he suspected. Maybe it was what it looked like—Flynn was an available man, in town on business, and he was looking for some company from a beautiful woman. Nothing necessarily sinister about it.

But Danny felt big-brotherly toward Sam. Sometimes. Now, watching her nodding and smiling and laughing at whatever Flynn was saying, was one of those times.

Then Flynn noticed Danny watching. He caught Danny's eye, gave the briefest of nods, and excused himself, almost leaping into an elevator just as it closed. Sam turned around, as if looking for whatever had chased him off, and saw Danny.

Danny closed the distance between them. "Hey, Sam."

"Hi, Danny. What's going on?"

"I couldn't help noticing you talking to that guy Flynn. He works for the German security outfit."

"I know," Sam said with an odd smile. "You weren't spying on us, were you?"

"Me? No, no. Just happened to come along and saw you there."

"There's not something wrong with that, is there? He seems like a nice guy. Cute too."

"I guess," Danny said. "I was just wondering what you were talking about."

"What did you think we were talking about?" Sam had a way of speaking in an arched tone that made a man sorry he had ever said a word, and he could hear it coming fast.

"I thought maybe he was hitting on you."

"And is there anything about me that would make you think I'm not used to that?"

Time for damage control. "No," Danny said with an uneasy laugh. "I'm sure you get hit on all the time."

"So I look easy to you?"

"That's not what I said, Sam."

"You didn't have to say it. Is that what you meant?"

Danny put his hands up as if she might hit him. "No."

"I'm perfectly capable of handling myself when someone's hitting on me," she said. "In case you were worried about that."

"I'm sure you are."

"So there's nothing to worry about, right?"

"I wasn't worried, Sam. Just curious."

"Okay, Danny. Whatever." She turned on her heel, about to walk off and leave him feeling like an idiot. She had a knack for that too.

"Sam?"

She stopped, eyeing him over her shoulder.

"What were you talking about?"

Her smile made her eyes seem to twinkle. "He was hitting on me."

"Really?"

"No, I'm kidding. He was asking me about Wolf-gang's." Suddenly her expression turned serious. "You don't think I've lost it, do you?"

"Lost it?"

"My sex appeal, Danny. Why didn't he hit on me?"

"I don't know, Sam. You haven't lost it, believe me."

She twinkled again. "Danny, you've got to learn how to tell when someone's kidding."

"There will never be peace on Earth, as it is so often phrased," Heinrich Hartung said. Beth Newton's re-action surprised him; although he barely knew the woman, he had thought she was a hardened security professional. Yet when he spoke she looked crest-fallen, her thin lips parting, nostrils flaring, her dark eyes going wide and liquid. "Not that there will not be peaceful periods," he quickly clarified. "Or even lasting peace between former antagonists. But a per-manent, global peace? Never."

Beth had spotted him sitting at a table by himself,

lingering over a dinner from the Montecito's buffet, and had politely asked if she could join him. Although he had enjoyed the few moments of solitude—and marveled at the sheer number of food options the buffet offered—he was also happy to get acquainted with the Olympic champion who now worked for the American Secret Service. She was pleasantly attractive and fit, after all, with an athletic build and neat blond hair. Her eyes, of a brown so dark they looked almost black, were a startling contrast with her pale skin and light hair, and Hartung realized he kept stealing glances at her, not out of lust—he was, after all, old enough to be her grandfather—but just from the sheer pleasure of viewing such a unique woman, like a work of art rarely displayed in public.

"But then what are we all working for?" she asked. Somehow their conversation had veered quickly from casual discussion of their host city and the splendors of buffet fare to geopolitics and Klaus Aickmann's upcoming speech. "Isn't an enduring peace in the best interests of everyone?"

Hartung paused, a forkful of salmon almost to his mouth. "It would seem that way, wouldn't it? But of course it is not. When I say that peace is impossible, I don't mean traditional conflicts of state against state. It is remotely possible that we won't see any more of those, at least in the near to intermediate future. Instead, we will see, as we always have, conflicts of smaller groups, stateless groups—against each other and against existing nations."

He put the salmon in his mouth, chewed rapidly,

and continued. "Your country, of course, is young and optimistic—although recently it seems that your optimism has been tempered by an almost European sense of despair, and that instead of exporting hope around the world you export gloom and fear. And you are young, as well. But Germany is old." Hartung chuckled. "And I am old. I have seen much, I'm afraid, and if I speak with a certain pedantry, please forgive me, Miss Newton. The curse of age is that we believe we must be right all the time."

Beth smiled politely and speared an asparagus stalk with her own fork. Hartung went on. "Too many times in our history we have seen that people can be led in directions that would seem to be contrary to their own best interests. Seventy years ago, more or less, we allowed ancient hatreds and prejudices to be stoked by a madman, and we all know how that turned out. Not well for anyone, eh?"

"Sounds about right," Beth said.

"Since that time, of course, Germany has not been an antagonist against any other sovereign nation, except in the very limited sense of supporting multinational coalitions taking on bad actors. But we have not been exempt from conflict. Far from it. In some ways we seem to have been at the forefront of the modern approach to warfare. The seventies saw, for us, the Baader-Meinhof terrorist gang and the tragedy at the Munich Olympics. Once again, we saw up close the terrible sorrow that conflict can bring, but while this conflict had a different face, it was still simply ancient hatreds flaring up in new ways. Now, of course, the United States and several

other nations have felt firsthand the pain of these
sorts of attacks, and your response, as might be expected, has been a dramatic change in your national
mood.

"This, I think, is part of why Herr Aickmann loves
Las Vegas so much. As do I, and many other Euro-
peans. We may seem to you like a dour group, but we
have always loved that American optimism I mentioned. The can-do spirit."

"The American Dream," Beth said.

"Exactly. Americans have always believed, I think,
that they can reinvent themselves. It explains your
westward expansion, no? One can move to a new
place, traditionally to the west of the last place, and
start over. Life can always be improved upon. One's
status quo is always subject to change, to elevation.
In Las Vegas this still holds true, more, I believe, than
in some other parts of your country."

"Probably, yeah," Beth admitted. "The big jackpot
is always possible here, right? Sudden wealth that
can change your life. And even for people who aren't
gamblers, Las Vegas has been growing so steadily that
people can leave behind dead-end jobs in other
places, come here, and find new careers and new
lives."

"Precisely my point," Hartung said. "Once, your
entire country was that way, moving always to the
west. The weight of history—of *having* a history, in
fact—has perhaps caught up with you. Now the rich
get richer, the poor grow ever poorer, the middle class
is squeezed, and as a result the national mood becomes ever more European. You need Las Vegas, if

only to remind yourselves of what you once repre-
sented and to what, if you try, you may still aspire."

Realizing that he had dominated the conversation
to excess, he forked some garlic mashed potatoes into
his mouth, chasing them down with a swallow of
mediocre beer. Germany could make many things
well, and excellent beer was one of its most illustri-
ous accomplishments. By the time even good German beer was bottled and shipped and refrigerated
and sold in the States, however, it had lost a good
deal of its flavor.

Perhaps depressed by his view of her country, or
otherwise anxious to change the subject, Beth Newton did so, talking about things she enjoyed in Las
Vegas away from the casinos. Hartung let her, happy
to watch her animated face as she described the roller
coaster at New York, New York, indoor skydiving,
and the natural beauty of the Red Rock Canyon area,
outside the city.

Finally Beth finished her meal and excused herself, but Hartung remained in the restaurant, thinking that perhaps he would return to the buffet line
for dessert and coffee. He sipped at his pale imitation
of real German beer and allowed his mind to wander
back to the earlier conversation, and to the fears that
had prompted it.

He had spent years running Klaus Aickmann's security operation. There had been threats, of course.
One didn't achieve Aickmann's position in the world
without making enemies, some powerful and some
not so. It took no power to load a gun and point it,
though, and a lone, deranged assassin was not vul-

nerable, as were organizations, to infiltration and in-
telligence-gathering operations.

Never in those years, however, had he been as
worried as he was right now. The CD that showed
what appeared to be a plan of attack was unsettling.
Another possibility—that the CD was a ruse, meant
to distract them from the real attack—he found
equally troubling.

Would Aickmann's enemies strike at him here?
And why not? In Europe, his assassination would
rock the continent. In Las Vegas, it would rock the
world.

Hartung had to be prepared for a major terrorist
incident. He was not alone—the Secret Service had
people on the scene, as did the Montecito itself. But
he didn't know those people. He believed he could
trust them, but only to a point.

In the end, it would be up to him and his group to
protect Herr Aickmann from whatever threat might
materialize here. Until that threat did materialize, he
had to remain alert, ready to see its first inklings
when they appeared.

To that end, he made a decision. Strong coffee, not
another weak beer.

He returned to the buffet line to see what dessert
options might be available to go with it.

10

The ringing of Mike's phone drew his attention away from the computer screen. "Hello?" he answered, still distracted, figuring it would just be Linda Lou Snead again.

"Mike, you're still working?"

Mike allowed himself a smile as he pictured Sarasvati Kumar, the casino's drop-dead gorgeous Indian statistician, who kept the executive team apprised of which way the numbers were moving at any given moment. As with other members of the management group, Ed had given her more and more responsibility as she proved her abilities. Which was fine with Mike, because the more time she spent out of her own office, the more he got to see and interact with her. He imagined her big brown eyes looking into his, her delicate hands touching his face, and then he blinked and stopped imagining so he could concentrate on what she said. "Yeah, Sarasvati. Burning the old midnight oil, trying to track down this missing equine joy juice."

"I'm sorry, Mike. Joy juice?"

Mike gave himself a mental slap in the face. "I'll explain later. What's up?"

"I wanted to see if you are still intending to come to the concert tonight."

The concert. Big and Rich, Cowboy Troy, and Gretchen Wilson. It had entirely slipped his mind. The casino would be rocking for sure. "If I can, definitely. Wouldn't want to miss that lineup." Big and Rich and Cowboy Troy had played a dynamite set for the new Montecito's grand opening, but Gretchen Wilson had never appeared onstage here.

"I'll be there too," Sarasvati promised. "I hope I see you there. Good luck with your . . . your search."

"Thanks," Mike said. He dropped the phone back into his pocket and pushed away a lingering afterimage of Sarasvati's lush curves. The computer screen waited, and Linda Lou Snead, Leroy's wife, had been bugging him almost every hour for progress reports.

Since he hadn't been lucky enough to spot someone stealing the vial on the digital playback, he had decided on a different approach. At the level of Cavanaugh's Virtue, he figured, only a handful of quarter horse breeders operated. Another, larger handful probably hoped to attain that level, or had specific programs under way that they expected would take them there. The likeliest suspects would come from this second group—those with less money and more desperation—but he couldn't afford to discount the first batch. And of course, the possibility remained that the prize horse's seed hadn't been stolen for financial gain at all, but instead to humiliate Snead or to destroy his business. If that was the case, then the perp was probably a peer and competitor.

A third group—breeders who might want to ramp up their stables and reputations but so far had shown no signs of producing championship animals—he decided to write off altogether. Any of those people, coming up out of nowhere with a horse that approached Cavanaugh's Virtue's abilities after the news of the theft broke, would be automatically suspect. Of course, it was possible that the thief would sell the semen somewhere offshore, where such suspicions would be lessened or ignored, but he would work that angle later if he had to. That opened up a whole new, impossibly vast range of possibilities, and if he started in on that, he'd never get anywhere.

Mike had spent the last couple of hours online, amassing all the data he could on the horse-breeding business. Which breeders had raised champions, which ones had realistic ambitions in that direction, and most significant, which ones combined both traits to become competitive threats to Snead. He had tentatively ruled out some who hadn't come to the Stampede at all—tentatively, because they might have sent agents to do their dirty work for them, although he believed anyone involved with this crime would have wanted to handle it personally. More than a million dollars' worth of anything could prove awfully tempting, so trusting hired hands and flunkies with it seemed unlikely.

His winnowing had left nine people, in the first and second groups, who were attending the convention and who might stand to profit from the theft in a big way. Five came from group two, those who hadn't quite cracked the major leagues but who had come close and could reasonably be expected to produce winners down the line. Any of these would have to show the lineage of champions they bred, but

Mike guessed that such documents could be faked if necessary. Three were from group one, competitors of Snead's at about the same level of accomplishment. The last was a breeder from South Africa who had fielded some disappointing animals along with a couple of potential winners, but who had yet to collect any major purses.

The Montecito's surveillance room never slept. Tonight a crew of six observed the bank of monitors and checked in regularly with security guards who walked the casino floor and guest floors. The surveillance job required the diligent attention of an air-traffic controller, combined with the gut instincts of a veteran cop. Most who did it well—and Danny didn't put up with those who didn't—had backgrounds in law enforcement, the military, or both. The task could also involve long, dull hours with little action beyond switching from camera to camera, so adventure junkies tended to burn out fast, if they managed to get hired in the first place.

A surveillance operator named Larry passed by Mike's desk carrying a cup of coffee, on his way back to his station after a scheduled break. "You look like you're working it pretty hard, Mike. Can I grab you a cup of joe or something?"

"Thanks, Larry, I'm good."

"Cool. What's cooking?"

Mike scooted his chair back from the desk, taking advantage of the interruption to try to restore some circulation to his limbs. He shook his arms from his shoulders as he answered. "Somebody stole a jar of horsey baby paste from a dealer in the hall."

Larry had been about to take a sip of coffee, but he caught himself, moved the cup from his lips. "Did you say 'baby paste'?"

Mike gave a weary nod. No matter what he called the stolen substance, somebody complained. "Horse semen, Larry. Believe it or not, it's a big deal."

"I know," Larry said. "It's just—that's a disgusting way to put it."

"Sorry, dude."

"Yeah, no prob, Mike. Later." Larry walked back toward his own station, shaking his head sadly as he went.

This is the worst, Mike thought. *The worst.*

Still, he needed to flex his legs a bit. Danny was still working in his office, so Mike, bracing himself for whatever cracks his friend might make, went in.

"I thought you had plans tonight," Mike said as he entered, flopping into a chair.

"I did too," Danny replied. "But you know, stuff happens."

"Tell me about it."

Danny tossed a smirk. "And I don't mean horse stuff."

"You can leave that alone anytime, Danny. What's going on?"

"It's this Aickmann business," Danny told him. "I thought we were ready to go, but there's been a new twist. Now there's a semicredible threat, which means I have to come up with an entirely new plan to counter it." He beckoned Mike behind his desk and showed him a crude digital animation.

"And you think this is a diagram for a hit?" Mike

asked when it finished. "The crossfire is automatic weapons spray to cover an escape?"

"We think it might be. We have to act as if we believe it."

"That would be suicide."

"For some of them, yeah," Danny said. "But some would probably get away, if it played out like it shows here."

"Could be," Mike said. "Where did it come from?"

"One of Greg's guys found it on the floor, stuck in between some slots."

"Lucky find."

"I'd say so. How common is the kind of software that someone could use to make this?"

Mike grinned. Now Danny was speaking his language. "Something that simple? Probably done in Flash animation. There are plenty of programs that could have made that, but none of the others are so widely used. Flash has been around since—"

Danny raised a forestalling hand. "Never mind, Mike. I don't have time for the lesson. Just that it's common, that's all I need to know."

"It's common. Real common. That's not gonna help you narrow down its origins, Danny."

"Okay, thanks."

Feeling dismissed, Mike stuck his hands in his pockets. "Well, I guess I'll get back to my missing horse puckey."

"That's not what horse puckey is."

"Okay," Mike admitted. "I guess that one was a stretch."

"And I hope you don't call it that in front of the

women," Danny said. "That could be construed as creating a hostile work environment, you know?"

"Danny, my friend. It's a bottle of ball-bearing oil from a champion racehorse who spent the last, happiest years of his life injecting it into female horses the old-fashioned way. I'm trying to be sensitive to people's feelings, but no euphemism in the English language is going to change that fact."

"I guess you're right, Mike. Good luck."

Mike wandered back to his waiting computer, muttering to himself. "He guesses I'm right. He *guesses.*"

He sat down, scooted his chair back in, and went back to reviewing the footage of his nine suspects, trying to follow their every move since the last time Leroy Snead knew where his most prized possession had been.

This is so much the worst.

Charles Hooper hated country music of any sort, so while most of the members of his team not currently on duty went to the concert, he sat in the Opus bar nursing an apple martini—shaken, not stirred, James Bond–style, except of course for the apple part.

It wasn't just country music that he hated. He was in his late forties, a child of the rock generation, but seemed to have inherited his father's musical tastes. He was not, in general, the passionate sort, he knew, but he had a few secret passions, including spy fiction, root beer floats, fast driving, and big-band music. His wife, whose musical tastes had cemented around eighties hair bands, kept A Flock of Seagulls

CDs in her Camry, while he kept Glenn Miller and Tommy Dorsey and Les Brown in his. At home, they stuck to TV or talk radio just to avoid conflict.

Hooper supposed it was his old-fashioned leanings that had sent him into government service in the first place, in days when most of his classmates had been more interested in jobs on Wall Street or Madison Avenue. He had gone into the military, worked his way up, been tapped for intelligence work, and when he got out after his third hitch, it was to a post with the National Security Agency, where he had put in nine years before shifting to Treasury and the Secret Service. Along the way he had married twice, the last time to the former Kelly Cristol, had the requisite two kids, and bought a house in McLean, Virginia, with a quarter acre of wooded lot and a yard that had to be mowed once a week.

He had half expected his life to end in a Central American jungle, a rain-swept Serbian alleyway, or a presidential motorcade, but he had survived all of those assignments, and the ones he tended to be given now were more like the current one. Babysitting jobs, for the most part. Except this one showed promise of becoming much more than that. If the disc the Montecito's security people had found was genuine, then his life might end in a spray of automatic-weapon fire in a Las Vegas ballroom—a somewhat absurd and surprising change from his earlier expectations. That was the thing about life, he guessed. Anytime you thought you knew for certain what you'd see around the corner, you were likely to be wrong.

In the midst of another sip of martini, Hooper felt a presence close to his left arm. Someone small and light on her feet, or he would have noticed her approach sooner, perhaps reflected in the angle of the martini glass. Because a cloud of warm, woody perfume enveloped him, overwhelming the crisp, fruity aroma of his drink, he knew she was female. The scent was Niki de Saint Phalle, Hooper guessed, but he wasn't as expert on fragrances as he had once been, and more women wore Niki in the daylight hours than at night.

He swiveled slowly on his stool, setting the martini glass down.

A woman leaned toward him from her own stool. She had piled a mass of lustrous brown hair on her head, with a few strands dropping down to frame a pretty face so casually that they had to be entirely intentional. Her brown eyes were luminous and huge, but with lines at the corners that he guessed, given her relative youth, indicated that she was a longtime smoker. She parted thin lips, which lipstick didn't quite succeed in giving more weight to, in a friendly smile.

"I'm Angela," she said.

"Charles." He had always been Charles, even as a young boy. Maybe if he'd been Chuck, or even Charlie, he sometimes thought, he wouldn't wrestle with depression, with those black moods that sometimes gripped him in the dead of night, making his heart race and his breathing shallow. Charles was not an easygoing name, and a heavy weight to hang on a small child.

She extended a slender hand with rings on every finger. He shook it gently, hoping he didn't cut himself. "Pleased to meet you, Charles." She continued leaning toward him, her blouse gapping open. He didn't peer down the gap. Her body was thin, almost girlish, and he wondered if she was an addict. "What are you up to tonight?"

He tapped the stem of his martini glass. "Just having a quiet drink."

"Want some company? A quiet drink sounds nice to me right now."

Hooper waved the bartender over. "Lady wants a drink," he said when she arrived.

"Hi, Erika," Angela said. "Rum and Coke?"

"Angela." Erika glanced at Hooper, who nodded his agreement to pay for the drink. Without further comment, she moved off to mix it.

"You staying at the Montecito?" Angela asked.

"Yes."

"By yourself?"

He knew she was asking if he had come with his family, or if he was sharing a room with friends. "I'm here with some business associates," he said.

"Where are they?"

"At that concert."

"So you're here all by yourself."

Erika brought Angela's drink, set it down. "Run a tab?" she asked.

"No, I'm not staying," Hooper replied. He carried a separate wallet, but he also kept five twenties folded up in his leather badge case, behind his Treasury Department ID card. He drew that from his jacket pocket, opened it, and removed one of the twenties. Sliding it across the bar toward Erika, he said, "There you go, Erika, thanks."

She thanked him in return and stepped away.

Hooper left the badge visible until he knew, by a stiffening of her muscles and the rushed downing of her sweet drink, that Angela had seen it. Then he folded the case and tucked it away.

"Thanks for the drink," she said. "I hope you have a great night, Charles."

She slid from the stool and clip-clopped away as fast as her stiletto heels would carry her. Erika returned to pick up the empty glass and ran a bar rag across the ring it left on the polished wood. "That was choice," she said, grinning at Hooper.

"The no-rejection rejection," he said. "One of my specialties." He drained off the last few drops of his martini and shoved the glass toward Erika. "Thanks again. Good night."

Erika bade him good night, and as Hooper left the bar, he saw that she was still smiling.

So, in fact, was he.

That had been the closest to fun he'd had all day.

11

The house was, as expected, rocking.

Cowboy Troy had opened the show with his wild country rap performance, then Big Kenny and John Rich did a set featuring incredibly tight vocals and a driving beat. Gretchen Wilson took the stage after them for her first-ever Montecito appearance. After a phenomenal set that closed on "Redneck Woman," the stage went dark. A couple of minutes later, to thunderous applause, the lights came up again with Troy, Big, Rich, and Gretchen all onstage together with their bands. They launched into "Here for the Party" and everyone in the room leapt to their feet. The place smelled like perspiration and perfume, tinged with booze, tobacco, and excitement. All three acts had played together for more than thirty minutes so far and showed no sign of slowing down. Danny thought the show might just go on all night.

He only wished he could really enjoy it.

He had worked until curtain time on his response to the disc Greg's man had found. In principle, the hit seemed like an easy enough plan to defend against. Simple tactics often worked against simple attacks, so that's what he tried first. The trouble was, everything he came up with left some huge questions unanswered.

He couldn't figure out a way around the inescapable

conclusion, which he and Greg had both reached independently and everyone else seemed to agree with, that nobody would try such a blatant, simplistic offense unless they had some guarantee of getting around the anticipated security constraints. Since those constraints would obviously include metal detectors, the potential attackers must believe they had a way to get their weapons past those detectors and into the ballroom. Until Danny knew how they meant to do that, all of his defensive measures could only be half formed, guesses made on insufficient data. Aickmann, he had been informed, would not agree to cancel the speech or to speak from behind a bulletproof screen, which left Danny with a serious problem.

He watched Mary, Delinda, and Sam dancing to the blaring music. Sarasvati stood near them, looking about expectantly—probably for Mike, Danny suspected. The mutual attraction between the two of them seemed to have heated up lately. Even wheelchair-bound Mitch rocked out, moving his upper body and pulling spins and wheelies on the floor. Danny wanted to join them, to give himself over to the music. That would require shutting down the part of his mind obsessing over the Aickmann situation, however, and he couldn't make that happen.

Finally he walked out of the concert, happy to see that it continued to rage even though he couldn't stay. He had been given contact information and a schedule for the Secret Service team and for all of Heinrich Hartung's operatives. Knowing he would want their input and assistance, he picked two who were on duty at the moment and called them.

Apparently he would have no peace until this was figured out.

If nothing else, he could make sure they didn't either.

"You did what, Leroy?"

She stood before him, hands on her wide hips—the weight she had put on these last few years had swelled her womanly parts, tightening her skin like a summer sausage—and a furious scowl twisted her pretty features. Her blond hair seemed to have been flattened a little, during the day, but that sometimes happened when she wore her red cowgirl hat. She would tease it up again in the morning, he figured. Linda Lou was as proud of her hair as if it alone had been responsible for the Miss Beakins Oil Filter pageant she had won in her teens, and in fact she kept the comb she had used that day in a case at home, along with the sash and tiara in which she had strutted down the runway on her victory walk.

As Snead had feared, Linda Lou exploded when he told her about the oil deal that went south. He didn't feel like he had much choice, though. If they couldn't recover the stolen vial, then the company's finances—and with them, the Snead family's personal fortunes—were on the line in a serious way.

A lawsuit could potentially recover some of the lost revenue. If he and his lawyers played their hands right, they might even get more out of it than the auction would bring, if only because the Montecito would settle for a significant sum in order to keep the theft out of the newspapers. But a lawsuit, or even settlement negotiations, could drag out for months. Snead Enterprises wouldn't have months remaining without the auction income. Snead wasn't sure he could hold off their creditors for weeks, much less months.

"Look, Linda Lou," Snead said. He had broken into the Beam after all and had brought the bottle up to their room with him. Now he sucked down a quick snort and slammed his glass down on the polished wooden table. "I did it because we were hurting financially, and we needed some cash coming in from somewhere. You know Todd Albert. He's never steered us wrong before, so I trusted him."

Linda Lou sat down on the edge of the bed, and the stern expression on her face collapsed into a fit of giggles. She rolled backward, pounding her fists against her heavy thighs as she laughed. Snead poured more of the Jim Beam into his bathroom glass, watching and wondering what had possessed her. If there was something funny about this whole situation, he had missed it, and he wouldn't mind being let in on the joke.

Finally she turned on the big bed, put her elbows against its surface, and rested her head on folded hands. "Do you really think I don't pay attention to the books, Leroy? You do remember who you're married to, right? I ain't some ditz who can't read a column of numbers and see what makes sense and what don't."

"You . . . you knew?" he asked. He put a hand on the table to steady himself. Although his chair had not actually tipped forward or spun around on its axis, he felt like it had. Maybe it was just the Beam hitting him hard, but he didn't think so. "Why didn't you say anything?"

"Because I wanted to know when you'd get around to tellin' me, sweetheart." He detected just a hint of condescension in her voice. Maybe more than a hint, but at the moment he didn't entirely trust his own judgment. "I figured sooner or later you'd have to, so I thought, why spoil my fun? I guess you were hoping tomorrow's auction would put all those worries behind us, right?"

Snead nodded. "That was pretty much the plan." He believed he was balanced enough now to make a grab for the glass, and did. "I knew we could get enough for Cavanaugh's Virtue's seed to more than make up for those losses."

"But now that's gone too."

"You can't put that on me, Linda Lou," he said.

"You were the one who didn't want to keep it in the hotel safe. 'It'll be fine in the booth,' that's what you said."

"I wanted potential bidders to be able to see it!" Snead reminded her. "It's always easier to bid on something you've laid eyes on."

"It was a vial, Leroy," Linda Lou said, her exasperation clear as day. "It could have been full of ranch dressing or anything else. Nobody asked to sample it, did they?"

"No," Snead admitted. "No, they didn't do that."

"Then the real stuff could have been locked up safe. But that wasn't good enough for you. And now it's gone, and our chance at a million bucks right along with it."

"Maybe it'll still turn up."

"Sure, maybe," she agreed. "And maybe Cavanaugh's Virtue will come back from the dead and win some more races. I've been keeping on top of that hotel detective or whatever he is, Mike Cannon. You know what he has so far? Diddly-squat."

"It hasn't even been a day, Linda Lou."

"And the trail gets colder with every hour that goes by. I know you watch TV, Leroy, you ought to know that."

"They got cameras everywhere, Linda Lou."

"Have you even talked to him? He said the cameras didn't show anything. You'd have been better off keeping the vial right out in the open instead of inside the trailer. They don't have a camera inside your trailer, do they? And the way you set up the trailer, you blocked the camera that is there from seeing the doorway."

Snead downed the rest of the glass. She was right, he couldn't deny that. All the way down the line, he had screwed things up. It had all been Cavanaugh's Virtue's fault for getting that infection and dying in the first place—nothing Snead could have done would have prevented that. But after that, he had made one bad move after another. What was the saying? Scared money never wins.

The money he had thrown at that oil deal had been scared half to death.

Now that he was closing in on desperate, he had thought about playing the quarter slots or video poker and praying for a big jackpot.

That, Snead knew, was the thinking of a loser, a man who'd had it all and thrown it away. No, small-time gambling wouldn't help him save his business or his marriage.

He needed something else, some other big score.

He didn't know yet what it would be, but he had to figure it out soon.

He looked at the glaze of contempt on his wife's face and poured another drink.

"Looking for someone, Sarasvati?" Sam asked, shouting to be heard over the raucous music.

Sarasvati had been turning in a slow circle, eyes skimming over the crowd, as if watching a bird in flight. Sam was pretty sure she knew the answer to the question before she asked it, and Sarasvati's answer confirmed her guess. "I thought that perhaps Mike might come down," she said. "He told me that he planned to."

"Mike?" Delinda broke in. "Last I heard he was too busy to do anything."

"I heard he had some dinner sent up to his office," Mary added. "Because he couldn't take the time to run out and eat."

"I know he's busy," Sarasvati said. "Nevertheless, I hoped—"

"Don't go hoping for too much where Mike's concerned, sweetie," Sam interrupted. "I love Mike. He's the nicest guy in the world, but as long as I've known him, I haven't seen him in a relationship that lasted more than about twenty minutes."

"What about Nessa?" Mary asked, naming the casino's former pit boss, who had practically been a sister to Delinda.

"I said relationship," Sam countered. "Not puppy-eyed longing."

"Sam's right," Delinda said. A sad look always overtook her when Nessa's name came up, because Nessa had had to go into hiding to protect herself and her father. "They almost got together, but never really made it happen long enough to be called a relationship."

"I guess that's true," Mary said.

"He does still mention her sometimes," Sarasvati said. "I have wondered if he has really let go of her in his heart."

Sam let her gaze roam over Sarasvati's lush figure. Sarasvati tended to keep it under wraps, certainly more than most of the other women in Las Vegas, but she couldn't disguise it. "Honey, he's a man. Whether or not he's still pining for Nessa, he wouldn't let it get in his way if he had a chance at some of what you've got."

Sarasvati smiled shyly, casting her eyes toward the floor. "Do you really think so, Sam?"

"Definitely," Delinda said. "There's no question about that. The only question is, do you want more of a relationship than that? Nobody can really guarantee what'll happen, of course. But if you just want a fling, I'm sure that can be arranged. There hasn't been a man made yet who wouldn't be up for that."

Sarasvati looked mildly scandalized. Sam realized they had not included her in enough of their group activities for her to really understand the kind of women they were, or to learn what long experience had taught them about guys. "Surely some men—" Sarasvati began.

"She's right," Mary said, cutting her off. Of the three friends, it figured that Mary would take her side. She wasn't quite as naive as Sarasvati, but there was a romantic streak in her as wide as the Great Plains. "Not every guy would jump into bed with any woman at the drop of a hat."

"Not any woman," Delinda said.

"But there is at least one woman for every guy," Sam jumped in. "One woman whose bed they'd jump into, no questions asked. You wouldn't even need the hat-dropping part. And I have a feeling, Sarasvati, that you're one of those for Mike."

"I don't even wear hats," Sarasvati said.

"I think you can forget about the hat part," Delinda said. "There are plenty of articles of clothing you could drop that would get Mike jumping."

"But he didn't even come to the concert," Sarasvati said.

"I'm sure he would if he could," Mary assured her.

"Especially if he knew what we were talking about here," Sam added.

"He's met us, hasn't he?" Delinda asked. "Of course he knows."

"Like they're not talking about the same thing," Sam said.

"Only, I think, with less of the relationship stuff," Mary said.

"That's probably true." Sam noticed that Sarasvati had already resumed scanning the crowd. *Girl's an optimist,* she thought. *Gotta give her that.*

12

Danny bit back a yawn. He had downed two cups of coffee before the morning meeting Ed had called, but they hadn't had much effect. More people had gathered in Ed's office for this meeting than for the one last night. Heinrich Hartung had brought Stefan Zerweck, who Danny had pulled away from a winning blackjack streak the night before (after promising not to tell Hartung where he'd found his employee), and Garrick Flynn, the former ranger. Charles Hooper's contingent included Tim Turro, a veteran agent who had spent six years on the security detail for the previous president of the United States, and Beth Newton, a martial arts expert who had earned three gold medals in Olympic shooting events. Turro had been walking the hotel's perimeter when Danny reached him the night before, and he had joined Danny and Zerweck in the suite reserved for Klaus Aickmann.

Danny sat while Ed made the introductions, then rose when Ed directed the group's attention toward him. Danny had made photographic enlargements of some of the critical frames from the computer animation, and a member of his surveillance staff had combined those with actual photographs of the corresponding parts of the ballroom. The stack of poster board that resulted from their efforts leaned on an easel near the conference area in Ed's office.

"Last night," Danny began, "Tim, Stefan, and I did a walk-through of Herr Aickmann's suite. We swept it for listening devices and for hidden explosives. We didn't find anything inside—not even dust. The guest-room attendant who cleaned that place deserves a raise."

This drew a few chuckles, and Danny went on. "After that we swept the ballroom. Again, we found nothing out of the ordinary. We brought in a maintenance worker with a ladder who opened up some of the ceiling panels, in case potential attackers thought they could hide above the ceiling and drop down during Herr Aickmann's speech. We saw no evidence that any such plan has been tested or put into operation, and the panels themselves wouldn't hold a person's weight. Someone very light would have to negotiate the struts between panels, which is almost impossible. Nevertheless, before and during the speech we'll have people securing the access points through which anyone might be able to enter that area.

"Which leaves the ballroom itself." He pointed to the first sheet of poster board, showing a wide shot of the ballroom, with the podium at which Aickmann would speak front and center. Below the photo was the initial image from the video, showing the single dot and the lines that indicated walls and seating areas.

"This bottom image is from the video that I believe you've all seen by now. The top one is the ballroom in which Herr Aickmann will speak. As you can see from this picture, while simplified, the bottom image is a pretty accurate rendition of the room, and the dot is in the exact location of the podium. What this leads us to believe is that the disc we found is a credible threat, because no one would go to such lengths for some kind of gag. It also points, once again, to an inside job, because very few people know what the podium placement will be."

"Although, given the layout of the room," Turro added, "it's kind of a natural placement. It could be a reasonable supposition, not specific knowledge."

"Could be," Danny admitted. "But we have to treat it as if it is specific knowledge, because it's just not safe to assume it's a guess." He saw Ed nod at that. Ed didn't meet his gaze, but Danny knew Ed had seen him notice. He appreciated the support, however subtle, and prepared to continue.

Charles Hooper raised a hand, stopping the conversation. "You're right about the possibility that there's a participant on the inside, McCoy," he said. "Speaking to that, I'd like to get the personnel jackets of all the Montecito employees."

Ed's head swiveled toward Hooper as if it had been on a string and Hooper had yanked it. "Do you have any idea how many that is?"

"I'm sure you'll tell us, Ed."

"We have more than four thousand people on staff here," Ed said. "At peak hours, such as during Aickmann's speech, there'll be fifteen hundred actually on the premises. We've vetted them all thoroughly. And do you actually think you can go through that many files—much less running any checks of your own—in the time we have until the speech?"

"We don't know until we try," Hooper replied. "As far as your vetting, can you honestly say you've never had one surprise you? Never had to fire one for stealing or cheating or abetting someone else who was stealing or cheating?"

"No, of course not," Ed said, almost snapping the words. "It's human nature. When that many people work anywhere, a few bad eggs are going to turn up. You get rid of them when you find them. But if we had any people with terrorist leanings, I think we'd know."

"I don't believe," Heinrich Hartung interjected, "that I am willing to risk Herr Aickmann's life on the basis of you thinking you know who you have. I will also dedicate two of my people to helping Mr. Hooper's people go through the files."

Ed hesitated. Danny could read the anger on his face. He hated to be second-guessed, but Danny figured the bigger factor was that personnel files were confidential. On the other hand, anyone that Hooper and Hartung assigned to check them would be screaming through them, without time to abuse the confidentiality. All in all, this was a battle that it was probably better strategy to avoid.

As Danny expected, Ed gave in. "Fine," he said, although he didn't sound fine with it. "I'll make our records room available to your people. But let me just say that I think it's a waste of your time and resources."

Hooper and Hartung nodded their acknowledgment of his protest. "Now," Ed went on, "I think Danny still has more to show us."

With the group's attention on him again, Danny

whisked the current board away to reveal the next, a reverse angle showing the doorways at the back of the hall, again with the corresponding video image below. Seven dots showed on the animated image.

"Here we can see that these seven dots correspond very precisely with the doorways into the ballroom. From the way they appeared on the video, we believe the attackers intend to stagger their entrances. The first two come in through these doors"—he indicated two, then tapped the other doors in the photo, in sequence—"then two more through these, and finally three through these." He touched two more of the dots again. "According to the video, these two individuals will fire the shots intended to assassinate Herr Aickmann, creating a crossfire effect. Then these other three will spray the covering fire. Finally, they all make their escape, each one exiting through the door he or she entered through initially."

He moved that poster, showing a final one. This was a diagram he had worked up showing an overhead view of the whole room, with colored *X*s indicating where he planned to position security personnel.

"This one shows what I think our response to this threat should be. These *X*s represent our people—red for Montecito, blue for Secret Service, and green for Herr Hartung's group. Outside each of the seven doors, of course, we'll have the screening already agreed upon—metal detectors and manual bag searches, and matching IDs with the names on the invitations. Inside each of the seven doors, one person from each team will be stationed, armed and ready to respond in the event that the attackers somehow get through the screening with weapons. Anyone showing a weapon of any kind will be taken down by any means necessary, up to and including deadly force."

"Damn right," Ed said. "Anybody dies in the Montecito, it's going to be one of the bad guys."

"Finally," Danny added, "I'd just like to say that I think—I hope—all these extra precautions are unnecessary, thanks to the great work done by the Montecito's security team in finding the disc that tipped us off. No one would have left it where it was by accident—it had to have been intended for someone else to find, as a way of passing on the plan's details to a colleague or subordinate. Since that someone didn't find it, there's a very good chance that the whole operation will already have been called off. They know we're onto them, or at the very least they know their security has been penetrated in some way. This has to make the would-be assassins nervous about their chances of success, especially since there's so little time left to reconfigure their plan. I believe they went from overconfident to underprepared in a heartbeat, and I wouldn't be surprised to find that whoever is behind this has already checked out of the hotel—if they were staying here—and left the city."

"Let's hope you're right, McCoy," Hooper said. "We can't relax our guard, but I'm inclined to agree with your assessment."

"As am I," Stefan Zerweck said. His English was almost without accent. "As Danny pointed out, we saw nothing out of the ordinary last night. The ballroom is as secure as a room can be with a large audience present. Herr Aickmann's route into the casino, to his suite, and to the ballroom are equally secure. I believe that any attempt on his life would be made after the speech, while Herr Aickmann is enjoying himself in the casino. We have much less control of his surroundings then."

"True," Garrick Flynn agreed. "He is more vulnerable then, when we can't dictate who else is in the casino and what his movements might be. But while it's true that someone of his stature is always a target, the fact is that this kind of assassination is usually meant as a statement just as much as, or more than, a simple murder. And to really make a statement, in front of the press and the world, they'd have to hit him before or during the speech. After is anticlimactic, and hardly worth the risk, from a terrorist's point of view."

"If you can apply reasonable thinking and logic to the actions of terrorists," Hooper put in. "Which I'm not sure is the case."

"I think we can agree that the likeliest time for any attempt is during the speech, but that the threat remains high throughout his visit," Ed said. "We'll be on top of him—as I know all of you will—from the time he arrives in Las Vegas until the time his plane taxis out on his way home. I never say never, but I think it's pretty safe to say that Herr Aickmann's stay here will be unmarked by any drama greater than his speech and maybe winning a few hands of blackjack." He offered a beaming smile. "Losing a few would be fine too."

"This is how we want it as well," Hartung said, with a smile that, on his huge head, looked like a crack that had opened up. "Although perhaps without the losing."

"Thanks, Danny," Ed said. "That's good work. We can't know if they have some sort of backup plan they've put into operation, but the best we can do is stay vigilant and alert. We're still working to find out if there's anyone in the casino, or in Las Vegas, who is especially likely to pose a threat. Anything that does come up, we'll deal with."

Danny sat down again, glad that his part was over and had gone smoothly. He was pretty sure he'd covered everything, and he had worked it all out with Tim and Stefan, but you never knew when a fresh eye might spot problems that hadn't even occurred to you.

"Herr Aickmann arrives in six hours," Ed said, bringing the meeting to a close. "Everybody knows what they need to do, so let's get out there and get it done."

13

Not expecting much, Mary allowed Delinda to drag her into the exhibit hall first thing in the morning. Her ears still rang a bit from the concert the night before, and her face ached from smiling nonstop for hours as the bands played. But she had told Delinda she would check out this picture—and the cowboy who owned it—so here she was, trying her best to be bright-eyed and bushy-tailed, just in case the guy was everything Delinda claimed.

On the way in, she spotted Sam talking to a couple of cowboys. Sam, in her backless silk top, snug pants, and Jimmy Choo pumps, looked out of her element among all the Wranglers, boots, and hats. She caught Mary's eye and cut her conversation short. "Burl really wants to do it," Sam said. "So I'd personally appreciate anything you can do to make it happen. Appreciate it a lot."

She broke away from the cowboys and joined Mary and Delinda.

"What's going on?"

"I'm going to introduce Mary to a guy she'll be crazy about," Delinda said.

"So she says," Mary said. "It doesn't usually seem to work with me, though. Whenever someone tries to fix me up, I figure it's just because they like the guy themselves and want an excuse to see him again."

"Like Delinda ever needed an excuse?"

"It really is about you, Mary," Delinda promised."
You'll understand when you see the picture."

"What is it a picture of, Delinda?" she asked as
they made their way down the long aisles.

"Didn't I tell you that part?" Delinda asked. "It's you."

"Me? There's a picture of me in here?"

Delinda stopped in the middle of the aisle. She had
given up on the western look, instead wearing a cop-
pery Sheri Bodell dress with an uneven hem, tight
across the bodice and flaring at the bottom. She wore
Manolo sling-backs with it, and copper bracelets jin-
gled at her wrists. "It's not really you, apparently, unless you're like that guy who sold his soul to the devil
so he'd never age, and all his sins would show up on
a picture. Except the picture doesn't look very used
up, either, so if that's what happened, I guess you
really are just squeaky clean. Anyway, it's on a calendar from 1962. But I'd swear it's you anyway. You
just have to see it."

Mary's expectations dropped another notch lower.
"Great," she said to Sam in a low voice. "People usually misjudge who my type might be, but they're always way off when they think someone looks like
me. Which, for reasons I can't understand, happens
distressingly often. The person in the picture will
probably have reddish hair, and might even be female. If I'm lucky."

"I don't know," Sam said. "Someone told me once
I looked like that hot chick from *General Hospital,* and
I can sort of see it."

Mary ignored Sam's comment, her mind already

starting to work over the things she had to get accomplished before the big chuck wagon cookout. Not paying attention, she almost lost Delinda in the crush of people jamming a booth that contained cavalry antiques from the days of the Apache wars, but then she spotted her inside a booth across the aisle, standing beside a tall, handsome man in a taller white hat.

"This is Mary and Sam," Delinda said when they made their way into the booth. "Mary's the one I told you about. And this is . . . umm . . . who are you?"

The man tipped his hat. He looked to be in his mid-thirties, maybe, suntanned and clean-shaven. His eyes were the pale blue of summer sky, his jaw square and solid. "My name is Streeter, ladies. Some folks call me Rocket, 'cause that's how I used to shoot off a saddle bronc's back, but my given name is Will."

"Pleased to meet you, Will," Mary said, sticking out her hand. He gave it a firm shake.

"Same to you, Mary."

He shook Sam's hand as well, but his gaze seemed riveted to Mary's face with an intensity that made her feel uncomfortable. "So, Delinda said something about a picture?"

He held the stare for a moment longer, then seemed to register that she had spoken. "Oh, right. It's in the case here. I think you'll find it kind of curious." He moved behind a display case, then brought out the calendar Delinda had mentioned. "Here you go."

"Thanks." Mary took the calendar. She felt Delinda move in close behind her, looking over her right shoulder, smelling like mint and citrus.

"I told you, Mary," Delinda said, before Mary had even had a chance to examine the thing.

"Geez, she's not kidding," Sam said. "It is you."

Mary shushed them and went back to looking at it.

The back panel was a single piece of card stock. A reproduction of a painting had been glued to the top third, and individual sheets for the months were stapled below it.

Looking at the painting felt strangely like looking into a mirror.

The woman depicted wasn't her, of course. She didn't own a fringed blouse like that, or the tiny shorts—both were cute, though. She didn't have a six-shooter, either. She was pretty sure she had never sat on a rail fence in just such a cute, coquettish fashion.

Other than those things, and the way the woman in the picture wore her hair . . . well, she had to admit that this time Delinda was right. It really did look like her.

Stunningly like her.

"Who is this?" Mary asked.

"I wish I knew," Will said. His smile looked sincere, but his eyes seemed distant, his gaze finally leaving Mary's face and shifting toward the high ceiling. "Like I told your friend here, I've had that calendar for years. I never could bring myself to sell it. But I've never learned who she really is, if she's anybody. Might be the artist just painted what he thought was the ideal woman."

Mary felt her neck and cheeks starting to go pink. "Or maybe his worst nightmare," she said with a laugh.

"I'm sure that's not it."

"See, I was right, wasn't I?" Delinda said. "That girl could be you."

"I have to admit, it almost could be," Mary agreed.

"Almost?" Sam asked. "It's like she's your evil twin. Unless you're the evil one."

"Mary's not evil," Delinda said. "Anyway, the other one has the gun."

"It's very close," Mary said.

"It is. The picture lacks a little something—life, I guess, like she's too perfect, too flawless, to be quite real," Will said. "I always thought she was the ideal woman, but I guess to truly be ideal she'd have to be flesh and blood."

Now Mary knew she had gone completely crimson. The guy was every bit as cute as Delinda had promised, but she didn't want to have to try to live up to his fantasy about the woman on the calendar. "That's probably always true," she said, hoping it was noncommittal without being rude.

"I reckon it has to be," Will said. "A woman in a picture can't smell good or hold your hand or kiss you. And if you bring her breakfast in bed, I've found, she's hardly ever grateful."

I'm not sure if that's romantic or creepy, Mary thought. *Maybe a little of both.* "Okay . . . I really need to get to work, Will. It's been great meeting you, and seeing . . . her."

"Do you work here at the Montecito, Mary?"

"I manage the hotel," she replied. "And today I'm wranglin' the chuck wagon feast."

"Great. Maybe I'll see you later on, then. Never have gotten over my taste for beef and beans."

Mary backed out of the booth, Delinda and Sam close beside her. "See you, Will," Delinda said.

"Nice to meet you," Sam said. "Even if you completely ignored me," she added under her breath.

When they were halfway up the aisle, Delinda grabbed Mary's arm. "What did I tell you, Mary? Is he yummy or what?"

"He is pretty yummy," Mary admitted.

"He likes you."

"You think?" Mary asked, trying to drip sarcasm.

"Oh yeah. He likes you. He calls me ma'am. He calls you Mary."

"Which is, after all, my name." Mary dodged a full-size, taxidermied pony being wheeled down the aisle on a cart.

"Yes, and my name's Delinda, not ma'am, but he doesn't care about that. He told me he's always had a crush on the calendar girl, and you're as close to her as humanly possible."

"Which is part of what's weird," Mary said. "I don't think he likes me, I think he likes her. And yes, I do look like her, but I'm not her. I'm me."

"He'd like you too. I can tell these things."

"Oh, you can?"

"That's right. In high school I met a guy who was just right for my friend Katie, and I hooked them up even though she swore he wasn't her type."

"And it worked out?"

"Sure." Delinda paused, chewed her lower lip for a second. "Well, partly. He's out of jail now, and Katie has a new identity in another state. For a while, though, it was hot and heavy. Never mind, maybe that's not a good example. But I can still tell he's right for you."

"He is kind of sweet," Mary said. They had reached the door of the exhibit hall. "Odd, but sweet."

"I'm with Delinda," Sam said. "There's something there."

"We'll see," Mary said. "I have to get to work. Are you going to get Wolfgang for me, Delinda?"

"I'll ask Gunther," Delinda said. "Not Wolfgang." She mimicked Mary. "We'll see."

Oh my God, Will thought when Mary, Delinda, and Sam left his booth.

He'd had a thing for redheads, particularly of the curvaceous variety, pretty much his whole life. He had obsessed over Ann-Margret movies as an adolescent: *Bye Bye Birdie, Viva Las Vegas,* the bean bath sequence from *Tommy* (at certain stages, *especially* the bean bath sequence from *Tommy*), and that fantasy image had never left him. He still remembered a dream he'd had in his late teens, of a redhead he met in a grassy meadow dotted with orange poppies. Her hair had almost matched the poppies, her eyes the color of the sky behind her head, and she had worn a simple white sundress. They had walked toward each other, each cutting a swath through the grass, and although he had never seen her before, when they came together and looked into each other's eyes, he had the sense that he had always known her and would know her forever. They held each other, the swells and valleys of her body firm and youthful under the simple cotton dress, and Will had been overwhelmed by feelings of destiny, of romance, and of eternity that had stayed with him after he awoke, angry not to be in the dream anymore.

Even now when he thought of that dream he felt a bittersweet melancholy, knowing that none of the buckle bunnies or truck stop waitresses or cosmetology students he had known (which were, for some reason, the sort of women he kept meeting) would ever be the one from the dream even if they were physically similar—which, truth be told, most of them were, because that's what he gravitated toward. Carlotta had been none of those things—she had a college degree, managed an insurance office, and her hair was black as fresh asphalt. He had thought maybe he was turning a corner, growing out of old habits, and look how that had wound up.

When he first came across the calendar with the pinup painting of the cowgirl on the fence, he had been struck at once by how much she resembled his dream girl. Not just physically—her eyes were the wrong color, although otherwise the two were almost identical—but he even thought he had a sense of her personality from the way she held herself, from the smile that hinted at some secret connection to the viewer. Nothing, he believed, would ever come closer to giving his dream girl physical form, which was why he had priced the calendar so far above market value. Selling his treasures earned him his living, and he had decided long ago that he couldn't pick and choose which ones to keep and which to sell, not if he hoped to eat three squares and sleep under a roof. Not putting a price tag on the

calendar would have gone against his entire philosophy of business. But no rule said that price had to be
reasonable.

Besides, as long as he kept her in the glass case, he
could look at her any time he wanted. When he was
at home in Wind River, he kept her in a place of
honor on the living room wall, and he transported
her to events in a special leather briefcase he had
bought just for that use.

Now that he had seen Mary Connell, he knew the
calendar girl would no longer be the ultimate. Mary's
eyes were the color of the pinup's, not of the dream
girl's, but other than that she *was* the girl from the
dream. Put her in a simple white sleeveless dress,
drop her into a meadow, and he could re-create the
whole thing for real. When he had shaken her hand,
he had felt an almost electric charge, as if the dream
meeting—that sense that they had known each other
forever—had been duplicated exactly. Will didn't believe in past lives or reincarnation or any of that nonsense, but he wasn't sure how else to explain the fact
that he had dreamed of this woman decades before,
remembered the dream so vividly, let it determine his
choices in companionship, and led him to cherish a
painted calendar picture for so long.

Mary Connell, though, was no painting. She was
flesh and blood. Chances were good that she had a
boyfriend, even a husband. Will knew Vegas was
loaded with beautiful women—he had seen many
since he'd arrived who would have looked at home
on the pages of a fashion magazine, or, in some cases,
a skin magazine—but even with that competition

around, he believed Mary would have been snapped up early.

And even though he had felt an instantaneous connection, that didn't mean that she had as well. As a flesh-and-blood woman instead of a painting, she would have opinions of her own on the subject. She might have seen a dumb redneck standing before her, a used-up cowboy without sense enough to settle down somewhere. He couldn't deny his own nature, after all. At best he could hope and pray that, against all odds, Mary might find used-up cowboys attractive.

Will was no gambling man, but sometimes, he figured, a man had to play his hand as it was dealt him.

Meeting Mary and letting her walk out of his life—or worse, getting back in his pickup and driving north—was not an option. Not without making an attempt to get to know her better.

Whether she would respond, he couldn't guess. But he had to try.

If he didn't, the girl on the calendar would never let him forget it.

"I see you got rid of the hat."

Danny, distracted, touched his head as he turned, as if maybe he had been wearing a hat without realizing it. Mary stood behind him, dressed down in cowgirl casual, a mischievous smile illuminating her sweet face. "Oh, the cowboy hat from yesterday," he said as comprehension dawned. He grinned at the memory. "I think Ed was jealous because I looked so manly in it."

"You looked like a little kid playing dress-up," Mary said.

"And you don't?" He cast an admiring look at the way her soft denim clung to her curves. "Not like a *little* kid, I guess. Anyway, you liked it when we used to play dress-up together. Me in my dad's shirt and tie, you in one of your mom's old dresses. Those tea parties you used to throw."

"I did like it," Mary said. "I still do. Still doesn't mean you should be wearing cowboy hats in public."

He had been walking the casino's inside perimeter to clear his mind after the meeting, in hopes that if he had missed anything, it would come to him after he got away from it for a while. Mary had stopped him at the entrance to the wide corridor leading to the convention center. As he walked he had been churning the elements of the situation over and over, like sand and water in a cement mixer, wanting to form a new, cohesive solution out of it all. He saw a chance, with Mary, to escape his own thoughts for a while, and recognized the potential value. "You have time to walk for a couple of minutes?" he asked.

She looked chagrined. "Not really, Danny. I mean, I'd love to, but I'm kind of running around trying to get this chuck wagon thing together. I feel like that chicken with the head cut off you always hear about."

"Oh yeah, the chuck wagon," Danny said. "How's that going?"

Mary chewed on her lower lip for a second before answering. "On second thought, maybe I'd rather *be* the chicken. Headlessness does have its advantages."

"Okay," Danny said, recognizing that she really did need to get going, and in the opposite direction. "I guess I'll see you later."

She gave him a peck on the cheek and scurried off. He continued into the broad hallway, watching the people going toward the exhibit hall and meeting rooms, and others coming back, some already laden with merchandise. He had only taken a few steps when he was brought short by a piercing scream. Scanning the hallway, he spotted its source.

The guy looked like a young executive on the rise, wearing a slate-gray business suit with faint chalk pinstripes, a white shirt with French cuffs and precise round gold cuff links, a yellow silk tie with red and black diagonal slashes, and Italian leather shoes. The ensemble, including the power haircut and the top-of-the-line mobile phone, must have set the guy back five grand, easy.

The only thing out of whack was that, at ten in the morning, he was plastered. Seriously drunk, leaning against the wall, knees bent as if they had buckled under him.

He shouted so loudly into his mobile that Danny wondered if the other party even needed a phone to hear him. "How can you frickin' say that, Juliet?" he screamed. "How can you say you love me and then pull crap like this?"

Juliet must have said something in reply, because phone guy went silent for a moment. His face crumpled in, as if he had lost control of his own muscles. "No!" he shrieked in reply. "That's not . . . that's not how it works!"

A family passing by shot him dirty looks, to which he responded by flipping them off. Danny had been willing to cut him some slack if he was just going to argue with Juliet and then move on, but he didn't want a belligerent drunk on Montecito property. Particularly if the fight with Juliet, whoever she was, made him even angrier than he already seemed to be.

He approached the man, giving him plenty of time to see that Danny was coming. The last thing he wanted was to startle him and wind up in a brawl. The guy noticed him, and his demeanor changed. "I gotta go, it looks like they're about to frickin' throw me out of here. You think about what I said, Juliet. Think long and hard or you'll find out what it's like living on the street."

He folded the phone and dropped it into a pocket just before Danny reached him, then he tried to swivel out of Danny's reach. The motion sent him lurching into the wall. Danny caught him by one arm. "Let's go, pal," he said, his voice soft, gentle. He didn't want to be antagonistic, but he wanted the guy gone. "Are you staying in the hotel?"

"I look like a tourist to you? I live here." He named one of the high-rise condo buildings that had been going up overlooking the Strip. If he lived there, it confirmed Danny's impressions of his financial status.

"Outside, then," Danny said. "I'll get you a cab." He started to head back toward the casino. To get to the valet area and taxi stand they would have to skirt the casino's edge and out the main entrance, and

Danny hoped the guy wouldn't cause a scene along the way. Just before the end of the convention center access hall, he saw a tall man making a call in a phone booth. It took him a second to realize the guy was Garrick Flynn, the American working for Klaus Aickmann's private security force. The one he had seen talking to Sam by the elevators. Flynn caught Danny's gaze, nodded an acknowledgment. He looked questioningly at Danny, who realized Flynn was asking, nonverbally, if he needed help with the drunk. Danny responded with a shake of his head, and Flynn went back to his call.

Handling drunks was a regular part of Danny's job. This one had turned out to be decidedly meek, compared to some. Maybe he realized he'd made a spectacle of himself, or it really had been the argument, not the booze, that had wound him up. He seemed deflated now, his sleeve feeling empty in Danny's hand. They made it to the valet stand, where Danny poured him into a cab. The guy gave the driver his own address and waved off Danny's offer to pay the fare, validating Danny's impression that he hadn't really been as bad off as he seemed.

Just the same, Danny was glad to see him leave. And gladder still that the event had proven a worthwhile distraction, stealing his attention—for a little while, at least—from the Aickmann problem.

He had to get back to it. When he did, however, it would be with a fresher point of view, and that couldn't hurt a bit.

14

Ed Deline had been right about the impossibility of checking all the employee files before Aickmann's speech, of course. Even a team of speed readers couldn't get through four thousand jackets that fast, especially if discrepancies turned up that had to be checked out. And how would they spot potential troublemakers, anyway? Criminal records? Anyone who might be involved in an assassination attempt was probably smart enough to lie about their record, in which case they would either not have been hired, if they had been found out, or they wouldn't have been found out, in which case no notation would exist in the file.

But Hooper had felt like he had to try something. Short of lining up the hotel's employees and gazing into their eyes, trying to read their souls, he didn't know what. His superiors in D.C. had been adamant that nothing had better happen to Klaus Aickmann during his visit to Las Vegas. Relations with the European Union had been sketchy enough for the past few years. The fact that Aickmann had come to the United States, rather than a European capital, to make his speech indicated a possible thaw. An attack on him, whether successful or not, could kick those relations back into the deep freeze.

And it would take Hooper's career down with it.

He had put in enough years to see retirement on the near horizon, promising time to spend with the grandkids he hoped to have one day, maybe some extended fishing trips, and a chance to write a history of the big-band era, like he'd always wanted. If he let anything happen to Aickmann, he might instead find his golden years spent wearing a red vest and greeting shoppers at a store entrance, just trying to make ends meet.

Fortunately, the Montecito's personnel files were computerized and searchable, and despite his problems with Ed—decades in the past, but not forgotten by him, and from some of the looks Ed had shot him over the past couple of days, he didn't think they had slipped Ed's mind either—the Montecito staff had been helpful and efficient. He'd had his agents start by pulling everyone who had had disciplinary issues noted in the past year. That narrowed the field down to a few hundred. It wasn't perfect, he knew—if someone had gotten hired specifically to be on the scene for Aickmann's speech, he would probably have tried to keep a clean record in the interim.

Since Aickmann's visit had been confirmed only two months before, he also told the agents to focus on the newest hires. Another couple of hundred to check.

Even with Hartung's people helping, the task was Herculean.

If something went wrong, however, Charles Hooper would be the one wading in crap.

"Eustace T. Barnes," Mike said.

"Where do you get these names?" Danny asked, a

smirk on his face. "Is there a clown directory I don't know about?"

"Eustace T. Barnes," Mike repeated, sitting on the leather couch in Danny's office that he had claimed as his own, "hates Leroy Snead."

"Like I said . . ."

"Eustace T. Barnes breeds horses. His best stud, Sentimental Fool—"

"Mike, the horses in your stories have better names than the people."

"Sentimental Fool," Mike continued, disregarding Danny's interruption. "Has come in second to Cavanaugh's Virtue nine times. He won plenty of races, but he could never beat Cavanaugh's Virtue. As a result, Barnes's stud fees were lower than Snead's. Barnes paid more for Sentimental Fool's sire and dam too. He didn't quite take a bath on the horse, but he didn't make anywhere near as much as he thought he should have. Now Sentimental Fool's health is fading and he doesn't seem too interested in the ladies anymore."

"Aren't there pills for that?" Danny asked.

"I don't know that it's so much an equipment problem as a lack of enthusiasm," Mike said. "Fool's done the deed with plenty of frisky fillies, but commitment to the cause is flagging. Barnes thought he had a few more years of those stud fees, and now it looks like he'll take a financial hit there too."

"This is fascinating stuff, Mike. I'm glad you've become so well versed on the ins and outs of horses." Danny laughed. "Ins and outs, that's pretty good."

"Choice, Danny. Really."

"But the thing is, Mike, Klaus Aickmann arrives in less than two hours. He's a human, and a rich, powerful one. I have to get back on that."

Mike got the message. He would rather have been on that too. Danny had been frustrated for days, trying to coordinate the conflicting desires of the Germans and the Secret Service. If not for the Snead case, Mike could have helped him out, and he wouldn't have been the butt of nearly so many jokes.

And besides, Danny hadn't had to put up with Linda Lou Snead breathing down his neck.

"Just trying to make sure you're in the loop, Danny. Eustace T. Barnes. Remember that name, not that you're likely to forget it. Officially a person of interest, as far as I'm concerned."

"Bring it home, Mike."

"Roger that." He rose, walked to the door of Danny's office, and stopped, the slender fingers of his right hand clutching the jamb. "Listen, I'm up to my eyeballs in rice pudding—so to speak—but if there's anything I can do to help you out on this Aickmann thing, just give a brother a holler."

"Thanks, Mike," Danny said. "I'll do that."

Mike went back to the desk in the surveillance room at which he had spent most of the day reviewing footage. He had definitely eliminated five of the nine suspects on his list, because they hadn't been anywhere near Snead or his booth during the time that the vial must have been stolen, nor had anyone else to whom Mike could link them directly. Neither had Barnes, for that matter—he seemed to have spent most of the day yesterday in his suite, in the company of a woman with bright red shoulder-length hair, leopard-print pants, stiletto heels, and a very pronounced sway in her boo-tay.

Bringing Barnes's face up on-screen, he ran a search for other occasions on which Snead's competitor had showed up on camera. As usual, it was slow going. With so many cameras in the building, anyone who spent time—as Barnes did—in the exhibit hall, the casino, the restaurants and bars, on elevators and lobbies, spent literally hours on camera.

Most of what Mike watched, sped up as much as possible without losing the sense of what happened, was perfectly innocent. Barnes wasn't exhibiting, but he spent plenty of time in the hall, shopping and schmoozing. There were social events associated with the Stampede, in which he took part. Mike did notice some surprising moments—a hushed conversation at one point with Linda Lou Snead, another time when Barnes seemed to lock eyes with someone across the room at a cocktail party. Mike paused that and brought up another screen, forwarding through footage until he found the same moment as captured on the camera on the other side of the room.

Linda Lou was there, looking out of the camera's range, with what looked like a secret smile playing around her lips.

Nothing Mike saw was definitive, but there was enough to make him feel like he was on the right track.

Then he found another bit of footage that almost sealed the deal.

It was from the night before the secret sauce had gone missing. Barnes had been playing video poker

in the casino when Leroy Snead had spotted him
there. Snead stormed over to him, his fists balled and
his brow knotted. Words turned quickly into shouting. Barnes jumped up from the machine and Snead
got into his grill. Mike wished he could hear the argument, but from the looks of it—Snead poking his
finger into Barnes's chest, Barnes swatting it away—
it was one that had taken place many times over a
long period.

Finally, Barnes had enough of Snead's poking and
grabbed Snead's hand in his fists. Mike was sure a
brawl would result, but a security guard, a sturdy-
looking sister with a cool head and fast hands, noticed the altercation and stepped into the frame,
prying the two men apart. She did a good job, easing
Barnes and Snead away from each other and sending
them in two different directions.

Without knowing just what the fight was about,
Mike still didn't have a smoking gun he could put in
Eustace Barnes's hand. But his considered judgment,
especially now, was that Barnes had to be the prime
suspect.

He still needed that smoking gun, though, if he
wanted to prove his case. *There has to be a way,* he
thought, *to pop the perp with the protein.*

Hartung left the meeting dissatisfied. He called Stefan
Zerweck to him, and together the two walked down
to the casino level and strolled around the floor. He
noticed Stefan's gaze darting toward the gaming tables, blackjack and roulette especially, and wondered
if his top man had a gambling problem. If so, he

would have to be alert to the possibility that Stefan had become indebted to enemy agents and was in on the plot against Herr Aickmann.

So far, however, he had no solid evidence pointing in that direction. He considered himself a good judge of people and had made a point of learning to read their faintest, most subconscious tics. Tells, he understood people called them in Las Vegas. Stefan, he believed, was interested in the tables but probably not to any dangerous degree. And he needed to trust his best man as long as he could.

"What did you think of Herr McCoy's presentation?" he asked Stefan. They walked closely together so they could speak in low tones and still hear each other over the incessant racket of the casino.

"He covered everything pertinent, I thought," Stefan replied. "As he said, he consulted with me and we tried to identify all the potential weak spots in the room. We both thought we had come up with adequate defenses."

"'Adequate' is hardly good enough," Hartung chided. "Imagine it was not Klaus Aickmann at risk but your own child. Or Germany itself. Would you feel then that 'adequate' defenses would suffice?"

Stefan chewed over the question for a moment instead of answering right away, which Hartung approved. It meant he was thinking, not simply reacting.

"Perhaps not," Stefan finally said. "But McCoy and Turro and I were quite thorough, I believe, in our inspection and our discussion."

Hartung halted next to a particularly noisy slot machine with animated elves dancing about its screen. "Here is my concern, Stefan," he said, lowering his voice so much that the other man had to lean close in order to hear. They were speaking German, but any enemies of Herr Aickmann might also know that language. "What if the CD is a phony? What if we're spending our time and energies looking for ways to defend against a plot that isn't real, while the true threat lurks elsewhere?"

"We covered more than the ballroom," Stefan said. "We examined his suite, the entrance, the path he will take, everything."

"I'm confident that you did," Hartung said. "Nonetheless, the attentions of our compatriots in this effort, the Secret Service and Montecito security, will be focused on the occasion of Herr Aickmann's speech. We can't afford to make that same mistake. We must be vigilant at every moment, from his arrival in Las Vegas until his departure. I want the airport checked. I want to know every mechanic who touches his plane while it's on the ground. I want to know what the traffic patterns are like between the airport and here, and if we can have traffic stopped or redirected."

"I'll work on that, sir," Stefan said.

"See that you do."

He dismissed the man with a nod and watched him cross the casino floor. This time Stefan did not slow at the gaming tables but went straight toward one of the exits, drawing a telephone from his pocket as he walked, no doubt to call the rest of the team and alert them of the modification to their plans. Dieter Klasse had already been assigned to help Hooper's people work through personnel files, but others could assist Stefan with his tasks.

What Hartung hadn't told Stefan was that a nightmare had awakened him at four o'clock that morning. It was a dream that had recurred at various times of his life, one that always left him in a cold sweat, clutching at his bedding as if that could rescue him. Freudians would have a field day with the nightmare, he knew, since it involved himself walking into a dark tunnel—forced into it, chased, really, by some force he could never identify, and although it began as a leisurely stroll in the park, by the end of it, when he discovered a wall blocking his escape, the tunnel not being a tunnel after all, he awoke shivering and clutching frantically at his sheets. The dream usually accompanied disaster of one kind or another, and Hartung had long since learned not to ignore its portents.

Since the first time, early in his espionage career when it had come the night before an operation that had turned fatally bad, the same dream, with only minor variations, had come on at least a dozen occasions. The second and third times, he ignored it and things went bad. After that he began to recognize that it meant he should reexamine his plans, reconsider his preconceptions. Sometimes he was successful at finding the problem area, sometimes not, but always, without fail, a problem area existed. The dream seemed to be his brain's way of telling him that another path might exist, if only he knew where to look for it.

The fact that it had returned this morning worried him. He could still search for another path, go over the plans again and again until he found the potentially fatal flaw.

But he didn't have much time in which to do so.

Herr Aickmann would arrive within hours. From that moment, there could be no more reflection, no careful study. There could only be reaction to external events.

And that, he feared, could result in Herr Aickmann's death.

The cold sweat returned, and he had no time for a second shower.

"Mary!"

"Yes, Ezra?" The chuck wagon cook had already run her ragged. She was glad she'd worn jeans, boots, and a snug denim shirt with pearl snaps and sawtooth pockets, because she had begun to feel like a ranch hand instead of a hotel manager.

"I need more mesquite, conflab it!" he grouched. "And where's that flour I asked for?"

"I'll look into it, Ezra." Mary flipped open her phone to check on the additional supply of mesquite, which had been ordered but had not shown up yet. The answer turned out to be "stuck in traffic on the Strip," something which happened with more and more frequency as Las Vegas's permanent population boomed along with its tourist business. Jake, Mary's most recent ex-boyfriend, had complained often that Las Vegas smelled like exhaust and money. Sometimes Mary agreed, but she wasn't sure money had an odor of its own, and thought it leaned more heavily toward the exhaust side.

"It's on the way," she told Ezra after she hung up. Smoke billowing from the fire pits stung her eyes, tearing them up. It smelled good, though—aromatic and appetizing, the opposite of exhaust. If she and Ezra both managed to survive the day, she realized, she just might be able to enjoy the food.

"On the way ain't *here*, is it?" he grumbled.

"No, it's not."

"I thought you folks ran a business here. I ran a chuck wagon this way in the old days, I'd've been lucky if'n the cowboys didn't strip me naked and stake me down on top of an anthill, Apache-style."

"I'm sorry, Ezra," Mary said, wiping her eyes with her fingertips. "Nobody thought the mesquite would burn so fast, or the traffic would be so bad at this time of day."

"Excuses don't cook the vittles, Miz Connell."

"I know that."

"And what about that flour? Biscuits ain't gonna cook up too well without it."

"Checking on that next," she said.

"And I need some jalapeño chiles too."

This was the first time she had heard about jalapeños. "How many?"

"Seven or eight bushels oughta do."

"Bushels." She would have to take notes if this kept up.

Ezra whipped his tattered hat from his head and slapped it with his other hand. "Yes, bushels. You got corncobs in your ears, Mary?"

What is it with Ezra and corn? she wondered. At least he seemed sober today. Although judging by his mood, she thought she might prefer him drunk.

"Okay," Mary said. "I'm going inside to order some chiles and check on your flour. I'll be back in a little while, Ezra. Try not to have a stroke." She left him, mumbling something she couldn't hear and didn't care to. On the way in, she called Delinda.

"Has he asked you out yet?" Delinda said when she answered.

The question caught Mary off guard. "Who, Ezra?"

"No, goofy. Rocket. Will Streeter, your cowboy admirer."

"I haven't heard from him since this morning," Mary said. "I imagine he's busy trying to sell things, and I've been busy dealing with the Emeril of the cattle drive. Speaking of which, when is Wolfgang going to come out and help me?" *Couldn't hurt to try again,* she figured.

"How does 'never' sound?" Delinda replied. "But I did talk to Gunther. You know him, though—he said he might do it, if he had time, and if Benito didn't create some catastrophe in the kitchen that he had to fix, and if he felt like it, and if I slept with him."

"Do it, Delinda," Mary urged. "If ever there was a time when you—"

"I'm not sleeping with Gunther," Delinda interrupted. "He knows that, he just feels like he has to ask every now and then in case I've gone temporarily insane and agree."

"So what you're saying is I'm pretty much on my own?"

"Pretty much, Mary. Sorry."

"I still think you should reconsider the sleeping-with-Gunther thing."

"Good-bye, Mary."

"'Bye." She closed the phone and fatigue washed over her. She didn't like the feeling. It was much too early in the day for that, and this one promised to be a very long day indeed.

15

"Aickmann's limo is five minutes out," Danny reported, closing his phone.

"Good," Ed said. They stood in the front entrance lobby, on reddish-brown marble floors with the Montecito logo displayed in white marble. The logo repeated in stained glass over the three sets of frosted-glass double doors. Ed glanced around at the security personnel in place, essentially invisible to the paying guests but ready, he hoped, for anything. "Nothing's worse than this waiting. The sooner he gets here, the sooner this will all be done and we'll have our hotel back."

"Got that right," Danny said. "I can't wait for the Secret Service and Aickmann's people to be out of my hair."

"Makes two of us." Ed didn't say anything about it—he rarely went into any detail about his CIA days with his staff, even Danny—but one of the reasons he had left the agency was because he had become fed up with the second-guessing, the backbiting, and the political maneuvering that seemed to accompany large bureaucracies. Charles Hooper had worked his way up in the Treasury Department by being good at those sorts of games. Ed hadn't been bad at them, he had just lost patience with the whole process and found the games a waste of his energy and efforts. It looked as if Heinrich Hartung was another skilled bureaucratic gamesman. Being around the two of them made Ed feel like he was back in the agency, and he didn't like the sensation at all.

He was about to say something else when a raucous commotion from the casino floor interrupted him. "What the hell is that?" he asked. Both men rushed toward the floor.

A dozen cowboys—who had not, from the looks of them, yet finished the drinking they had begun the night before—ran through the casino, whooping and hollering and beating the air with their hats.

Noisy enough, and distracting to the serious daytime gamblers, but they were not the source of the furor.

Among the cowboys, snorting and thundering and releasing loud, anxious moos, ran ten or twelve cows.

The Montecito's aisles were wide, but not wide enough for a cattle stampede. People dove under gaming tables or leapt up onto banks of slot and video poker machines. Others dashed before the cattle like runners in Pamplona. An elderly woman wearing a dark cowboy hat, Ed noticed, kept punching the buttons on two side-by-side slots as the tip of a bull's horn sliced the air mere inches from the back of her head.

In the flashing, blinking, indirect colored lighting of the casino's interior, the whole scene took on an air of unreality. The cowboys, in their hats and boots and jeans, looked like characters from another century, laughing as they sprinted until tears ran down their tanned, sun-beaten faces. The cattle, wild-eyed with terror at their strange surroundings and the raucous din of the casino—accentuated now by shrieks of fright from the players—raced along on the path dictated by the cowboys, but threatened to outpace them at any moment. They sported hides of black, brown, white with brown spots, or almost pure white. Some had long horns, some no horns at all. But they all weighed in the neighborhood of two thousand pounds, and they menaced everyone around them. The pounding of their hoofs on the carpeted floor sounded like a hundred drummers.

"What are you staring at?" Ed asked Danny, slapping him on the arm. "Let's go!"

"Do I look like a rodeo clown to you?" Danny asked.

"Just get some help over here."

Danny flipped open his phone and called the surveillance room. "Get every available body on the floor, now," he barked. The call finished, he and Ed charged onto the floor, on what looked like a collision course with the onrushing herd.

Security guards rallied toward them. Ed wasn't sure what they could do—if they stood in front of the herd, they'd just be trampled. But in a couple of seconds he saw what Danny had in mind.

Danny and the others, joined by Garrick Flynn of Heinrich Hartung's security team, had started running ahead of the herd and the cowboys, clearing a path. They pushed people out of the way—as gently as they could, but forcefully, knowing that the risk of being sued for trying to protect their guests outweighed the risk of being sued for doing nothing—and opened up a route toward one of the emergency exits, which led out into a parking area.

The cowboys, who had begun to realize what they had started, shouted and slapped the animals' flanks and led them down the route Danny had chosen. Ed made it to the double doors just in time to hurl them open before Danny, Flynn, and the other guards raced through. Outside, they flattened themselves against the building on either side of the doors. Emergency Klaxons blared.

On their heels came the cattle, bursting from the doorway into the bright Nevada sun. The cowboys followed them out, intent now on trying to control their charges. Ed glanced over to see Danny on the phone again, urging someone to locate more cowboys, with ropes, to round up the agitated beasts.

Fortunately, this section of the lot had been dedicated to the stock trailers and the pickup trucks of those who had brought animals for display—Danny, Ed happily noted, had picked the right door for multiple reasons—so when the cattle started running into the vehicles, Ed figured the owners could sue one another for damages. This would still be a legal nightmare, he knew, and he decided to bring Cathy Burson and her legal team into the loop at once.

Dusting himself off, Danny returned to his side. "What a mess, huh?"

"It sure is," Ed said. "I want every one of those guys responsible ID'd and held for Metro."

"Done," Danny said.

Ed glanced past Danny at Garrick Flynn, who stood outside watching the cowboys trying to bring the cattle under control. "Crap!" he said. "Aickmann!"

"Right!" Danny agreed. Ed ran back in through the open doors, followed by Danny and Flynn.

Charles Hooper, Heinrich Hartung, and some of their operatives waited in the lobby. Hard-faced men in plain suits had to be the team that had traveled here with the billionaire. In their midst, arms crossed over his chest, a look of profound dissatisfaction on his face, Klaus Aickmann glared at Ed.

"There he is," Hooper said. "That's Big Ed Deline."

"Herr Aickmann," Ed said, swallowing his consternation. He had wanted to meet the man the moment he set foot on Montecito property, not on the wrong side of an embarrassing lapse of decorum. "Welcome to the Montecito." He put out his hand. After a moment's hesitation, Aickmann took it, gave a brief shake. His fingers were thin, with prominent knuckles, and shaking hands with him felt like holding a handful of bones.

"Mr. Deline," he said. "It is a pleasure to be here, in Las Vegas and at your beautiful hotel. Your waterfall"—he inclined his head toward the doorway—"is magnificent."

"Thank you," Ed said. The waterfall spilled from just under the Montecito's giant illuminated marquee sign and fell almost fifty stories, making it one of the world's tallest waterfalls—the tallest man-made one anywhere, unless you counted certain dams. Since it had become such a recognized symbol of the resort, like the Mirage's volcano or the Bellagio's water show, Ed had to admit that it had been one of Monica Mancuso's better ideas.

Aickmann had a Leonine mane of thick white hair

above a heavy brow. His prominent nose jutted forward, an assertion of his notable position. In spite of his verbal enthusiasm, his thin lips remained set in a frown. His bearing exuded power, as did the expensive pin-striped suit he wore with an open-collared silk shirt over his lean, muscular physique.

"I apologize for the scene that met you when you came in," Ed said. "I had intended to greet you at the car, but you know how it is." He shrugged. "Sometimes an emergency demands one's attention."

"And a very interesting emergency, at that," Aickmann said. His accent was soft, more British than German, as if he had been schooled in England. "I do not believe I have ever seen cows inside a casino before."

"It's a first for me too, believe me."

"So it was not intended for my benefit? A demonstration of the Old West for your foreign visitor?" A subtle crinkle at the corners of his blue eyes made Ed realize he was joking.

"Not at all," Ed said.

"Still, poor timing, Mr. Deline," Hartung said, sidling up behind Aickmann. "With all of our emphasis on security, I would have thought that you and Mr. McCoy would have allowed others to handle your runaway animals."

"We did what we had to do," Ed countered. "Herr Aickmann was secured by your people and Mr. Hooper's, as well as our own. It was unfortunate but unavoidable, I'm afraid."

"No, Hartung's right for a change," Hooper said. "You should have had additional staff standing by in case something like that happened. What if it had been a diversionary tactic? My people were ready, but with yours distracted, do you think Hartung's could have backed us up alone?"

"Backed you up?" Hartung responded. "It appears you've forgotten who has primary responsibility for Herr Aickmann's safety."

"Please, Heinrich," Aickmann said, putting his long, lean fingers on his security chief's shoulder. "Arguing, I think, serves no one's interests."

"He's right," Ed said. "We need to stay focused on the job."

"You should have taken your own advice about five minutes ago, Deline," Hooper said.

"Gentlemen, please," Aickmann said again.

"Let's get you to your suite, Herr Aickmann," Ed suggested. "Then these gentlemen and I can work out whatever differences we may still have."

"Very well," Aickmann said.

"It's right this way." Ed started toward an elevator, with Aickmann trailing behind and the others following him. Bellmen had loaded his considerable piles of luggage onto a couple of rolling carts. Ed had already stashed Aickmann's key cards safely in a pocket. Some guests didn't have to go through even the painless VIP check-in procedure, and he was one of them. It pained Ed to know that Aickmann, wealthy as he was, would not have to spend a dime for his stay here, and that the Montecito would eat the cost of the man's lodging and meals. With any luck Aickmann would lose enough at the tables to make up for it. Ed could, at least, bill the Treasury Department and Hartung's company for the rooms their people occupied, and he intended to charge them for every bag of nuts consumed from their minibars.

A couple of security people waited inside the elevator with a control key, and once Ed, Aickmann, Hartung, and Hooper were on board, one of them closed the doors and pressed the button for the forty-ninth floor.

"I'm sure you'll be comfortable in this suite, Herr Aickmann," Ed said. "It's one of our very best."

"I have investigated it personally, Herr Aickmann," Hartung added, speaking English for the benefit of their hosts. "It should be adequate for your needs."

Adequate. Ed held his tongue. Aickmann would like the suite, he knew. If Hartung felt the need to inflate himself by belittling others, Aickmann was smart enough to recognize that.

The elevator doors opened at the forty-ninth floor, where more security personnel waited. Aickmann and his party would occupy an entire wing of this floor. Ed led the procession between the ranks of guards to the door of Aickmann's suite. "I'd like to assure you once again, Herr Aickmann, that your security is absolutely guaranteed while you're on Montecito property. And any other need you may have will be met as well. All you have to do is ask me or any member of my staff."

"Very well, Mr. Deline," Aickmann said. He stopped in the entryway to the suite and made a slow circle. The place was as big as some private homes. The walls were a rich chocolate brown, the carpet slate gray. Original oil paintings graced the walls. A giant plasma-screen TV dominated one wall, with a sound system beneath it. A plush sofa and a couple of comfortable chairs flanked a coffee table. A full bar hugged another wall, across from a floor-to-ceiling picture window facing the Strip. "This will do nicely, I think."

Ed showed him where the bedrooms were, showing off more full-length windows, more plasma, more luxury. He decided to let Aickmann discover the plasma screens, Italian marble, and gold fixtures in the bathrooms for himself. "Again, let me know if there's anything else you need, anything at all. I'm sure you'd like a few moments to get settled in."

"Yes, that would be appreciated," Aickmann said. "The flight, I'm afraid, was long and wearying. There was quite a bit of turbulence in the air."

More than a little down here too, Ed thought, but he didn't say anything.

"Good. Herr Hartung, Mr. Hooper, if you'll come with me down to my office, let's leave Herr Aickmann in peace."

Hartung grumbled, but Aickmann dismissed him. They left Aickmann in his suite with a butler, two guards who would use the suite's second bedroom, and the bellmen bringing in his luggage, all of whom had been thoroughly vetted. One of the bellmen was a member of Danny's security staff and wore a gun under his uniform jacket. Cameras watched the door, and no one could access the wing without authorization.

Klaus Aickmann was as safe there as in his own backyard. Maybe safer. No one, Ed believed, would get to him at the Montecito.

16

"Hi, Will."

"Howdy, ma'am."

"It's Delinda."

"Okay, howdy, Delinda."

She smiled. That wasn't as difficult as she had feared, given that the cowboy sometimes seemed determined to redefine "strong, silent type." "Can I ask you some questions about that calendar?"

"Knock yourself out," Will Streeter said. "Don't know as I can answer 'em, but I'll take a crack at it."

"Do you know anything about the painter?"

Will considered for a moment, sucking in his cheeks and looking up toward the rafters overhead. "I did a little research into that, a few years back. His name was Steve Toyon, and he did a lot of advertising work in the late fifties and early sixties. He was based in Albuquerque, but painted for some national campaigns out of New York too."

"Is he still alive?" Delinda asked.

"Nope."

"Do you know when he died?"

"In the mid-seventies."

"There must have been some business records."

"There were. For a while I thought I had a line on them—I've been through all this, Delinda, trying to figure out who that model was—but it turns out they were put into storage in a place that burned to the ground in 1980. Nothing's left."

Delinda had felt a moment's hope, but his words dashed that like a crystal goblet thrown to the concrete. At this rate she would never find the model who looked so much like Mary. She couldn't even explain why it had become so important to her to try. Every now and then she came across the *New York Times* crossword puzzle, and she couldn't stop until she had solved it, so maybe it was just a matter of wrapping her brain around a problem until it was done.

"He must have had friends or family who knew his models," she pressed.

"I thought that too," Will said. "But he painted literally thousands of pieces, for all sorts of commercial uses. I never found anyone who remembered anything about this particular model, or the painting itself."

"What about at the oil company?"

"Cassaday Oil went out of business in '69," Will said. "But I checked their corporate records just in case. They hired Toyon through a commercial art broker in New York—also out of business. Their records and the broker's never showed the model's name, just the dollars and cents, delivery date, that sort of thing. The deal between Toyon and the model—if there really was a model and she wasn't just a figment of his imagination—was strictly between them."

"You really have researched this."

He pulled off his hat, scratched at the back of his head, then straightened his hair and replaced the Stetson. "I've sure tried."

"Thanks for the info," she said. "I hope you have a great day in here."

"Business is steady so far," Will said. "Sorry I couldn't be more help."

As Delinda walked away, she wished he had been more help too. It sounded like Will's thorough search had hit a dead end.

Then again, he didn't have the resources of the Montecito.

As she hurried toward Mystique, Delinda dialed the surveillance office. Mitch answered. "Mitch, just who I was looking for. It's Delinda."

"What's up, Delinda?"

"I need a favor," she said. "I need you to find out anything you can about an Albuquerque artist named Steve Toyon, who painted a picture for a Cassaday Oil Company calendar in the late fifties or early sixties."

Mitch blew out a sigh. "For a second there I thought you were going to throw something complicated at me."

"Thanks, Mitch! Love ya!"

Delinda hung up. Daddy might not appreciate her using the company's employees for something like this, but Mitch had sounded bored. Anyway, she was sure it wouldn't take him very long, and what else did he have to do but stare at the monitors all day?

Delinda smiled, convinced she'd handed Mitch a welcome change of pace.

Danny stayed on the floor until the maintenance crew had come in with shovels and pails, scooping up what they could of the cow pies deposited by the panicked animals. A second crew came behind them with disinfectant, industrial vacuum cleaners, and carpet shampooers. Yellow caution tape had been stretched along the path the cattle took, to keep the guests out of the way. The shampoo and liberally applied air freshener masked the odors until the hotel's ventilation system could whisk them away. Another crew quickly replaced the few gaming tables that had been damaged, hauling them down to the Montecito shop where they would be repaired and repainted.

He was surprised to notice Garrick Flynn still on the casino floor too, watching the cleanup. Not every one of Hartung's operatives was on duty at every moment, so possibly Garrick had been down here on his off time. Danny stopped next to the man, making every effort to appear casual. "What a mess, huh?"

"You said it," Garrick replied. He wore a dark gray suit that might have come straight off a catwalk in Paris or Milan, with a rich blue shirt and a silk Hermès tie. His muscular bulk strained the seams of the suit. "Not really how you wanted to greet Aickmann, was it?"

"For sure," Danny said.

"It was kind of funny, in a way," Garrick went on. "Watching those rich people screaming at the cows like they were some kind of monsters or something."

"Rich people?"

"I don't know, all the gamblers. I guess I just assume they're rich because they throw their money away at the tables."

Danny had met other people with the same prejudice, although most of them stayed far away from Las Vegas. "They're not rich," he said. "I mean, sure, a few are, but they mostly play in the high-roller areas, not out here. Mostly these are just middle-class people who save up some money for a trip to Vegas, know how much they can afford to lose, and are willing to take that risk to be here. If they win, great—then they tell their friends and come back next year. We think of it as entertainment, not throwing money away. Some people buy season tickets to football games, some go to the beach, some stay home and watch TV. We like to think we've come as close as possible to perfecting the art of hospitality, and people who play here enjoy themselves and take advantage of our full range of activities, not just gambling."

Flynn looked at him as if he had just sprouted antennae. "Sorry," Danny said. "Didn't mean to go off on a lecture, Flynn. It's just that these people are my guests as well as my livelihood, and I don't like seeing them misrepresented."

"No problem, McCoy. Thanks for setting me straight."

"Sure," Danny said. "Can I ask you something? Record like yours, you could have had any intelligence job in the country, or worked for any private firm. Why work for Hartung?"

Flynn smiled, his teeth white and even, dimples carving his cheeks. "I guess I could," he said. "But my first posting out of basic was in Mannheim, and I got to like Germany. Besides"—he touched the lapels of his expensive suit coat—"I'd never be able to afford this on a civil service salary."

"I guess that's true," Danny said. He liked wearing nice clothes too, and he had chosen the private sector after his hitch in the marine corps had ended. Part of his reason had been that he wanted to stay in Las Vegas. He loved his hometown, which he perceived as the most vital, exciting city in the country. Other places clung to the past—Washington with its monuments, Philadelphia with its historical center, Boston, even New York. Vegas not only looked to the future, it grabbed onto tomorrow with both fists and yanked itself forward. "Well, I have to go check out some footage. Good talking to you."

"Likewise," Garrick said. When Danny left, Garrick remained on the casino floor, watching the action return to normal.

In his office upstairs, Danny played back the footage of the beginning of the stampede. Drawing on multiple cameras, he was able to piece together the entire progression, from the drunken cowboys going outside to the temporary stockyard and releasing the cattle from their pens, to the ones who held open the side door that gave them access to the casino.

At no point did it look like an intentional distraction, meant to cover an attempt on Aickmann. No attempted hit had taken place, which only furthered Danny's theory—that the stampede really was simply intoxicated fun that got out of control. He still thought it odd that Garrick Flynn had been on the floor—not gambling, and not preparing for Aick-mann's arrival, but just kind of roaming around watching people. "Rich people," as he had called them, and for whom he seemed to feel nothing but contempt. Nothing in the footage tied Flynn to any of the cowboys, though.

Danny forced himself to view the footage over and over, looking for any anomalies that he might have missed on the first run-through. The fifth time, as he worried that his eyes might glaze over entirely, he spotted it.

The four cowboys at the beginning, outside in the stockyard and opening the door, were not the same ones who ran through the casino with the cattle. They appeared to have been drinking with the others, and they all went into the stockyard together, but once the animals were inside, the four who seemed to have insti-gated things had not followed. Instead—seemingly in-stantaneously sober—they had let themselves out of the stock area and headed for the parking lot.

He captured good shots of their faces—as good as he could get with big cowboy hats shielding them—and ran them through video IQ. No information turned up on any of them. He tried facial recognition, but came up equally blank. As far as his software could determine, the four men didn't exist. All he knew about them was that they were not currently on the premises.

The cowboys who had followed the cattle inside had all been taken into custody. Danny would call Detective Jernigan, who had caught the case, and make sure he pumped them for information about the four who had left the scene. He had a feeling it would turn out that they had just met while out drinking and didn't really know anything about the missing foursome.

All of which made the stampede considerably less innocent than he had thought at first. He would have to tell Ed about this.

And Ed, he had a feeling, would not be thrilled.

17

"Miz Connell!"

Mary decided she now understood why early cowboys had been a wandering breed of man. If there had been many chuck wagon cooks like Ezra, people must have fled in droves, always on the move, searching for an outfit with a less ornery cook.

"Yes, Ezra?"

"You think you can round up some more bacon grease?"

"I thought you had bacon grease," she said.

"I did. It's gone. I ain't never cooked chuck for so many people before and it didn't go as far as I thought. You might get me some more bacon and I could fry it up for the grease. I just thought it'd be easier if one of the restaurants had some grease they didn't need."

Mary nodded, reaching for her phone. "Bacon grease. Check." She was about to call Delinda when she saw Gunther striding toward them with a broad smile on his face. Gunther had driven Delinda mad as head chef of Mystique, but the man knew his way around pots and pans.

"Thank you, Mary," he said in his thick Austrian accent. He wore his chef's whites, a tall hat on his head, and an apron tied snugly around his waist.

"Thank me? Thank you!"

He shook his head furiously and waved his hands. "No, no, thank you. You have saved me from a lifetime in prison. If I had stayed in my kitchen for two more minutes with Benito, I would have killed him. That Gypsy boy has worked at my side for years, but he still doesn't know how to brown veal. Can you believe it?"

"Just barely," Mary said.

"So I am grateful to you for bringing me out here where I do not have to watch Benito disgrace me, himself, and the art of cuisine." He sniffed the smoke that hung in the air. "What is that, is someone burning tires?"

"That's what I asked you out here for," Mary said.

"I know nothing of tires."

"It's not tires," Mary said, beginning to wonder if all chefs were insane, or if it was somehow the effect she had on them. "It's Ezra's chuck wagon cookout. For the last night of the Stampede."

Gunther sniffed again. "You claim that is food? That is not food, that smell."

Ezra came around the end of the chuck wagon, hat in hand, red-faced, sweat running down his cheeks. "Hooey," he said. "Gets a little warmish there when you're flippin' over fifty steaks. Just got another hundred to go."

"One hundred and fifty steaks, this man is destroying?" Gunther asked. He looked appalled.

"Destroyin'?" Ezra repeated. "Who in tarnation is this feller anyhow? I don't like the sound of his voice."

"This is fine," Gunther shot back. "I do not like the smell of your . . . I don't know, I cannot call it 'cooking.' Or perhaps it is simply the smell of you."

"Look, mister," Ezra said, face turning even redder. I don't know if you've ever made vittles for so many folks, but it ain't easy."

"I do not make 'vittles,' " Gunther said. "But I have prepared fine meals for full restaurants every night for years."

"Ain't the same at all," Ezra declared. "People in restaurants wait their turn, and you control the number of tables you got. I got seven fifty-five-gallon drums of beans goin' out here. You wouldn't know what to do with that."

Gunther turned to Mary. "He cooks in drums. I do not even know how to respond to that. Isn't there a law about people like this? Should he not be put away where he can do no harm to society? Killing Benito would be less of a crime than cooking in drums."

I should have known better, Mary thought. *I should have just kept on top of it and never asked for help. If they don't stop, I might have to kill them both.*

The more Charles Hooper thought about it, the more he believed Danny McCoy was right. The kid probably didn't even know himself how right. After all, he probably thought the people he worked with were on the up and up, or he thought that his department and Montecito's personnel department had checked out new hires thoroughly.

The trouble was that dedicated terrorists seldom

worked alone. Their circles of professional acquaintances included people who could fake documents or even entire background histories. Getting hired wouldn't be a problem—they could gin up excellent résumés and letters of recommendation, and phone calls to "previous employers" would be met with realistically effusive praise. A truly dedicated terrorist with an experienced support network could gain access almost anywhere.

Hooper sat in his cabana at Bello Petto, the hotel's topless pool, thinking over the problem. He had a great view from his lounge chair of exactly the kind of woman who raced his engines: a lean hard-body with small breasts and a narrow behind, tanned and athletic-looking. Her dark brown hair was cut short, and oversize sunglasses hid much of her face while still exposing a perfect nose and full, delicious-looking lips. Stealing glimpses at her as she read a paperback novel with a red cover—he couldn't make out the title from this distance—offered a pleasant distraction from his real worry, and he was pro enough not to let it become anything more than that.

He had become convinced that the plot against Klaus Aickmann was legitimate. Further, he felt, with absolute certainty, that it was, as McCoy had said, an inside job. No other scenario fit all the facts. Watching the topless woman shift in her chair, scratching her left thigh before returning to her book, he ran down what he knew for sure.

One of the Montecito's security guards had found the CD and turned it in to Danny. It had been found in a public part of the casino floor, where just about anyone could have deposited it or picked it up. No surveillance footage existed showing anyone dropping it off, though.

To Hooper, that pointed in only one direction. Someone in the surveillance office had doctored the footage, or switched off the camera that would have captured whoever planted the CD at just the right moment. A few seconds of missing footage out of the twenty-four-hour coverage would never be missed. The other possibility—although less likely—was that someone had learned to gauge the sweep of a moving camera and had managed to drop the disc at precisely the right moment to avoid being seen. Unlikeliest of all was that the drop had occurred at that moment through sheer coincidence. Since McCoy wouldn't provide access to all the footage and camera data, he didn't know if the camera in question was stationary or mobile, but either way those latter scenarios seemed less likely than the first.

Just to complicate things further, Hooper knew that he couldn't really trust McCoy. Or Deline. He didn't know Danny McCoy from Adam, and although the kid had an impressive record, that too could have been faked. Maybe he had been in Iraq—but fighting on which side? Charles Hooper hadn't reached this point in his career by trusting people without verification.

And Ed Deline? As far as Hooper knew, he had always been an American hero. But he was a relic, a soldier whose conflicts had faded into history. Who knew what he had been into since his retirement from the company? Even trusted agents could be turned—Hooper stole a quick glance at the reading brunette, knowing that one technique enemy states often used to recruit spies was sending the target's own "type" in to develop a relationship—and here in Las Vegas for these past years, Ed was hardly immune to temptation. A surreptitious relationship with someone other than his wife, a gambling debt, a promised career boost, all these things could be used by the bad guys.

So he couldn't trust either of the Montecito's top two men.

He had to get into the surveillance room, had to get a look at that footage for himself.

And he had to do it without either of them finding out.

It wouldn't be easy.

That had never stopped him before.

Sam had started to think that Kaylie Hammer was a reasonable human being. A little headstrong, perhaps. Easily distracted, but basically sane, especially for a six-year-old child.

That was before.

She had managed to get Kaylie, Marcella, and Byron together for an early dinner at Wolfgang's. After dessert, the plan was that Sam would send a babysitter up to their suite to stay with the girl while Marcella and Byron went to see Elton John together. Sam knew that Byron would never sit through the whole concert and would return to the Montecito alone, ready to gamble.

Now, however, Marcella looked chagrined. Byron

had scooted back to a blackjack table, as if afraid of his own daughter's tantrum. Dressed in Disney Princess pajamas, Kaylie stood in front of the elevators, her hands bunched into tiny fists, her head thrown back, letting out a wail that could have been heard in Tonopah. Kaylie's eyes were clenched tight, but tears still bubbled out of them. Her face had turned purple, causing Sam to wonder if she would pass out from lack of oxygen.

That would not, she decided, be altogether a bad thing.

"I thought she was going to bed," Sam said.

"She was. But she can't find Mr. Fuzzkins."

"Mr. Fuzzkins. Oh, the rabbit?"

"I want my bunny!" Kaylie shrieked. In an emergency she could stand in for a siren.

"We have dozens of stuffed animals in our shops," Sam said. "I'll find her a rabbit. I'll do better than that, I'll get her one of each. Take her up to the room and I'll bring them up in a few minutes."

Kaylie released another wordless, piercing scream. "She has other animals," Marcella explained. "But she loves Mr. Fuzzkins the most."

"Do you want me to send housekeeping up to search the room?" Sam asked. Guests walked past, covering their ears with their hands, making faces at the racket. "He's probably just buried under something, or stuck in the covers."

"We searched the room, top to bottom," Marcella replied. "He's not there."

Sam opened her mouth to make another suggestion, except that she hadn't quite figured out yet what it would be. Before she had a chance to wing it, Byron Hammer rounded a curve, stalking toward them. Maybe he'd had a change of heart, or maybe Kaylie's screams had penetrated the casino. "It's okay, honey," he said. "Sam will fix it."

Kaylie looked at her father. Her breath hitched, and then she let out another shattering wail. A bubble of snot formed at her nostrils.

"Sam will fix it," Byron repeated, directing it to Sam this time. "Won't she?"

"I'm afraid I don't know where Mr. Fuzzkins is hiding," Sam said, still trying to keep things light.

"He's not hiding, he's been stolen," Byron said with absolute seriousness. "And I want him found, Sam. Now. Kaylie needs him to go to sleep. As you can see, she's overtired herself."

She's over-something, Sam thought. Somehow she refrained from saying that aloud.

"You *will* find him, right?" Byron said.

Sam read the unspoken threat in his eyes. Either she found him or Byron Hammer took his considerable business elsewhere, never to return.

"Do you know where she had him last?" Sam asked, addressing the question to Marcella.

"I'm not a psychic," Marcella snapped. Even her usual veneer of patience had eroded under Kaylie's assault. "I have no idea where the damn bunny is or where it's gone. The last time Kaylie remembers seeing it was on the elevator."

"I miss Mr. Fuzzkins!" Kaylie squealed. Sam didn't know how much more she could take before her ears started to bleed.

"Okay. I will find Mr. Fuzzkins," she said. It wouldn't be the first promise she had made with no idea as to how she might possibly keep it. For the first four years of her career as a casino host, that had been a daily occurrence. "Why don't you take Kaylie to your suite, where she'll be more comfortable, and I'll find her bunny and bring him up?"

Byron folded his arms angrily over his chest. "See that you do, Sam."

Marcella pointedly glanced at her wristwatch. "The sooner the better."

"Understood," Sam said. That part she didn't need to be told. Anything that would shut the kid up sounded good to Sam.

And, as Marcella had said, the sooner the better.

18

"You had an argument with Eustace Barnes the other day," Mike said. Leroy Snead sat on a folding, leather-backed director's chair inside the horse trailer in his booth. The trailer was more luxurious than some RVs Mike had seen, and would hold eight horses in elegant splendor and comfort. The air inside smelled like booze, but none was in evidence, and Snead seemed sober. He had turned the horse trailer into a temporary office, using a small wooden table to hold sales meetings and write orders. A locked display case off to one side had held the vial containing Cavanaugh's Virtue's final output.

Mike stood in front of the table, clutching a printed image from the surveillance video showing Snead and Barnes in each other's faces. In the photo, Barnes jabbed a thick finger against Snead's chest. Veins stood out on Snead's neck and his face was twisted into a mask of pure hatred.

"There are days I don't have arguments with Eustace Barnes," Snead admitted. "Generally speaking, they're the days I don't see him. But sometimes we get into it on the phone, so that's not an absolute."

"You don't like him."

"Am I speaking English, Mr. Cannon?"

"I'm trying to build an impression of the relationship, Mr. Snead. What is it you don't like about Barnes?"

"Have you met him?"

"Haven't had the pleasure," Mike admitted.

"When you do, just be sure you have time for a shower afterward. If there's a slimier character walking around without a shell on his back, I don't want to know about it. He once tried to get his nephew hired on at my place just so he could keep tabs on my breeding program."

"What did you do?"

"Found out the kid was his nephew, and told him to tell his uncle that he could read about the program in the *Daily Racing Form*. Look under 'winners,' I told him."

"But you didn't get physical with him."

"I can get physical if I need to." Snead slapped his own upper arms, as if to demonstrate his musculature. "And I could take Barnes any day of the week. But I won't waste my sweat on his kind if I can help it."

Mike turned one of the other chairs around and straddled it, letting the picture of Snead and Barnes flutter to the table. "You mind telling me what this fight the other day was all about?"

Snead hitched himself up in his chair, wiped a big hand across his forehead. His hat rested on the little meeting table, beside Mike's picture. "The usual. Mostly they're about him telling me that he's better than me, that his animals are better than mine, and that he'll prove it right soon now."

"And you didn't think maybe it would be worth telling me about this when you told me someone stole your bottle of buttermilk."

"Sorry?"

"Right," Mike said, remembering that this was the one guy who didn't dabble in euphemism. "Your horse semen."

"It didn't even cross my mind," Snead replied. "Like I said, I fight with that bastard all the time. And I wouldn't let him near my booth, much less inside this trailer."

"But he could have hired someone to sneak in here and steal it."

"Could have, but I don't think so. Whoever took the vial had stones, Mr. Cannon. Big brass ones. And that don't describe Eustace Barnes. That old boy ain't got the brains of a spare tire nor the testes of a gelding." He tapped a stack of order forms sitting on the table beneath his hat. "Now, if you don't mind, I got me some math to do, and that ain't my strong point, if you get my drift. If I don't get enough orders to make up for what I'm losing in that auction, I could be finished."

Mike knew that he had been dismissed. He also found it surprising that Snead wasn't more interested in the results of his investigation so far, and so uninterested in Mike's suspicions about Barnes. He left the horse trailer and headed for the exhibit hall's exit, still trying to parse out why the man seemed so detached from everything. He had not made it all the way out when he heard the quick clacking of heels on the tiled floor, and then felt long-fingernailed hands grasping his arm.

"Mr. Cannon!" He turned to face Linda Lou Snead, knowing before he did so who had attacked him. She had a breathless way of speaking, as if she had just finished running a quarter mile underwater. And she came surrounded by her own cloud of perfume, like an ambulatory flower show. Short and curvy, she had applied lipstick as red as a fire truck and teased her blond hair out so much that her matching cowgirl hat floated on top of it like an autumn leaf on a tidal wave. "Mr. Cannon," she said again in that wifty voice, southern accent on full bore, "have you found our precious Virtue's seed?"

"No, ma'am, I haven't," Mike admitted.

"Can you tell me what avenues you're pursuing?" she asked, still holding his arm in that clawed grip. "Have you been working over some suspects? I know y'all have those back rooms where you can take rubber hoses to the bad guys, right?"

Mike tried for a sympathetic smile. "No, Mrs. Snead. I mean, yes, we have back rooms. Sometimes we even use them for interrogations. But working guys over with rubber hoses went out of style the same time the mob got out of the casino business."

She put a hand over her mouth. "The Montecito isn't mob owned?"

"Not at all."

"I thought sure it was. That Mr. Deline looks like—"

"People sometimes think that about Ed, but I assure you there are no mob connections in his past or present. And he's not the owner anyway, he's president of operations."

"Well," she said, narrowing her eyes as if she didn't

quite trust Mike. "This comes as a surprise, I have to say."

"Sorry to disappoint you."

"Still, you have been working on our case, right?"

"Of course. Nothing but."

"That's good. Leroy is just beside himself. That horse meant everything to him."

"I know," Mike said.

"So who have you been looking at? If you want, I can go over some mug shots with you. If you think it'll help."

"A few different people," Mike said. "I'm not really comfortable naming names until I can do a little more investigating." Leroy Snead's immediate dismissal of Mike's Eustace Barnes theory had shattered his confidence, and he didn't want to repeat any of his guesses to Linda Lou.

"I can be a lot of help to you if you let me," she said. She ran her long crimson nails up his arm, purring like a southern-fried Marilyn Monroe impersonator. "Leroy trusts me implicitly with his business affairs—we're a real partnership, not just husband and wife. He has no secrets from me."

Mike didn't get where she was going with this kind of talk, but he didn't like it. He had promised to report to Leroy, not Linda Lou. If they were full partners in the business, then he supposed she had every right to ask for information, but it seemed odd that she was so much more adamant than her husband had been.

And he found her interrogatory technique exceptionally strange. Maybe Leroy had no secrets from her, but, he wondered, did she have any of her own?

"Look, Mrs. Snead," he said, gently shaking his arm free of her clawing grasp. "I'm trying to run down some leads, and when I have something certain I will definitely let you and Mr. Snead know. Until then, the innocent parties are entitled to their privacy, so I'm really not comfortable talking about them."

"I understand perfectly, Michael," she said. Nobody called him Michael, and he didn't want Linda Lou Snead to start.

Mostly, he didn't want Linda Lou around at all.

"Thanks, Mrs. S. Soon as I know anything real I'll be in touch." He backed away from her, lest she dig those claws into him again. She pursed her bright red lips at him as if to blow a kiss, then turned and walked away, hips swaying like a palm tree in a hurricane. He remembered his view of Sam's departure, the day before, and Linda Lou suffered by comparison. *These people,* he thought as he watched her go, *are just a little bit weird.*

An hour before the exhibit hall was scheduled to close, Will noticed, some of the vendors had already started packing their goods. Every show he had worked had some like that: folks so anxious to hit the road for home that they closed early, hoping to get loaded up and out the doors as quickly as they could. He understood the urgency. If sales had been weak, the cost of a hotel room for that last night could make the difference between profit and loss for the entire show. And some vendors had families at home, or livestock, and needed to get back in a hurry.

At this show, for him, sales had been brisk, and he

had moved a couple of high-ticket items. The first day's receipts had covered his booth rental and travel costs, even including staying over this last night. Today had been about making a profit, which Will considered he had accomplished only if he exceeded the cost of the goods, including his original purchase price, storage, and transportation, and made enough to pay himself a little something besides.

That goal had been accomplished by noon. He could afford to close up early, but as long as potential buyers roamed the aisles, he had no intention of thwarting their shopping and maybe losing another good sale.

Then, straightening his display after browsers had picked through it, his gaze landed on the Cassaday Oil calendar and a sudden realization struck him. Yes, he'd be staying at the Montecito one more night—but only one. After that, he might never see Mary Connell again. For all he knew, her shift had ended and she'd already gone home for the day.

He didn't want to just drive away from Las Vegas without at least making a decent attempt to get to know her. Maybe nothing would come of it. Probably. But he had to give it a shot. He'd ridden many a bronc and earned nothing but applause, but he kept getting back on, and once in a while landed in the prize money. You couldn't win if you didn't ride.

Bob and Shirlene sat in their booth, the weary glaze that often overtook show vendors showing on both their faces. Like Will, they appeared determined to stay open until the last shopper had been chased away at the end of the day.

"Bob?" Will said. Both of his neighbors reacted, turning toward him, awareness animating their features again.

"What's up, Will?" Bob asked.

"I was wondering if you guys would mind watching my booth for a few minutes. I'll be back in time to close up, but I might be gone for a little while."

"Need a little pit stop?" Bob asked.

"Something like that. I'd really appreciate it."

"It's no problem, Will," Shirlene said. "You go and find her and take all the time you need."

"Thanks, Shirlene," Will said. He could feel his cheeks heating up. He didn't know he'd been so obvious. Then again, maybe she was just attuned to such things. Bob, after all, hadn't seemed to grasp Will's real intent. "I'll be back as soon as I can."

Confident that his booth would be looked after—but as nervous as a young cowboy climbing onto the back of an unridden horse—Will left his merchandise behind to try his luck in Vegas's biggest casino.

He had gambling in mind. But nothing to do with money.

Delinda knew her reputation was that of a party girl, on the flighty side, who didn't take life too seriously. To a large extent, the reputation was true, and she had come by it honestly. She didn't take many things seriously and saw no reason why she should. She was young, healthy, and beautiful, with a genius IQ and survival instincts—perhaps inherited from her father—that had kept her out of real trouble for the most part.

She did, however, take her job very seriously indeed. She had been put in charge of the Montecito's food services, and she wanted her customers to be served good, healthy meals at prices they could afford, so they would want to come back for more. She paid her staff well, emphasized fresh local ingredients whenever possible, and tried to treat each customer like an honored guest. By doing so, she hoped to turn a good profit for the resort and earn a good income for herself.

Sometimes turning that profit meant doing certain jobs herself instead of paying others to do them. She didn't mind a little hard work as long as she saw a good reason for it, which was why she had gone down to the Montecito's internal florist, looking for some new arrangements for Mystique's back wall, and now returned to the restaurant pushing a steel cart laden with fresh blooms.

She had almost reached Mystique's entrance when she heard a voice calling her name. She didn't recognize it and she didn't want to lose her momentum with the heavy cart, so she kept going and the voice called again, with greater urgency.

This time she stopped the cart and looked.

Mary's cowboy crusher came toward her, hat in hand, his hair smashed down in a perfect ring around his head. "Sorry, Delinda," he said. "I couldn't tell if you heard me."

"Everything okay, Will?" she asked.

"Yeah, fine. Show's going fine. I was just wondering . . . do you know where Mary is? I mean, if she's still here someplace."

Oh, I'm good, Delinda thought. *I could have a second*

career as a matchmaker. "She's probably down by the chuck wagon," Delinda said, pointing toward a nearby door to the Montecito grounds. "Go out there and down the hill, you can't miss it. There's a fence to keep people out, but just let yourself through and you'll find her."

"Thanks, Delinda. You need some help with that cart?"

Ordinarily she wouldn't have turned it down. The thing was heavy, and he had volunteered so it wouldn't be sucking up payroll dollars. But she didn't have far to go, whereas if he wanted to get anywhere with Mary, he would have miles ahead of him, metaphorically at least. That girl didn't give in easily, Delinda knew. Vegas was full of guys passing through, and if Mary had been interested in that type, she could have had her pick of them. So far, she had passed every time.

Maybe Will would be the one to break that streak. Delinda had been right about him liking Mary, after all, and she didn't seem immune to his charms either.

If this works, Delinda thought, *I'll definitely have to consider hanging out my shingle. Delinda's Date Factory, maybe. Or Hookups "R" Us.*

Las Vegas could always find room for one more entrepreneur.

19

Mary wondered if the smell of burning mesquite would ever come out of her clothes and hair. Worse, she wondered if she would ever be able to flush the sight and sound of Gunther and Ezra fighting from her mind. When she had agreed to take this job, she had envisioned a wide variety of tasks and situations, but nothing quite like this one.

With any luck, it wouldn't be repeated for another hundred years. Unless medical science made some major breakthroughs, that would make it someone else's problem.

She stood off to one side, trying to keep the smoke out of her eyes and prepared to dodge any objects the two chefs might throw. From the corner of her eye, she saw a figure pass through the security gate and start down the hill. Ready to tell whoever it was that the chuck wagon hadn't opened for business yet, she turned and realized that the figure looked familiar. When he had passed through shadow and into the light, she recognized him as Will Streeter.

"Hi, Will," she called, adding a little wave. He responded by touching the brim of his hat and continued down the slope toward her. A few feet shy of her, he stopped, touched the hat again.

"Hello, Mary," he said.

"Is the show over?" she asked.

He checked his watch. "Another twenty minutes or so. Sure smells good around here."

"I guess so," she said. "I think I'm immune to it by this point."

"That's too bad," Will said. "I was thinking it'd be a great place to have dinner. And"—he hesitated, casting his gaze at the sky, then back to Mary's eyes, catching and holding them with his—"and if you'd be interested, I'd love to have your company."

The offer came as no surprise. He had been interested since the moment he saw her—earlier than that if you counted his fascination with the calendar model.

Which was precisely why she held back. Will seemed nice enough, and he'd no doubt be an interesting dinner companion. But did he think he was having dinner with Mary Connell, or with a painting somehow magically brought to life? If the latter, then what expectations would he bring to the table with him?

Maybe she'd wear the little fringed blouse sometime, but Mary Connell didn't twirl six-guns for any man.

Still, the way he stood there, the toe of his right boot digging nervously into the dirt, the look of hopeful expectation on his face . . . she couldn't quite bring herself to turn him down.

It's only dinner, she decided. *Even if he turns out to be a complete nut job obsessed with that sheet of paper, we'll be surrounded by people. And I know where Ezra keeps the big knives.*

"Sure, Will. That sounds like fun. We should be open by six or so, so any time after that would be great. You'll be able to find me right here."

"Thanks, Mary," he said, sounding surprised. "I guess I'll see you here, then."

He didn't make any move to leave. "I guess so," she said. "Umm . . . shouldn't you be getting back to your booth?"

He blinked a couple of times and broke into a smile. "Yeah. Yeah, I guess so." Backing away, as if he didn't want to lose sight of her for a moment, he said, "I'll see you later, Mary."

She gave him another wave, then turned toward Ezra and Gunther.

For a change, their angry sniping came as a bit of a relief.

"It's just like you figured, Danny," Detective Jernigan said. "None of these good old boys know who the other four cowboys were. They met in the bar earlier that night. Those four, they said, were buying round after round, and they were the ones who instigated the stampede. Of course, this could just be a way for the ones in custody to deflect blame onto the ones who got away."

"Could be," Danny said. He sat at his desk, where he had been working the phone when Jernigan called. Scribbled notes filled a sheet of legal paper in front of him. "But I don't think so. I think those four had something specific in mind, and they duped the cowboys into helping out. If you look at the video, those four really don't have much interaction with the cattle. They wear the clothes but it doesn't look like they really know what they're doing."

"I can't comment on that," Jernigan said, "since I wouldn't either. But I'll take your word for it. All I know is that these guys I have in here feel like they were used. They admit to helping with the scheme, and they understand that it was a stupid stunt. One of the stupidest stunts ever. But they don't want to be looking at a lot of jail time, when they're also the ones who got the cattle out of the casino with no one getting hurt."

"I'll talk to Ed," Danny promised. "I know he wants to see somebody do hard time for this, but he wants it to be the right people."

Jernigan agreed to hold the men until Danny called back. Danny hung up the phone and returned to the notes he had scrawled on his pad with a blue pen. He had been calling guys he had known in Iraq, people who might also have run into Garrick Flynn. There seemed to be more to Flynn than he had yet been able to determine, and he wanted to know what the man's real story was.

He had managed to find a guy who knew a guy who knew another guy. He had been about to phone that other guy when Detective Jernigan's call had come through. Now he located the number on his pad and dialed it.

A masculine voice answered, thick with sleep. "Yeah?"

"Hey, sorry if I woke you," Danny said. He checked the clock on his computer. Almost six in the evening in Las Vegas, so eight in Maryland, where he had called. "My name is Danny McCoy. I was a lieutenant in the Corps, but now I run surveillance and security for the Montecito Hotel and Casino in Las Vegas."

"Okay." The man on the other end of the line cleared his throat. "I was asleep."

"I figured," Danny said. "Is this John Solomon?"

"That's right."

"I'll keep it brief, John. I heard from Kevin Sassen that you might have known a guy named Garrick Flynn, over in the Gulf."

"Sure, I knew Flynn."

"He a close friend of yours?"

"You've been over there?" John Solomon asked. He sounded a little more alert, but his voice remained gravelly.

"Yeah."

"Then you know every guy in your unit is a close friend, at least while you're there. The more heat you take the closer you get, right?"

"That's right," Danny agreed. Just talking about it brought back painful memories he would rather forget, images of dust and heat and fear, smoke rising from mud-walled buildings, the whine of bullets and the roar of mortar shells. In his mind Iraq would forever smell like fire, sweat, the metallic stink of blood, and the antiseptic bite of field hospitals.

"After we got back," Solomon said, "Flynn and I both moved to the D.C. area and took jobs with Coleman Security."

Danny jotted the name down on his pad. "That's one of the contractors providing private security consultants in Iraq, right?"

"That's right. None of us wanted to go back there, but the money was so good, you know? Hard to turn down twenty large for a month's work. And we had better equipment and better wheels than we did when Uncle was footing the bill."

"I hear you," Danny said. He had been called back to duty there once, and it would take more than twenty thousand dollars to get him to return to that theater again. Voluntarily, anyway. But when Uncle summoned, you went. That's what "duty" meant. "Did Flynn go back too?"

"Yeah. For a while, anyway."

"Why just for a while? Did something happen?"

"Look," Solomon hedged. "I don't want to get anybody in hot water."

"He's not in any trouble," Danny assured him. "I'm just trying to get a sense of who the guy is."

"Well, he ended up going home early because Coleman fired him. He got into it with about four of us, mixed it up at our base in the Green Zone. One guy went into the hospital for three months and had to drink his meals through a straw. Flynn was lucky he only got fired and not charged with attempted murder."

"He took on four of you?" Danny asked, surprised. "I mean, he's a big guy, but—"

"It's not like he went through it unscathed," Solomon said. "We all got in some shots. But he was like a madman, like he was possessed or something. We were worried about him, didn't want to mess him up too bad. I guess now if we hadn't gone easy on him, it might have spared Levon some grief."

"Levon is the guy who ended up in the hospital?" Danny scribbled the name down.

"Yeah. He got shipped out to Wiesbaden, but he's home now."

"Got a last name?"

"Is it important?" Solomon asked. "I mean, we all got a right to privacy, don't we?"

"If it becomes important, can I call you back?"

A moment's hesitation, and then Solomon said, "Okay, sure. If you really need it."

"What was the fight about?" Danny asked, happy with the concession Solomon had made. He still didn't know how this information might help, but if there was the slightest chance that Flynn might go nuts in the Montecito, he needed to know about it.

Solomon hesitated again, and for a second Danny feared he had hung up. There was no dial tone, though, just the empty, hollow sound of a live connection. "He got kind of strange," Solomon said after a while. "I guess it started when we were over there with the rangers, on our first tour. It was almost like he became some kind of fundamentalist, like some of those guys we were fighting there."

"He became a Muslim?" Danny asked, confused.

"No, not like that. Not even religious, really. Just . . . super straight. Prudish, almost. He was always talking about how the world was falling apart, and blaming it on booze, drugs, sex, porn, rock music, whatever his beef was on any given day. Before, he joined in, partied, drank on his days off. He's not a bad-looking guy, you know, and there were always girls around him, it seemed like.

"But then after we were in country for a few months, he started to change. He got withdrawn, at first, like he was always thinking things over without telling anyone what was on his mind. Then he started speaking up, and that was worse. He used to give us crap about almost everything we did to stay sane over there. I mean, we're shooting people and he's worried about some guy putting a centerfold up on the wall beside his bunk. I thought maybe it was just combat stress, you know? When we got back to the world I figured he'd mellow out some. And he seemed to, for a while. So I thought he was over it and would be okay to go back."

Solomon paused, and it sounded like he took a drink of something. Danny wanted him to keep going but didn't want the guy to think he was pushing too hard. He stayed silent, figuring Solomon would spill whatever he was comfortable with.

"But I was wrong," the man said finally. "He wasn't. He got worse the longer we stayed. Got so he would barely speak to any of us except to bitch us out, because he disapproved of us so much. I remember he said Sonny was one of society's dregs one day. Isn't that something? Society's dregs. I mean, who talks like that?"

"Pretty strange," Danny agreed, just to keep Solomon going.

"Finally, the day came that he snapped. Flynn saw Levon looking at some pictures his girlfriend e-mailed him, of herself, you know? Au naturel? He just came freakin' unglued. Went berserk, and when we tried to pull him off Levon he started in on the rest of us. Me, Sonny, Levon, and Dale."

Danny jotted the names down. "And so Coleman canned him and shipped him home?"

"That's right. Word got out too. Spread fast. No other security company would hire him after that, even though he didn't get charged with anything. I heard he went overseas and found a gig, though. I'd hate to be around when he goes off again. You said you're in Las Vegas?"

"That's right," Danny said. The implication of Solomon's question worried him.

"Seems like the kind of place he would freakin' hate. Like I said, I'm not out to jam him up, but I'd keep an eye on him if I were you. Two eyes."

"Will do," Danny said. "Listen, thanks a lot for talking to me. It could be a big help."

Danny hung up the phone and sat at his desk, hands linked behind his head, staring at the paper. He had only made a few notes during the conversation, but he didn't need notes to remember the high points.

Garrick Flynn worked for Hartung because he couldn't get a job in the United States. He couldn't get a job because he had assaulted the last crew he'd worked with. He didn't like sex, drugs, or rock and roll, but he was here in a Las Vegas casino, where two of the three were commonplace, and if you substituted booze for drugs you had the hat trick.

Sounded like a recipe for disaster.

20

"Herr Aickmann, you must cancel your speech."

Aickmann's thick eyebrows arched up his high forehead, pushing rows of ridges above them. "Excuse me, Heinrich?"

"Cancel the speech," Hartung repeated. "We can concoct a reasonable excuse, a flu perhaps. You can return to Germany and give the speech there, where I can better ensure your safety."

Aickmann paced to the floor-to-ceiling window of his suite's living room. Hartung winced, wishing the man would keep well away from it. A sniper outside with a high-powered rifle and a telescopic scope, an assassin with a rig to rappel down from the roof . . . "Do you have a particular reason to doubt my safety, Heinrich?"

"The plot," Hartung began. He had already explained to Aickmann about the disc the Montecito security guard had found, and described the precautions that had been taken as a result. "And then . . ." He let the thought trail off.

"And then what?" Aickmann moved away from the window. *Thank God for that much, at least,* Hartung thought. He sat in one of the chairs surrounding a low table that held some magazines and the remote control for the ridiculously huge television set. Aickmann walked to another of the chairs, but instead of sitting, he put his stocking foot on the seat and leaned forward, massaging his toes.

Hartung was at a loss. He couldn't tell his employer about the dream, or the stock he put in it. Not without making himself look like a superstitious fool, at any rate, which he had no intention of doing. Aickmann was an industrialist, a man of pure practicality, impatient with what he called "squishy thinking." And Heinrich Hartung was too old to look for a new job.

And, he thought sadly, *too poor to have none at all*. Three marriages, seven children, two homes, and a predilection for the finer things ate through his paychecks as fast as they came in.

"This place," he said, almost desperately. "Las Vegas. It's too chaotic. Millions of visitors every year, a large transient population, hotels and casinos open to the public without regard to who might be walking through the doors at any moment. Who knows who might be here? Or what they're plotting? If that CD was a fake, a distraction—or worse, just one plot of many—then the risk to you is too great. As head of your security division I'm afraid that I must insist—"

"As head of my security division," Aickmann said, cutting him off, "you work for me. Any insisting will be done by me. You are free to suggest, Heinrich, but not to insist."

"In the past you have always let me make decisions relating to your safety."

"In the past you have had good reasons for those decisions. Today you seem . . . what shall I say? Panicked? You sound like a frightened child, Heinrich, worried about monsters in the closet. It's not like you. And even if you could offer legitimate reasons, for which I'm still waiting, it's too late to cancel. This speech is important. Not just to me, but to Germany. To Europe. It has been scheduled. Distinguished guests will be in the audience. The press is arriving even now to cover it. For me to cancel it would send entirely the wrong message to our friends and supporters around the world, and would send a message of weakness to our enemies. No, Heinrich, there shall be no cancellation, no postponement. The speech goes on as scheduled. As to my safety, there and after, I leave that in your capable hands."

A faint smile played about Aickmann's lips. Hartung wondered if his employer was mocking him. Theirs had always been a relationship of mutual respect, each man knowing the other brought to it qualities and experiences that could help the other. Aickmann paid his salary but treated him as an equal.

Now the balance had shifted. In trying to press his case without having hard facts to back it up, he had allowed Aickmann to perceive him as immature. That happened, he knew, with old people—they regressed into childish behaviors, needed people to wipe their noses and remind them to brush their teeth. If Klaus Aickmann started to think of him in those terms, then his career would be over even if he saw Aickmann safely home this week.

"Very well," he said finally. "I must let you know in the strongest terms possible that I disagree with your decision, Herr Aickmann. But as it has been made, I will do everything I can to ensure that your stay in Las Vegas is—barring the obvious—uneventful."

Aickmann laughed without real mirth. "Uneventful? What fun would a Las Vegas trip be, then? Remember the city motto, Heinrich. 'What happens in Vegas, stays in Vegas.' I don't think uneventful is what they had in mind."

"Have you even been to cooking school, you ignorant country boob?" Gunther demanded, his clenched fists pressed against his hips. "Or did you learn in prison?"

"I learned out on the trail, like cookies have learned for generations!" Ezra shot back. He waved a hand as if the open prairie, not one of the nation's biggest cities, surrounded him. "I don't need no fancy degree to know how to whip up some chuck."

"And you persist in calling it 'chuck!'" Gunther shouted, his face red, tendons in his neck standing out in frightening relief. Mary stood on the sidelines, watching in horror. "It's an abomination. *You* are an abomination."

"I ain't no kind of snowman at all," Ezra countered. "And I sure ain't some Euro-jasper who thinks cookin' is like paintin' a gol-durn masterpiece, neither. I don't care how purty the grub looks on the plate, it's meant to be et!"

"*Et?*" Gunther mocked, leaning close to the shorter Ezra. "*Et?* You truly are a moron, aren't you? Are you even fully human?"

"Guys," Mary said, trying to squeeze in between the two of them. She waved her hands in the air, palms down, like she was trying to flatten sheets on an invisible bed. "Guys, let's just calm down, okay?"

"You best keep outta this, Miz Connell," Ezra said. "This is between me and this . . . this good-for-nothin' galoot. I swear he's just as chuckleheaded as a prairie dog. Don't even speak English right."

"I know English, Mary," Gunther said, waving her back. "For years I have been speaking English. I don't believe that what he speaks *is* English."

"I'm as American as the day is long!" Ezra yelled, his eyes narrowing with rage. He snatched hot tongs from the edge of a fire pit and brandished them at Gunther. "You take that back!"

Mary tried once again to rush between them, but this time Gunther shoved her aside, grabbing a rotisserie wand. "Stay back, Mary. If this barbarian wants a battle, then a battle he will have. I studied fencing at Heidelberg, you bumpkin! En garde!"

Guests weren't allowed near the chuck wagon until food service began, but Mary could see some watching from a distance through the orange webbed plastic security fence that had been erected to keep them away. They looked like they couldn't tell if they were watching a performance or an actual brawl. Mary knew she had to get them under control fast.

The two men glared into each other's eyes, breathing heavily, legs spread apart for balance. The whole tableau had a kind of primal savagery to it—two rival warriors facing each other down in the smoke of their cooking fire. Their weapons looked absurd, but they could do some real damage.

"Just cool it!" she demanded. "Both of you!" Both

men froze where they stood, the ferocity of her shouts startling them into stillness. She gave a terse nod of approval and ran for the hotel, whipping out her cell phone as she did and punching the speed-dial button for Delinda. The truce wouldn't last long. Tempers had flared too high for that.

Her friend came on the line a moment later. "Delinda!" Mary called breathlessly into the phone, still running and keeping an eye out for any handy security guards as she went. "Gunther and Ezra are about to kill each other!"

"Gunther wouldn't kill anyone," Delinda said. "Well, maybe Benito. But I think if he was really going to, he would have done it long ago."

"Maybe not kill, then," Mary said. "But they're pretty peeved and they're going at each other with barbecue utensils. You have lots of experience calming him down—can you get out here and talk to him?"

"I'm a little busy here, Mare."

"Delinda! How busy will you be if Gunther goes to jail for assault and you have to run the kitchen?"

Delinda gave a frustrated sigh. "Okay, okay, I'm on my way."

Mary had almost reached the hotel. She stopped where she was, panting, and leaned forward with her hands on her knees to catch her breath. There would be security guards just inside, but with Delinda on the way maybe she wouldn't need them. Delinda had wrangled Gunther for years, and if she couldn't control him, then they could bring in the big guns.

Watching for Delinda, she saw Sam storm past,

eyes turned toward the ground, like she was watching for snakes beside the path. "Hey, Sam," she said. "What's up?"

"Oh, hi, Mary," Sam said, startled out of her near-trance. She grinned. "Be vewwy vewwy quiet, I'm hunting wabbits. You haven't seen any wabbits—I mean, rabbits, have you?"

"I sometimes see cottontails on the grounds around here in the morning," Mary said. "But not today. If there had been any in the last couple of days, Ezra would probably have thrown them on the fire."

"Why does Ezra hate rabbits? And who's Ezra?"

"My chuck wagon cook."

"Oh, right. I saw him earlier. Is it just me, or does he really have flies for pets?"

"Flies?"

"They were buzzing around him like . . . well, never mind. Like something flies buzz around. I thought maybe he didn't know about soap and water."

"He's perfectly clean, Sam," Mary insisted.

"Okay, sure. Whatever. So no bunnies? Not real ones, stuffed ones."

"I haven't seen any bunnies, real or stuffed."

"Cool," Sam said. Her gaze returned to the ground, as if her rabbit hunt had never been interrupted, and she hurried off.

Delinda emerged from the doorway a minute later, rushing toward Mary as fast as her heels would let her. "Where are they?" she asked.

"Down by the chuck wagon!"

"You left them alone?" Delinda said.

"I didn't think they'd really kill each other," Mary explained. "Not for a few minutes, anyway. And I thought maybe I could find a security guard while I tried to reach you."

"We'd better hurry." Delinda's cheeks were flushed from the run. Even anxious and winded, Mary realized, she was stunningly beautiful. "The only thing certain about Gunther is that you never really know what he's capable of."

"Okay, I feel a whole lot better now," Mary said, breaking into a run alongside Delinda. "Thanks."

They passed through the gate in the orange fence, and as they neared the chuck wagon, Mary heard a wordless shout. It sounded like Ezra, but she couldn't tell what it signified. A few steps ahead of Delinda, thanks to her western boots, Mary cleared the end of the chuck wagon, half expecting to see one or both men on the ground, injured or worse.

Instead, Gunther and Ezra both knelt together beside one of the fire pits. "Hah!" Gunther exclaimed, scooping a hamburger patty off the grate with a long-handled spatula. "Like it wanted me to get it!"

"That's the way to do it!" Ezra said. A huge grin bulged his apple cheeks out over his brushy beard. "You're catchin' on, Euro-boy."

Mary stopped dead in her tracks, and Delinda slammed into her when she rounded the corner. "Oh," Delinda said, surprised. "I thought you said they were fighting."

"They were."

Ezra pointed to another burger near Gunther.

"Get that one," he said. "Can't let 'em cook too long over the fire. And you don't want to turn 'em too much—"

"I know, I know," Gunther interrupted. "You'll force out the juices. I have cooked many hamburgers, Ezra. Hundreds. Not over holes in the ground, no, this is true. But I know how to do it."

"Just didn't know if that was somethin' they teach you at them fancy cookin' schools," Ezra said.

"They teach many things," Gunther said. "You could not learn them all if you live another hundred years."

Ezra barked a laugh. "Boy, when I hit my first hundred you'll still be a whippersnapper."

Gunther joined in the laughter. "Whippersnapper! That is a good word, whippersnapper. Benito, he is a whippersnapper. Maybe too young for that, maybe just a whipper still. You should meet Benito one day, Ezra. You would enjoy teaching him some lessons. Perhaps with your fist or your shoe."

"I honestly don't know what happened," Mary whispered to Delinda. "When I left, they were at each other's throats."

"It's Gunther's fault," Delinda said softly. "Like I said, you just can't count on him."

Gunther rose from his kneeling position and moved to one of the drums of beans, stirring them with a long-handled wooden oar. "These are almost done, Mary!" he called. "When are the people allowed to begin?"

"If you guys are ready to go, I'll let them in," Mary replied. "They're lined up and anxious to chow down."

Mary turned to go back up the slope to where the crowd had been fenced off. Delinda stood behind her, shaking her head sadly. "Honestly, Mary, I didn't think you'd exaggerate like that."

"They were fighting," Mary insisted. "They had weapons of . . . well, weapons of meat delivery in their hands, and it looked like they meant to use them."

"Uh-huh."

"Why would I call you otherwise, Delinda? Just so you could see Gunther laughing? It's not that rare, is it?"

"I just don't know, Mary," Delinda answered. Her eyes had taken on a faraway look, as if she was trying to grasp a difficult concept. "Sometimes there's just no understanding you."

With Mike Cannon gone, Snead retrieved a new bottle of Jim Beam from the filing cabinet, unscrewed the lid, and helped himself to another long swallow. He couldn't afford to get seriously drunk, much as he'd like to, but he didn't see any reasonable way to stay entirely sober either. Instead, he just allowed himself enough to maintain a functional level so he could go about his business.

He needed to figure out a way to keep the company solvent even if the semen never showed up and his planned lawsuit against the Montecito failed. To that end, he had been running numbers over and over. Accounting tricks could help—numbers, he had learned, were malleable things, and at a glance one column of them looked much like another.

The tricky part would be when it came to writing checks, because the bank liked there to be money to back up these checks. Money, at a certain level, was also just numbers, but Snead Enterprises had not reached that level of financial accomplishment. He could skate for a few months, maybe, but no more than that.

Snead felt a belch rising in his chest. He covered his mouth and let it out, hoping the noise of the exhibit hall would cover it up. When it had passed, he thumped his chest once and leaned over to stuff the bottle back into its hidey-hole. While he swayed in front of the cabinet, bent over, one arm reaching down into the drawer, heels clattered on the metal step outside.

"Holy mother of God," Linda Lou's voice said, cutting into Snead like rusty hooks tearing at his flesh. "Was that you, or did someone let a goose in here?"

He released the bottle, which fell to the bottom of the cabinet with a slosh and a glassy clunk.

Linda Lou gave a knowing nod. "Drinking again? That explains the burp from hell."

"Just a little," Snead said. He tried to slide the drawer shut with his foot but couldn't get the right angle on it. Finally he left it open and returned to his chair and his stack of bills.

"Looks like a little," she said. "Mike Cannon came to see you, didn't he?"

"Yep."

"What did he tell you?"

Snead started to answer, but then a thought floated up from the liquid center of his brain. He tried to grasp it, couldn't, but it left him with the sense that he should not reveal everything, not even to Linda Lou.

Maybe especially not to Linda Lou.

If he had trusted her completely, after all, he would have told her about his oil investment in the first place. He would have told her about the company's true financial condition.

He loved Linda Lou, he believed. Unreasonably, out of all proportion to the love she returned. She had never betrayed him, but she wasn't the kind of woman who could just give herself over absolutely. She always had to hold something back emotionally, as if to do otherwise would somehow mean surrendering her own identity. Since she couldn't throw herself into the marriage with the same fervor that he had, he couldn't quite bring himself to confide the details of the business with her. Petty, he supposed, but he felt he had to have something to hold away from her, just as she reserved herself from him.

And the worse things got, the less he felt like sharing.

"Nothing," he said finally, realizing Linda Lou was staring at him like he was some kind of performing animal. "He's got nothing, and I told him I had to get this work done."

"You're paying bills?" He caught a mocking note in her voice. "With what?"

"You were never so concerned before."

"I never had cause to be, until I learned you were hiding things from me. Now I want to know what's going on."

"What's going on," Snead said, anger building inside him, "is that without the auction, we're screwed. I want to leave Cannon alone to find the vial, and if he can't find it, then I want to be able to sue the hotel. It's really pretty simple, Linda Lou. I'd think that even you could follow it." He knew the sharp edge that blurted from him belonged to Jim Beam, not to him, but he was powerless against it.

"You handle things your way, Leroy," she said with a dismissive wave of her hand. "I'll handle 'em my own. Since your way seems to involve staying on the sauce until the auction's over, guess who's likely to be more successful?"

She rattled the steps again on her way out the door. Snead sat at the table, not looking after her but instead staring at the pile of bills he couldn't afford to pay. "I can't imagine," he said quietly. No one could hear him, certainly not Linda Lou.

That was just the way he wanted it.

21

"Hi, Mike."

Mike Cannon spun around in his seat, acknowledging her with a quick nod. "Hi, Sam."

"You busy?"

Mike didn't hesitate before answering. "You know it."

"Put it aside. I have an emergency. The kind that comes attached to a whale who drops six figures every time he visits."

Mike's ready smile faded and he rubbed his forehead as if an ache was building behind it. "What is it, Sam?"

"What's so important?"

His gaze returned to his computer monitor. "Still looking for the missing mayonnaise," he replied, sounding distracted.

"Missing mayonnaise?"

"Horse gravy," Mike said, as if that clarified anything. "Love juice."

"What are you—eww, never mind," she said, as his meaning sank in. "I'm sorry I asked. But you have to drop it, because what I'm looking for is really important."

Mike tipped back in his chair, folding his hands together and laying them on his stomach. "What are you looking for, Sam?"

She held her hands apart about nine inches. "Its name is Mr. Fuzzkins, it's about yea big, and it's a disgusting, child-chewed, floor-dragged, ear-bitten stuffed bunny rabbit. I need you to facial it or whatever it is you do."

"You want me to use facial recognition on a stuffed rabbit?"

Sam sighed. "I don't know how you do your magic, Mike. All I know is that you can find people from up here when you need to. Now I need you to find a rabbit."

"It's not that easily done, Sam," Mike said. "To begin with, to use our system for that, we'd have to have an image of the rabbit. If we did, I think we might be able to search for it. But I can't just type in 'rabbit' and have it work."

"Does Casey Manning know that? Or Ed? Because I would think they'd want to upgrade, if that's true."

"I'm pretty sure that's universal to all existing surveillance systems, Sam."

"Seems like a serious oversight." She looked at the banks of flat-screen monitors, with images flickering across them showing virtually every square inch of the casino floor, hotel lobby, elevators, and the corridors of the guest floors. A few blank screens glowed blue amid the rest. Five surveillance personnel watched the screens with no unnecessary chatter. The room smelled dry and clean, with just the faintest hints of coffee, sweat, and the electrical odor of hot wiring. "But with these cameras you can see just about everything, right?"

"Very nearly." Mike looked as if he was about to

launch into an explanation of the system, and she wanted to forestall that if she could.

"Whatever you're doing, Mike, can't be as important as this," she said. "Most of what you do is boring anyway."

The tendons in Mike's neck seemed to tense, as if he thought maybe looking for a stuffed rabbit would also be boring. Sam knew it would be, which was precisely why she wanted Mike to do it for her. That, and she didn't know how.

"I would do it, but I don't know how to work the equipment," she said, allowing her tone to display the slightest hint of feminine incompetence. "Can you help me?"

"Pull up a chair," Mike said with a sigh. He sounded impatient. Sam didn't care as long as he did the job. Patience, she had long believed, was an overrated quality. "I'll show you how."

Sam sat, catching an edge of the table and sending her chair spinning. She laughed until the chair slowed and she saw the frown etched on Mike's face. "We don't really spin the chairs in here, Samantha," he said. "There's a lot of expensive hardware around."

"Sorry," Sam said, hoping she sounded chastened even though she really wasn't. She stopped the chair and pulled up to the workstation Mike indicated.

"Watch that monitor," he told her. "I'll throw some footage up there. Let me know if you see anything you want a closer look at. Do you know when the bunny rabbit was last seen?"

"I know it was in an elevator," Sam said. "I don't know when, or which one."

"That narrows it down," Mike said. He tapped on a keyboard and her monitor screen split into four equal boxes, each displaying a different elevator, with a time code stamped across the lower edge of each one. "I'll run these at fast-forward," he said. "If you see the rabbit, give me a shout."

"I will," Sam said. Somehow Mike had tricked her into doing the hard part herself. She stared at the monitor, afraid to blink because the images raced by, fast and jerky. People boarded the elevators, people got off. Some dragged rolling suitcases or carried shoulder bags. Two couples started making out on the trip, one getting far enough along that the woman had to button her shirt again when it came to a stop and a guest-room attendant got on, pushing her service cart. Finally, the time stamps reached the present. "Nothing yet," she reported.

"I'll put up some more," Mike said. "This can't take too long, though, okay?" He had gone back to whatever he was doing—thinking about it made her want to wash her brain out with bleach—instead of focusing on her needs. She hated that in a man.

Sam moaned but kept an eye on the monitor. In moments, three more elevator images flickered to life. She watched similar progressions of activity, silent vignettes of life. People headed down to the casino floor full of excited anticipation. Others returned to their rooms, ecstatic with their winnings or abashed at their losses. Some rode down toward the pools in swimwear and sandals, some to lunch, some traveled up laden with shopping bags.

After watching the speeded-up semblance of life

for about ten minutes, she saw Marcella and Kaylie Hammer board the elevator in the lobby. Marcella went to push the button for their floor, but Kaylie objected, and Marcella backed away to let her daughter take over. Mr. Fuzzkins dangled from Kaylie's left hand as she punched the button with her right index finger. The doors began to close.

Before they came together, someone outside the elevator must have pushed the call button. The doors slid apart again, and a family of five, dragging wheeled suitcases, stepped on board. Kaylie and Marcella huddled close together in the back. The family included three kids, one an infant and two, both boys, closer to Kaylie's age. One of them held two superhero action figures and engaged them in a pitched battle across the tops of his family's suitcases. When one of the heroes punched the other, the boy lost his grip on the loser, who sailed toward Kaylie's feet. The girl bent to pick up the toy and admired it as she handed it back. But, Sam noticed, she held the action figure in both hands, with Mr. Fuzzkins nowhere to be seen.

Marcella and Kaylie got off on a lower floor than the family—causing Sam to wonder who the parents were, since usually whales of Byron Hammer's caliber were on the highest guest floors available. Anyone with the money and connections to rent one of those suites, she needed to know. She made a mental note to find out, once the freaking bunny was found.

As Kaylie stepped off the elevator, Sam saw that her hands remained empty. Suitcases blocked Sam's view of the back of the elevator, where presumably

Mr. Fuzzkins lay abandoned on the floor. On the next floor, the elevator stopped again and the family got off without looking back. Now Sam could see the sorry-looking bunny lying there.

The bunny rode the elevator up and down on a couple more trips, ignored or unnoticed by the next batches of riders. Then three young men got on, one wearing a UCLA T-shirt, the other two similarly attired in casual shirts and jeans. They had, Sam could tell at a glance, been drinking heavily. They laughed at the slightest provocation or none at all, falling against the walls of the elevator and against one another. They air-boxed. Finally one spotted Mr. Fuzzkins, snatched him off the floor, and hiked him to one of his buddies. The three tossed the rabbit around like a football for the rest of their brief ride, and when the doors opened on the casino level, the one in the UCLA shirt tucked Mr. Fuzzkins under his arm and carried him out.

"Mike!" Sam shouted, realizing she should have called him as soon as she saw the rabbit. "Rabbit alert!"

He joined her at the workstation, but by the time he got there, Mr. Fuzzkins and the three college guys had moved out of camera range. "He was on this one," Sam said, pointing to the image on the upper right of her monitor.

"It's cool, Sam, I'll just back it up," Mike said. "Next time you might want to try reacting a little faster." He did as he promised, then paused it when Sam had the guys in view again. From his station, he did something to make the other images go away and enlarge the shot of the college kids. Then green lines traced the kids' faces, joined by tiny green boxes.

"Got 'em," Mike said. "The evildoers haven't been born who can evade the Cannon-man." Sam watched on the monitor as hundreds, maybe thousands of faces blinked past in less than a minute. The college kids' faces returned to the screen with legends reading NO MATCH beside them.

"They've left the premises," Mike said.

"I don't care about that," Sam said, afraid for a moment that they had taken Mr. Fuzzkins away with them. "Did the rabbit leave too?"

"Checking," Mike said. He switched her monitor to display an angle from near the elevator, but outside. She saw the guys walk into view, UCLA still carrying the bunny.

"Can you track that guy's movements?" Sam asked. "In the UCLA shirt?"

"Working on it."

Sam kept her gaze riveted to the monitor. Mike did his magic and the images blinked, one angle after another following the college guys around the casino at a frenetic pace. They stopped at a quarter video poker machine and played a few hands, Mr. Fuzzkins perched on top of the machine, posing as if looking down and watching the action. A good-luck charm he wasn't; Mr. UCLA lost four hands running. UCLA throttled the bunny, as if he had been expecting more help than he got, and the three of them moved on. They made a circuit of the casino floor, pausing now and then to watch the action at the craps or roulette or blackjack tables, pausing also to check out some of the scantily clad, beautiful women who were a fixture at every Las Vegas casino. On one of these occasions, UCLA held Mr. Fuzzkins upside down, by his ankles, as if the stuffed rabbit had asked for a better view under a long-legged lovely's short black skirt.

"This guy's a creep," Sam announced. "Worse than that, he's cheap. What's he played, like a buck so far?"

"A high roller he's not," Mike agreed.

"He isn't any kind of roller. It's too bad Mr. Fuzzkins can't bite him."

Finally a woman stopped to exchange a few words with the young men—a woman Sam recognized as a working girl, the kind who made a habit of asking men wandering aimlessly on the casino floor where they were going, which had become shorthand in Las Vegas for "I'm available at a price." Apparently a brief negotiation ensued, because she smiled and took the hand of one of the college guys, leading him out of the frame. UCLA tossed Mr. Fuzzkins on top of a bank of slot machines, where he vanished behind their lighted signs, and followed.

"Stop it!" Sam shouted. "Can you get me a live shot of those slots, Mike?"

"Coming up, Samantha," he said, having anticipated the request. Her screen flickered again and then an overhead shot of the casino floor became clear. Mike jogged a joystick and twitched the camera into place, pointing almost straight down onto the tops of the machines.

Mr. Fuzzkins lay curled in a ball atop the slots, as if he had climbed up to take a nap.

"I need a maintenance worker down there with a

ladder, pronto," Sam said. She allowed herself a quick smile, feeling a sense of accomplishment at having defused what could have turned into a huge problem. "I'll meet him there and get the stupid rabbit back to Byron Hammer's little monster."

She left Mike to make the call and rushed down to the casino floor, past a sea of blackjack tables and over to the dollar slots. By the time she reached the slots bank she needed (Elvis, Floppy Shoes, and Barkin' Bucks, forming a triangular shape on the floor), a maintenance worker had already set up a ladder. She tossed Sam a friendly smile as she approached. A spray of freckles dotted her nose and cheeks, as if someone had dusted her face with cinnamon, and she had tucked her long red hair under a baseball cap. "Rabbit rescue, at your service," she said.

Sam waited impatiently while the young woman climbed the ladder and fetched Mr. Fuzzkins. When she had, she tossed the rabbit to Sam, who shouted her thanks as she dashed toward the elevators, nearly taking out a cocktail waitress en route.

Inside the elevator, Sam punched the button for Byron's floor repeatedly, alternating with jabs at the DOOR CLOSE button. She had heard someplace that DOOR CLOSE buttons were usually not hooked up to anything, but just left there to reassure the impatient that they had some control over the speed with which they could get the elevator in motion. She had never asked anyone who might know if that was true for the Montecito or not, but since there seemed to be no correlation between pushing the button and the doors actually responding any faster, she suspected it was. Anxious, she pressed it anyway.

When the door opened, she charged from the elevator and collided with a bellman pushing an empty gold luggage cart. "Excuse me," Sam said hurriedly.

"Sorry, Sam," the bellman said.

"Rick, isn't it?" Sam asked as she made a sharp right around him and rushed down the hall. "You might want to be careful with that thing. You could break somebody's shins."

Rick pushed the cart around the corner and followed down the same hallway. "I'll try to be more careful," he said, sounding properly chagrined. The possibility existed, Sam supposed, that she had been the one at fault, lunging from the elevator without looking. But she had to hurry.

Almost to the Hammer family's suite, she saw that Rick still followed behind her. Struck by an unpleasant thought, she stopped, turned back to face him. "Where are you taking that?"

He gave her a suite number. Byron Hammer's.

"No," she said. "Go away. Take it back downstairs."

"I can't do that, Sam. The guest in that suite asked for a bellman to bring some bags down."

Sam held up Mr. Fuzzkins. "He doesn't need his bags to go down anymore. I have the rabbit."

Rick scratched his substantial nose. "I don't have any idea what that means, Sam."

"It means we don't need you up here. Now go, before someone sees you!"

Rick shrugged and reversed course. "I get in trouble for this . . ."

"If you get in trouble, you can blame me," Sam promised. "I'll take full responsibility, okay?"

"Cool, Sam. Thanks."

She waited until he had trundled back up the hall and she heard the bong of the elevator arrive to take him downstairs, then continued to Byron's suite. When she knocked on the door, Byron opened it almost immediately. Behind him she saw suitcases, fastened and ready to be picked up.

"You're going somewhere?" Sam asked, holding out Mr. Fuzzkins triumphantly. "That would make Mr. Fuzzkins very sad."

"Mr. Fuzzkins!" Kaylie screeched. She still wore her Disney Princess pajamas and her eyes were ringed with red, as if she had been crying nonstop since the last time Sam had seen her. She dashed toward Sam, shoving past her father's legs, and threw out her hands. When Sam released the rabbit, Kaylie enveloped it in a crushing hug. *No wonder it's so beat-up-looking*, Sam thought. *The kid's loved it to death.* "You found Mr. Fuzzkins!"

"I said I would," Sam reminded them. "Didn't I say that?"

"Thank you, Sam," Marcella said. Her normally perfectly coiffed hair hung in limp strands around her face, and she looked pale and drawn. "I really do appreciate this."

"I do whatever I have to in order to keep my favorite clients happy," Sam said. She pinned Byron Hammer with a fierce gaze. "You are happy, right?"

"Can we still get that sitter? And see Elton John?" he asked.

"Sitter's on standby," Sam assured him. "And Elton does two shows tonight. You'll be fine."

Byron glanced at the packed suitcases behind him. "I guess you came through just in time, Sam."

"Do you need me to send someone up to unpack the bags?" Sam asked. "The babysitter could do it, but she should be paying attention to Kaylie. And Mr. Fuzzkins."

"That would be terrific, Sam," Marcella said. "As long as they're unpacked by the time we get back from the concert."

"No problem," Sam said. Two of her favorite words in the English language, those, especially when they turned out to be true. "That's no problem at all."

22

Relieved, Mike watched Sam leave the surveillance room. He had reached the point where he hated to talk to anyone about the case he was working. At any rate, discussing it slowed down his actual progress, and he believed he had finally begun to make some headway.

The best investigators, Mike had heard, kept their minds free of prejudices or expectation, letting the facts fall where they may and only then building theories that fit those facts. For his part, Mike liked to amass data using a combination of personal interviews and technology, as he had done in this case. Now that he had done so, taking the investigation as far as he could, the time had come to create a plausible theory of events that he could verify. The scientific method, applied to criminal investigation. He smiled. Maybe he'd write a paper for one of the science journals he read regularly.

He electronically grabbed a surveillance image of Linda Lou Snead, then used it to search for other images of her, hoping to find one at the angle he needed. After almost half an hour of running through footage, he did. She walked toward an overhead camera, passed directly beneath it, and continued on past it. It was this angle, with her back to the camera, that Mike had been hunting.

Time for a little digital magic. He captured one of the images and opened it in Photoshop. He enlarged the image, then clipped her from the background so it wouldn't distract the eye. With the background gone, the casino's multicolored lighting became noticeable, so he corrected for that. Changing Linda Lou's hair color was no problem at all for someone with Mike's skills. He removed the color from her blond hair and made it bright red. He studied the image for a couple of minutes, satisfied with the way it had come out.

That part done, he electronically replaced her hair color in the rest of the video footage, dropping in the same red he had given her on the still image. He played it back. Now instead of a blonde sashaying away from the camera, he watched a redhead. *Looks good,* he thought. *Looks real good.*

But the naked eye could be fooled, he knew. He had no intention of making an accusation of this magnitude without more conclusive proof. He parked his newly retouched footage and brought up some he had viewed earlier, of the redhead who had seemingly engaged in afternoon hanky-panky with Leroy Snead's rival, Eustace Barnes. Playing that back, he allowed himself a satisfied grin. To the naked eye, the two bits of tape were virtually identical.

Time, then, for the real test. He brought up both bits of footage and played them with a gait comparison program running. MATCH, the computer readout showed. Mike played them a second time. MATCH.

Linda Lou Snead, then, had spent most of the afternoon of the theft in Eustace Barnes's room. She had worn a wig there, disguising herself to the naked eye. These facts, to Mike, indicated some kind of conspiracy. Infidelity happened in Las Vegas hotels, as it did in hotels around the world, and Mike figured that adults should be responsible for their own behavior. But why would Linda Lou, a partner in her husband's breeding business, consort with the company's prime competition? Simply a little afternoon delight? The timing made it questionable.

Just in case, he brought up the footage of the hallway outside Barnes's room for the rest of the days Barnes had occupied it. Linda Lou had not visited the room at any other time, with or without a disguise. Guest-room attendants had gone in to clean the room, but Barnes had no other visitors.

As a second test, Mike captured Linda Lou's and Barnes's faces and ran a search for any time they might have appeared on camera together other than the couple he had already found. This brought up a few occasions, but all public, mostly in the exhibit hall or bars and restaurants, and all having to do with the trade show itself. Nothing out of the ordinary, no secret meetings other than the one visit to his room.

Which only meant that they were careful. He still believed they had something going on that Leroy Snead didn't know about. A fling, at least. More likely, he believed, a criminal conspiracy. Mike was sure some fluid had been exchanged in Barnes's room that day, but what still needed to be ascertained was whether the fluid had originated inside Cavanaugh's Virtue, Eustace Barnes, or both.

"What is it, Danny?" Ed asked. "Aickmann's speaking in an hour, I gotta get downstairs."

"I just wanted to bring you up to speed," Danny said. "I've been working an angle I thought you should know about."

Ed had been on his way when Danny had appeared at his office door. He was in a hurry, but he had also learned to trust Danny's hunches, most of the time—unless his own gut contradicted them. Danny had good instincts and would have made a fine spook if he'd been so inclined, but that didn't change the fact that Ed put more stock in his own instincts than in Danny's. Ed was happy to hear what Danny had come up with, but he still had his own reaction to Charles Hooper to consider.

He settled back in behind his desk, picking up a gold pen. He thought Jillian had given him the desk set it came from for Christmas a couple of years back, but he was bad about remembering things like that. It might have been Delinda. It might have been the Maloof brothers. It might have been a birthday. Somebody should invent an implantable chip that would remind people of things like that when they touched the object in question. "What've you got?"

Danny sat down across from him, feet planted firmly on the floor, leaning forward with his hands resting on his knees. "I've been looking into Garrick Flynn," he said.

"That's the ranger working for the German group."

"Right. I thought it was strange that he happened to be on the floor when those cattle stampeded, instead of waiting for Aickmann's arrival or resting up for tonight. And I thought there must be a reason he worked for Hartung instead of an American security company."

"People make all kinds of employment decisions, for all kinds of reasons," Ed reminded him. "Maybe Hartung pays well. With Aickmann's billions behind him, he can afford to."

"Sure, I knew that was a possibility," Danny said. "But these days—ever since 9/11, really good security people can just about write their own tickets in the U.S. I figured there was probably more to it than a few extra bucks a month in his paycheck."

Ed turned the pen around in his hands. *Fine workmanship*, he thought. *Swiss.* He admired people who could make things, even relatively simple things, with care and pride. If the Swiss made nothing but chocolate, clocks, and pens, that would be all right with him, because they made those things so well. "And what did you come up with?"

"He did have a job here, but he got fired," Danny said. "He was working for Coleman Security, in Iraq. He got into it with some of his fellow Coleman operatives, even put one of them in the hospital. They canned him and sent him home. After that he couldn't get hired in the States, so he went to Europe looking for work."

"What was the fight about?"

"Apparently he's pretty uptight. Sex, booze, gambling—it all kind of freaks him out. More than kind of. The word one guy used was 'berserk.' "

"So this guy doesn't approve of sex, booze, and gambling, and he's here in Las Vegas," Ed observed, "where those things are in his face day and night."

"That's right," Danny said. "If Flynn couldn't keep the reins on his emotions in Iraq, under combat conditions, what's it doing to him to be inside a casino every day?"

Ed dropped the pen onto his desk. It landed with a satisfying thump. "You think maybe he's going to crack?"

"Or he already has and we just haven't seen it yet."

"If he put somebody in the hospital, I think we would have noticed," Ed said.

"Sure," Danny agreed. "I'm just saying we need to keep a close eye on him, that's all."

"You think Flynn is behind the assassination plot?" Ed asked. Someone had to be, and so far he hadn't heard any better theories. The closer it got to Aickmann's speech, the more he wanted to connect somebody to the CD. It bothered him that the CD didn't seem like Hooper's style—it smacked of amateur hour, and Hooper was a longtime professional— but he couldn't deny its existence. "Sounds like he's got a lot of baggage, but that doesn't make him a conspirator or an assassin."

"I don't know, Ed. I only know that from what I've heard he sounds like trouble. I'd hate to trust him to have my back—or Aickmann's—and have him turn out to be a flake, or worse."

"I hear you, Danny," Ed said. "Let's keep track of

him. Right now we've got to make one last final sweep of the ballroom and get ready for Aickmann's speech."

Danny rose quickly. "Right."

"I'll be down in a little while," Ed said, dismissing him. "Get started without me and I'll see you down there."

Danny gave Ed a curious look, but left the office without further comment. Ed waited until Danny's footsteps had receded into the distance, then took the handset from the phone. He wanted to make some calls of his own to see if he could learn anything else about Garrick Flynn or Charles Hooper. Danny had some solid contacts, no doubt about that.

But Ed's were better.

Danny had to pass through a gauntlet of security checkpoints to get into the ballroom. He was screened for metal objects, sniffed by a dog trained to locate explosive materials, and patted down by experts. Everyone he encountered knew who he was but they checked his identification just the same.

When the audience was let in, the checkpoints would be marginally more lax—guests would not be patted down, for instance. The people coming to this speech—mostly politicians and business leaders—would not stand for that kind of treatment. But they had to have special tickets, and they would have to show ID matching the names on those tickets, no matter how many times their faces had appeared on the nightly news. Danny had already instructed the staff to ignore complaints about that, or to refer people to him.

He expected to have a busy night.

Inside the ballroom, he found Tim Turro on the floor, making a spot check of the seating, examining the bottoms of the rows of dark blue plush-backed theater-style seats to make sure no weapons or explosives had been cached there. "Are you finding anything?" Danny asked.

"All clear so far," Tim replied. He stood up, dusting off his gray suit, and his eyes crinkled as he gave Danny a friendly smile.

"All those checks outside made me feel like a criminal," Danny said, returning Tim's grin.

"But that's good, right?"

"It's what we were going for. Trust no one, verify everyone." In the early stages of planning for Aickmann's visit, their catchphrase had been "Trust, but verify." After the discovery of the CD, that philosophy had undergone a slight revision.

Tim shrugged, spreading his hands wide. His face was open and forthright, youthful without looking immature. Danny knew it couldn't be real—not in his line of work—but on first impression, the man seemed incapable of guile. "I don't see anything at all untoward in here, Danny. Our guys have been over the place, your guys have searched it and had it on camera nonstop, Hartung's people have scoured it. Anyone making a move on Aickmann is going to be bringing their weapons in with them, not using anything that's already here."

"And theoretically the checkpoints outside will catch any weapons," Danny said.

"Theoretically. And if they don't, the people at the doors will grab anybody who shows one."

"So we're good?" Danny asked. A formality—he already knew the answer.

"I think we're good."

"Good." Danny looked at the dais, flanked by American and German flags. A podium with the Montecito logo on it stood in the center. Behind it six chairs had been lined up, with a railing behind those to make sure no one tipped over backward. The raised platform was made of blond wood. The audience seats had been arranged in twenty-five rows, thirty-six across, with two main aisles intersecting them, all of them fastened to a gently sloping ramp so nobody's view would be blocked by the row in front of them. The huge ballroom was two stories high. Danny and Ed, along with Hartung and Hooper of the Secret Service, would watch the speech from seats to the right of the dais, in constant communication with their security forces on the floor. "What do you think he's going to talk about?"

"Aickmann? He's been on a kick lately about Europe's place in the world. A unified Europe, he says, is working itself into position to take over the traditional U.S. role of world cop, world banker, and so on. The United States has been the only global superpower for years, but Aickmann believes that's changing, that Europe is joining the club."

"That's probably not going to be popular with some people here."

"Not at all," Tim agreed. He seemed to have given the issue a lot of consideration, and he went on, "In some ways I think it would be fine if they took on more of the burden that we've been carrying alone for so long. But with that burden comes a lot of influence, and I'm not sure we're ready to pass that on. The world stage may not be big enough for two superpowers anymore. And if it is, China and probably India might think they should be the second, not Europe."

Danny considered his words for a moment. Some of this ground had already been covered in meetings, but he felt comfortable with Turro and wanted his personal input in addition to the Secret Service's party line. "So in addition to foreign terrorists who might have it in for him, we've got to be on the lookout for homegrown ones who think he's a threat to our interests."

"That's the way it looks," Tim said. "I wish there was some indication on the CD which it might be."

"You and me both, Tim," Danny said. Garrick Flynn's image floated in his mind's eye. He was homegrown, and he definitely had his own agenda. "You and me both."

23

Thinking about Garrick Flynn reminded Danny of something he had forgotten, something that had been so unexceptional when it happened that he was a little surprised he remembered it now.

Except it shouldn't have been unexceptional. If he hadn't been distracted by the noisy drunk, he would have realized at that moment what had been wrong with the picture.

He knew Garrick Flynn had a cell phone. Every member of Hartung's group did, and he had all their numbers.

So why had the guy been making a call on a pay phone?

Land lines, Danny knew, could be more secure than mobile phones. Had there been some reason he needed a land line?

"I've got to go back up to my office for a while, Tim," he said. "See you later."

Tim bade him good-bye, but Danny, already rushing for the door, barely heard.

It took him ten minutes to reach his desk, because he had to stop by the phone booth in the hallway leading to the convention center and jot down the number.

Once he was seated, he went to work. He knew that he had seen Garrick Flynn at the phone somewhere around ten thirty. On a video monitor, he called up footage from a nearby camera. The angle on the pay phone didn't allow him to see what number Flynn had dialed, but he noted the precise time the call was made.

Time for a call of his own. He double-checked the number, since it wasn't one he dialed often. "Phone company, can I help you?" a pleasant feminine voice answered.

"Cindy, it's Danny," he said. "How are you?"

"I've been better," Cindy said. She sounded just as perky as she had when she answered, so whatever was wrong couldn't have been too bad.

"What's the matter?"

"This guy I knew in high school never calls me unless he needs a favor."

Oh, Danny thought. *That.*

He and Cindy hadn't dated in high school. For one thing, Mary had always been part of his life in those days. But there had been an unmistakable attraction between them, and they had flirted and teased even though they had never acted on it.

He wasn't with Mary anymore, though. He was, for the moment, free and loose. Cindy had been a real knockout in high school. No guarantee that she remained one, but chances were good.

On the other hand, she might have shaved her head and grown a mustache. Stranger things had happened. The only way to find out was to actually call her up and ask her out sometime. Not today, but sometime.

Focus Danny. He had an assassination to prevent.

"I know, I stink," he said. "I'll make it up to you, though."

"How?" Cindy asked. "Diamonds are always nice. So's platinum."

"You must have mistaken me for another Danny McCoy," he said. "I'm more the CZ and aluminum type."

"That's not the Danny I remember."

"Maybe we'll have to get together one of these days and compare notes," he said.

"I won't take that as a promise, Danny," Cindy replied. "But if you want to call sometime, obviously you have the number. At least during working hours. What is it you need?"

"There's a pay phone inside the Montecito," Danny said. He read her the number. "I need to know what number was dialed from that phone at ten thirty-seven this morning."

"You have a court order?"

"Do I need one?"

"According to the law, you do."

"I'm in charge of surveillance and security here, Cindy," Danny pressed. He hoped she didn't really want to play hardball. He could win, but it would take time, and that was one thing he didn't have to spare. "This is a security matter. A very, very important security matter. Someone's life might be at stake."

"Why does that sound like a cliché?"

"I know it does," Danny said. "But I'm not joking, Cindy. It's really crucial."

"I didn't think you'd call if it wasn't, Danny. It'll cost you lunch, though. You ready?"

He snatched a pen off his desk. "Go."

She read a number and he wrote it down. The area code was 702. "It's local," he said. "Can you give me the name and address of that customer?"

He knew she remained on the line because he could hear her breathing, but she waited long seconds before answering. "Did I say lunch? Sounds like I meant dinner. This is really pushing it, Danny."

"I know, Cindy. Look, if I had time, I'd go through channels, get a warrant. I don't. It's that critical."

"It's a residential number," she said. "It belongs to a Natalie Benz." She gave him an address in Henderson, which he jotted beneath the number.

"Thanks, Cindy. I owe you big-time."

"Damn straight," she said. "And don't think I'll forget it." Another couple seconds of silence, then she added, "And remember, I have your phone number."

After he hung up, Danny ran Natalie Benz's information through his databases. He came up with a driver's license, the photo showing a stringy-haired woman in her mid-thirties, and a criminal record with a variety of minor-league drug and misdemeanor charges. The mug shot showed the same woman, plain-faced, hollow-cheeked, and sad. He could find no indication of how or why she would know Garrick Flynn.

Only one way to find out, he thought. Although he had her number and he was in a hurry, he guessed this would be better done in person. He hurried outside to his yellow Camaro. In a few minutes, he was on the road to Henderson.

*   *   *

"Send those over," Ed said into the phone. "That'd be great, thanks." He hung up and tilted back in his desk chair, scanning his memory for another phone number. He could have looked it up, of course, but liked the mental exercise of trying to remember it. Every phone number he could recall years after learning it, he figured, stood for dozens of brain cells he hadn't lost yet.

As he slowly turned in his chair, the area code and prefix came to him. The final four numbers would follow quickly, but before they did, his gaze came to rest on one of the flat-screen monitors built into his office wall. It showed him a view of the surveillance office, which he liked to have in case Danny failed to ride herd on the crew.

The crew appeared to be hard at work.

Except for one of the guys, who was talking to Charles Hooper.

Ed heaved a sigh and rose from his chair. If his office had still adjoined the surveillance room, he could have had Hooper's scrawny neck in his hands within seconds. Now it would take a minute or two, and in the meantime his anger might cool.

He didn't want that.

He liked his anger white-hot, boiling-point hot. That was when it served him best.

Hooper was still near the surveillance room door when Ed got there. Instead of grabbing the man and throwing him out physically, he tried a different approach.

"Hooper," he said, voice soft.

Hooper turned.

Ed gestured "come here" with the index finger of his right hand.

Hooper hesitated. Color tinged his cheeks and ears, as if getting caught in here was somehow embarrassing. *It'll be a lot more embarrassing if I have to cuff you,* Ed thought. "Now," he said, his voice dripping quiet menace.

"Sure, Ed," Hooper said. Trying to sound casual about the whole thing, as if Ed didn't know he had no business coming to the surveillance room unescorted.

Ed led him out into the hall. "What's up, Ed?" Hooper asked.

Ed didn't answer, just kept walking. Hooper followed. They passed the receptionist outside Ed's office, who barely glanced at them, and went in. Ed closed the office door behind Hooper and waved him to a chair. Hooper sat, but Ed remained standing.

"What the hell are you doing in my surveillance room, Hooper?"

"If it's a problem, Ed, I'm sorry. We all have the same agenda here, right? I just wanted to check on something."

"On what? My people handle the surveillance, you know that."

"Just a thought I had. A hunch, I guess you'd say. Probably nothing to it."

"What was it?" Ed asked. Still on his feet, he paced around Hooper, who had to twist and squirm in his chair to keep Ed in view. "If it's good enough for you to check out, it must be good enough to share, right?"

Hooper shrugged, feigning nonchalance. Ed saw

through it. "You know how it is, Ed. When it's important, you want to check everything, no matter how lame-brained. I think this one was pretty lame, now that I think about it."

Ed grabbed a chair, spun it around, scooted it in front of Hooper's, and straddled it. He leaned over the back, his face just inches away from Hooper's. He could smell the guy's sweat. "I don't know how it is with you, Hooper. I never have known what to make of you. Not since that first time I met you, in the café in Nueva Ocotepeque, when you showed up with the dead guy, what was his name? Alberto?"

"I remember," Hooper said. To his credit, his voice was steady. The flustered bureaucrat dweeb who had been sitting in front of him had vanished, a steely professional in his place. "What about it?"

"And Ramirez," Ed said. "That's the real puzzle. What really happened to him? I mean, I know he got killed, I know his fingers were stuffed into his mouth, because I'm the one who found him there. But who set him up? I never have been able to figure that out."

"And you think it was me?"

"I'm just asking questions, not making guesses."

"If you have anything you want to say to me, Ed, go ahead and say it."

"I already said it."

"You want to know about a mission that you know is still classified? You're a private citizen, Ed. Even if I wanted to tell you, I couldn't."

"So there's something to tell?"

"I didn't say that."

"Sounded like it to me."

Hooper sighed. "What do you want from me, Ed? You want me to tell you that I killed Ramirez? You woke me up that night, remember? You would have known if I had been out of the room. Before you woke me you probably checked my shoes, looked for a bloody knife. I would have."

"I did," Ed said. "I didn't see anything. Doesn't mean you weren't involved."

"Ramirez was an ally of the United States, Ed. That's all you have to know."

He *was*. That sort of thing changed fast, though. Especially in those days, in that part of the world. Allies today were enemies tomorrow, and vice versa. Ed knew of terrorist leaders and other problem types around the world who had, at one time or another, been on the agency's payroll or were considered useful friends. Some of them had been armed, trained, and supported by the United States for years. Now they were among some of its worst enemies.

Ramirez's status could have changed in a day. A few hours. Or Ed's bosses at the CIA might have had a different view of his utility than Hooper's in the Pentagon.

Ed knew he'd get nothing from Hooper. But he hadn't trusted the guy before, and now he trusted him even less. He had risked his life to try to get Ramirez into El Salvador, and Hooper—unless he seriously misread the situation—had gone behind his back to take Ramirez out of the picture permanently.

It was the kind of betrayal that infuriated him. He told himself it was decades in the past, nothing personal, nothing he should worry about now. "Get the hell out of here," he said. "Get out of my office, Hooper.

And keep the hell away from my surveillance room, or I'll throw your ass out of my casino altogether."

"The United States government might frown on that, Ed," Hooper said, scooting his chair away from Ed's and standing up.

"They frown on a lot of things," Ed said. "Don't think I'll let that stop me."

As Hooper left, Ed tried to envision him landing on the pavement outside the front door. Maybe an overly enthusiastic valet would run him over with a Hummer.

For the first time in hours, Ed cracked a smile.

24

"Right in here, Mr. Snead." Mike led Leroy Snead into the surveillance room, past the crew intently watching the monitors. On one screen, he saw Danny and a Secret Service agent standing in the ballroom where the big speech would happen in another hour or so. He felt a brief pang that he hadn't been involved in that situation instead of this one. Danny got the better end of that deal, for sure. "Just have a seat over here."

Leroy Snead sat in the rolling chair Mike offered, removed his cowboy hat, and held it in his lap. His hair, flecked with gray, had been cropped close to his head. He touched the corner of his right eye with a blunt fingertip, as if wiping away a stray lash. "What are we here for, Mike?" he asked. "I got plenty I should be doing downstairs to get loaded out."

"I have to show you some footage," Mike said. "I wish there was another way to do this, but there isn't. Some of what I'll show you will be very disturbing, but I think you've got to see it for yourself."

"Son, I've delivered foals at three in the morning on the coldest night of the year. Ain't much disturbs Leroy Snead."

"That's good," Mike said. As unpleasant as spending a cold winter night helping to deliver a baby horse might be—Mike hoped he'd never have to find that out for himself—he guessed that the next few minutes would be much harder on Snead, emotionally speaking. "I know the loss of Cavanaugh's Virtue's seed is a terrible blow to you, and I've been working pretty much nonstop on the investigation. Now I've reached some conclusions, and I feel like you have a right to know what I've come up with."

"Damn right I do," Snead said. "You get the sumbitch on tape?"

"Nothing so concrete, Mr. Snead," Mike replied. "Just take a look at this." He sat beside the big man and pressed a button on the remote in his hand. The monitor on the desk blinked to life, showing an image of Snead's exhibit in the hall. "This is yesterday, before you noticed the theft of the vial."

Snead nodded and watched silently. On-screen, Linda Lou Snead entered the booth while Leroy and his booth attendants were all busy helping other people. Leroy Snead and his wife made momentary eye contact, she tossed a wiggle of her fingers his way, then disappeared into the trailer they used as an office. Mike stopped the tape.

"So what?" Snead asked. He touched his eye again. A nervous tic, Mike realized. Maybe the man already had a gut feeling about what he was about to see. "Linda Lou goes in and out of that trailer all day long."

"Keep watching," Mike said, his voice tight. He wanted Snead to see for himself, didn't want to have to lay it out for the guy. No way to tell how he might react. And people did, after all, have a long history of killing the messenger. Mike clicked the remote again and the image of the redheaded woman who Mike believed to be Linda Lou Snead appeared, walking down the hall toward Eustace Barnes's room.

"Who's that?" Snead asked.

"Ignore the hair," Mike said. "It's a wig. Does your wife have a pair of leopard-print pants like that?"

Snead hesitated, and when he answered, Mike heard a dry click in his throat. "Of course. Doesn't every woman?"

"Not where I live," Mike said.

"You sayin' that there's my Linda Lou?"

"Watch this." Mike split the screen and put the shot of Linda Lou walking toward the camera up on the right side, with the leopard-print redhead on the left. When Linda Lou passed beneath the camera and started walking away from it, he started up the left-hand image. In concert, both women moved toward the distance with the same pronounced hip sway. "I ran a gait comparison program, Mr. Snead. Those two are the same woman. They're both Linda Lou."

Snead's jaw remained firm, his eyes defiant. "Okay, so she put on a wig. So what?"

Mike brought the left-hand footage back to full screen and let it run. Linda Lou stopped in front of a door with the number 3729 on it and knocked.

"Whose room is that?" Snead asked.

Mike remained silent. Quickly, as if he had been waiting for her knock, Eustace Barnes opened the door. He remained clearly visible for less than a second, until Linda Lou moved into his arms, clutching him in a passionate embrace. Then they both stepped inside and she swung the door closed with her leopard-printed behind.

"Barnes!" Snead said. Another dab at his eye. His full lower lip had picked up a quiver, as if the muscles around it had suddenly atrophied. "What the hell was she doing there?"

"Your guess is as good as mine, but the footage doesn't lie, sir. She stayed in there for a couple of hours. This was yesterday, the same day the vial disappeared—right after she went into the trailer. If I had to guess, I'd say she stole it and took it to Barnes."

Snead's fist closed on the brim of his hat, crumpling it. "That no-good lyin' bastard," he muttered, more to himself than to Mike. "I'll rip his lungs out of his chest and smother him with them."

Technically, Mike knew, once his lungs had been ripped out he couldn't be smothered. But he thought it best not to point that out at the moment. "We can take care of this legally," Mike said, putting a reassuring hand on the man's shoulder. "Violence isn't the answer here, believe me."

"Maybe not where you live," Snead snapped, throwing Mike's own phrase back in his face. "Where I'm from that's how you handle this sort of deal."

"Mike," Mitch called.

"Yeah, Mitch?"

"Take a look at your screen." From his station, Mitch had taken control of the monitor in front of Mike and Snead. An image appeared there of Linda Lou, wearing the red wig once again, knocking again on the door of room 3729. A time stamp showed that this had occurred about thirty minutes before. "She's in there now. Hasn't come out yet."

"Right now?" Snead fumed. "I'm goin' up there, Mike, whether you like it or not."

"Hold up, Mr. Snead," Mike said urgently. "This is bigger than just you and Linda Lou. There's been a theft on Montecito property, and we're involved. Let's do this the right way. We'll go to Barnes's room with a security guard and we'll see what they've done with your vial." He figured with himself and a security guard along, Snead would be less likely to commit physical violence against Barnes, and they could restrain him if necessary.

Although, maybe we could accidentally let him get in a punch or two first. Barnes certainly deserved it.

Snead had clamped his lips together so tightly that they nearly disappeared. Whatever muscles had weakened a few minutes before had been strengthened by rage. His fists continued to mangle the brim of his hat. "Okay," he said. "We'll do it your way first."

Mike didn't like the implied threat of that last word, but he let it go. "Mitch, call Greg and have him meet us in the thirty-seventh floor hallway," he said. "Mr. Snead and I are going to pay Mr. Barnes a little visit."

Ed heard voices out in the hallway and looked up toward the door, ready to snarl at whoever was out there. He had been concentrating, and he didn't want to be disturbed. Then Jillian walked in and the snarl died, the anger vanishing. "What are you doing here?" he asked her.

"Hello to you too, Ed darling," she said, a hurt look flashing across her beautiful face.

"I'm sorry, honey. This is just not a very good time."

"Is it ever?" She crossed the office, planted a kiss on his lips. She smelled great. "I thought we'd have some dinner," she said, perching on a corner of his desk. "Before the speech."

"The speech?"

"Ed, it's all over the cable news and the papers. Klaus Aickmann? It's a big deal. History in the making, they're saying. I want to be there."

Ed loved Jillian as much as he had ever loved anything in his life. He wasn't always good enough about saying it, but that didn't mean he didn't feel it. She had been the one constant in his life, these last several decades, the reason he had been determined to survive every mission, because he always knew she waited at home. The thought of anything bad happening to her—anything at all—made him feel like he'd swallowed a small, hard ball of poison that slowly leaked into his veins, killing him inch by inch.

It was because he loved her so utterly, so absolutely, without condition or hesitation, that for the second time in the past few hours, he said, "Get the hell out of here."

"What? Ed—"

"I mean it, Jillian. I don't want you anywhere near this place tonight. And I especially don't want you near that speech."

Her brow knitted. "What is it, Ed? Is something going to happen tonight?"

"I can't tell you that, Jillian. You'll just have to trust me."

She made a tsking noise. "How many times have you said that to me?"

"And have I ever betrayed that trust?"

"How would I know?" she asked. "You think the CIA let me read your case files so I'd know you were really sharing an apartment in Prague with Frank instead of someone named Inga or Giselle?"

He wanted to clamp his hands to his head, but he knew her well enough to be certain that any show of exasperation would only make things worse. Instead, he tried to smile and hoped he didn't come off looking like a hungry shark. "Jillian, honey, just . . . please. I can't do this right now. Tonight when it's all over I'll tell you everything. But for now, just go, okay? Just go home."

He could tell by the brisk snap of her limbs as she rose and the clicking of her shoes as she headed for the door that she was angry. He hated that. Whatever he faced tonight during the speech would be better than trying to placate his wife.

The irony was that people were scared of him when they thought he was mad.

He had to believe those people had never pissed off Jillian.

25

The woman on the other side of the screen door might have been pretty once, Danny thought. But drugs steal beauty as easily as they do health, hopes, and dreams. She was tall, raw-boned, with sallow skin hanging loosely on her frame. Limp, straw-colored hair framed a face on which the nose and teeth looked too big. Dark circles surrounded blue eyes that seemed as if they would cave in at any time. For a change, the driver's license photo and mug shots had been complimentary, and he was surprised by how worn-out she looked in person.

"Are you Natalie Benz?" Danny asked through the bug-flecked screen.

"That's right. You're not from Social Services, are you?"

"No, ma'am," Danny answered. "I'm not."

"Cop?"

He smiled. Reassuringly, he hoped. "Not that either."

Her house was small, with faded aluminum siding. A painted brick wall around the patchy yard was decorated with gang graffiti. In the yard Danny saw a broken tricycle; between that and the Social Services question, he deduced that she had kids. And maybe wasn't doing the best job raising them.

"My name is Danny McCoy, ma'am." *I'm with the*

Montecito Hotel and Casino, he almost added, but he stopped himself in time and just left it at that. "You know Garrick Flynn, right?"

She thought about it for a moment, then nodded, her stringy blond hair wafting in front of her face. She blew it away. "Yeah, I know him. A little. Why?"

"I think he might be in some kind of trouble," Danny said. Not too far from the truth. "Can I come in?"

Natalie looked at him as if she could somehow determine his intentions from the cut of his hair or the way he held himself. Finally, she undid the lock and pulled the door open. "Don't know why I should care," she said. "Not like he's ever done much for us when we were in trouble."

She let Danny in, then released the screen, which slammed shut with a bang. As she led him down a barren hallway, he thought he could smell burned toast and spilled beer. A little blond head appeared in the doorway at the end of the hall. A girl. Toast and jelly remnants grimed a swath around her mouth; she had big blue eyes that measured Danny, much as her mother's had done. Before Natalie reached the door, she scooted out of the way.

Natalie ushered him into a kitchen, where the toast smell was especially pungent. Through another door, the toddler hustled away, clad only in a disposable diaper. "Meggie's in that shy stage," Natalie said, laughing hoarsely. "Better'n me, I guess—I can't remember a time I didn't like boys. Maybe she'll be able to keep outta trouble."

A scarred dinette set dominated the center of the kitchen. "Sit?" Natalie offered.

"Sure." Danny pulled out a chair, checked it for foreign substances, and sat down. "Thanks."

"You want a beer or anything?"

"No, I'm fine," he said. "I really don't want to take up any more of your time than I have to. I'd like to help Garrick, but I have a feeling that time is of the essence. Before I explain, you said 'us' earlier. Did you mean you and Meggie by that?"

"Meggie, and Glen too, I guess."

"Who's Glen?"

Natalie laughed again, and that laughter led to a smoker's cough that consumed her for almost a full minute. "Sorry," she said, sitting down opposite Danny. "I quit when I was pregnant with Megan, but it looks like maybe that was a few years too late." She studied Danny again. "He don't owe you money?"

"No, nothing like that. I don't know Glen. Glen Benz? Who is he?" he asked again.

"Glen Tidwell," she corrected. "I kept my own name. Glen's my common-law husband, I guess you'd say. Or was. I'm not sure what you'd call him now, except gone."

"He's gone? In what way?"

"In the way that he's hardly ever here," Natalie said. She pinched some crumbs off the table and dropped them over the side, onto the floor. "I mean, he was here today, for a while. Most of this week, I guess. But he ain't here now, and he hasn't been here much at all this last year or so."

"Sorry to hear that," Danny said.

She moved her shoulders in what might have been a shrug. "Guess I should've known when he didn't want to get married for real. 'It's just a piece of paper,' he said. 'What does a piece of paper prove?' I guess what it proves is that if you walk out on someone, they can get something from you. Not that we ever had much. Glen and me, we never were too good at keeping jobs, and we for damn sure didn't inherit anything like money or real estate from our families." She waved a bony hand around the drab kitchen. "As you can tell. I guess about all I inherited, besides a nine-grand Visa bill, was what they call an addictive personality. Me and Glen both got that. In spades."

"What's Glen addicted to?" Danny asked. He was beginning to think it was Glen that Garrick had called, not Natalie. He had been here this morning but was gone now. That had to mean something.

"You name it, he's tried it," Natalie said. She coughed again, holding her skinny fist in front of her mouth. "Coke, cards, chicks. Now it's religion. As for me, I got men, smokes, booze. Other controlled substances about which I should keep my big yap shut, I guess. You sure you don't want a beer? Keep me from drinking it."

Danny wanted to keep his senses alert, his reflexes sharp, since he didn't know what might be coming up. On the other hand, he wanted her to feel comfortable. He had the sense that she was getting around to the important stuff, and if he had to drink a little to hold her trust, he could manage it. He would sip and he could probably make a quarter bottle last through the rest of the impromptu interrogation. "Okay," he said. "One beer."

"Good." She rose, took one from the refrigerator,

cranked the cap off. When she opened the refrigerator door, a spoiled-meat smell drifted out, lingering even after she'd closed it. She set the beer on the table in front of him. Domestic, a discount-store brand. "Salut," she said, although she wasn't drinking.

He tipped the bottle toward her, took a swig.

"Glen," she continued, "he has some trouble with substances. But it's also behaviors, in his case. He gets obsessed with stuff."

"You mentioned religion a minute ago," he reminded her. "What did you mean by that?"

"That's why he left last year," she said. "He'd tried just about everything else, and nothing seemed to help him. So he decided he'd try church. Next thing I knew, he was packing his stuff into these three big plastic garbage bags and moving out, saying he couldn't live in sin anymore. Never mind that Meggie was losing her dad."

"What church does he go to?" Danny asked.

"You name it, he's tried it. I don't even know if he believes in God," Natalie admitted. She worked at a hangnail with her teeth for a moment. "But he believes in sin, that's for damn sure. Used to be an expert at it, and now he's against it."

"So the drugs, the booze . . . he's against all that now?"

"And the sleeping with a woman he's not married to," she said. "I told him we could get married, but I guess I'm not good enough for him anymore."

"I'm guessing he knows Flynn through one of these churches," Danny said. "Unless he's an Iraq veteran?"

She eyed Danny's beer longingly. He took another

sip, if only to keep her from snatching it off the table. "Your guess is as good as mine. He was over there, in the army, for a while. But he never told me where they met. Even though I'm just some old whore he used to sleep with, according to him, he still has no problem with using my place to sleep in sometimes. And sometimes he brings friends, like Flynn. One time, last year, Flynn was here for a week. He had nice clothes, fancy luggage, you could tell he could afford a hotel if he wanted one. Or at least to help out with the rent and groceries. But he and Glen kept to themselves, closing the door to the room Glen uses, talking into the night, taking walks together. I hardly ever saw either one of them, which really was okay by me. Glen kind of gives me the willies now, you know? Like there's a holy fire burning in his eyes and you don't know how he's going to let it out."

"Flynn called here this morning," Danny said. "Was he calling for Glen?"

"Yeah. He don't never call to talk to me."

"Did you overhear the conversation?"

"When he calls, Glen takes the phone in his room. We still call it that, his room, even though he hadn't used it for four months until this week. Anyway, I couldn't hear jack, not that I was trying to."

"What happened then?"

"Then Glen did what he's best at. He disappeared."

"And you don't have any idea where? Was he going to meet Flynn someplace?"

"Like I said, I didn't listen. And Glen gave up trying to explain things to me when I told him for about the millionth time that I didn't want to hear his opinion of my personal life."

He had abandoned his beer for a few minutes, and Natalie reached out suddenly, scooping it off the table. "I just want to smell it," she said. "Maybe taste it on your tongue, if you have some time to stay."

"I really should get going," Danny reminded her, not wanting to get into any lip-lock with Natalie. "Sounds like fun, but like I said, Flynn might be in a jam and every minute really might count."

She gave another shrug, as if being rejected was something she was accustomed to.

"Do you have a picture of him?" he asked before he left. "Of Glen?"

"I think I do," Natalie said. "There are a couple around here somewhere." A noise at the doorway alerted her to the fact that Megan was peeking in around the frame. "If Meggie hasn't eaten them all!" she added, lunging toward her daughter.

Megan screamed and ran away giggling. "Stay put," Natalie said, waving Danny down with her hands. "I'll be right back." She stopped at the door and eyed Danny solemnly. "I haven't always been the best wife, Mr. McCoy, common-law or otherwise. I make out like it's all Glen's fault, but hell, if I'd given him much to stick around for, maybe he would have. If he and Flynn are in some kind of jam, I sure hope you can help them."

Waiting at her kitchen table, looking at her mediocre beer—which he had no doubt she would finish as soon as he left—Danny felt dirty for having tricked her. Natalie Benz, he figured, had been used enough in her life. Now he had used her again.

For a good cause, he told himself. If Glen was involved in whatever Flynn's scheme was, maybe it would give them another angle to work.

And with time running very short, he would take any angles he could get.

26

"I'm not sure I've ever enjoyed a hamburger so much, Mary," Will Streeter said.

Mary dabbed at her mouth with a napkin, afraid she had enjoyed hers with a little too much enthusiasm. "I know I haven't," she replied. "I'm just glad Ezra and Gunther didn't kill each other making them."

Will looked past her toward the chuck wagon. She turned on the picnic table bench and followed his gaze. Ezra, in his element, rushed this way and that, checking on beans, flipping burgers and steaks. Gunther, who must have left Benito in charge of his own kitchen for the evening, seemed to be everywhere Ezra wasn't. They complemented each other's motions like they'd been cooking together for years. Between the two of them they had things well under control, and with Montecito servers dishing out the food, the line of hungry patrons had been fed, some even returning for seconds and thirds.

In the distance the glow of lights from other casinos on the Strip painted the bottoms of evening clouds, but from here trees blocked the view of the busy street. A huge orange moon brushed the tops of the trees, giving Mary the impression that she could climb the branches and leap right into it. That was an illusion, Mary knew, no more real than any feelings Will might believe he had for her.

The aroma of the food masked the city smells, and an acoustic band played traditional cowboy songs, covering the sounds of traffic on Las Vegas Boulevard. They might have been sitting in a forested glade, for all her senses told her, except for the bulk of the Montecito rising above the trees. "Those two look like old friends," Will said, nodding toward Ezra and Gunther.

"Hardly. But they pulled it off, that's what counts."

Will sipped from a bottle of beer so cold it left sweat rings on the picnic table, then returned his gaze to Mary. She felt it on her face like the brush of fingertips, as if it had physical presence. His attention flattered her, but she still found it a bit unsettling at the same time. "It's not just the burger," he said. "It's the company too."

"I'm glad we could get some time together, Will. For a while, these last couple of days, I wasn't sure I'd ever be able to sit down and enjoy a meal again." She wanted to guide the conversation into less intimate areas, at least for now. She wanted to believe that he was interested in her, not in a picture from decades before, but so far nothing about him had given her any such indication. "So how did the show go for you? It always seemed busy when I went by the exhibit hall."

"It was fine," he said. "Great, really. Good sales, great folks. Meeting you and Delinda and everyone, well, that would've been worth coming down here for even if I hadn't sold a thing. But I did, anyway."

"Delinda likes you a lot," Mary said, knowing it was disingenuous at best, but still hoping to stall any advances he might be intending.

"She's a terrific lady. Pretty and funny. Not my type, really—she's way too sophisticated for an old stove-in bronc jockey like me, but she'll make somebody a great gal."

He wore a clean blue western shirt with black diamond-shaped snaps and white piping. In his jeans and boots and Stetson, he looked every bit the rodeo rider he had been, although Mary couldn't make out the stove-in part. With his muscular build and upright posture, he looked healthy and athletic and a long way from used up.

Mary was about to respond when Will twitched his fingers toward something behind her. "Speaking of Delinda, there she is," he said. "That her mom with her? Or her grandma, I guess?"

Mary swiveled on the bench again. She had met Bette Deline, Ed's mother, before, and her return to Las Vegas would be a delightful surprise. But the old woman trailing Delinda between the picnic benches was not Bette, or anyone else Mary had ever seen. Something about her seemed familiar, although she couldn't put her finger on what.

"Maybe on her mother's side," Mary said. She had never met Jillian's mother, couldn't even remember if she was still alive. "I don't know her."

Delinda came straight toward them, beaming a smile like a million-candlepower bulb at them. She had changed clothes again, into a pale green dress with a cowboy and cowgirl print—on the kitschy side, for

Delinda, but still flattering to her slender figure, and perfectly in keeping with the weekend's theme. Her dangling earrings were shaped like gold cowboy boots and had diamond accents.

"Hi, Mary," Delinda said as she approached. Her tone was light, as if she could barely keep from laughing out loud, and Mary knew the old woman was meant to be a surprise of some kind. "Hi, Will. Are you two enjoying your beans and burgers?"

"Just about the best I've ever had, Delinda," Will said.

"Definitely," Mary added. "Who's your friend?"

Delinda held up the old woman's hand, as if she had forgotten she held it. "Oh, this? Her name is Taylor Malloy. Taylor, this is Mary Connell and Will Streeter."

"I'm delighted to meet you," Taylor said, releasing Delinda's hand and extending her own toward Mary. Mary took hers and gave it a friendly shake. It seemed as fragile and weightless as a baby bird.

"Will," Delinda said, letting the secret out at last, "Taylor here was the model for your Cassaday Oil calendar painting."

Will's jaw dropped in recognition as he studied the old woman's soft, lined face. Taylor's brown eyes sparkled with life, a smile curving her pronounced lips, her jaw delicate but still strong. That sense of familiarity grew, as if Taylor were a woman Mary had seen in movies during her childhood and never quite forgotten.

"And Mary," Delinda went on, "Taylor Malloy is your great-aunt, on your mother's side."

"You're kidding," Mary said, a sudden welling of emotion making it hard to get the words out. She hadn't let go of Taylor Malloy's hand yet, couldn't bring herself to tear her gaze from the woman's face. As soon as Delinda spoke, Mary realized that the reason Taylor seemed so familiar was that looking at her was like staring into a trick mirror that added decades to one's image. In Taylor Malloy's features, she saw herself. Or herself as she might look, a possible future Mary who she might or might not become.

"It's a great pleasure to meet you, Mary," Taylor said. Her voice almost seemed to crinkle, like a crisp new paper bag, and hearing it made Mary wonder if her own would take on that quality in her later years. The woman must have been seventy or more, but energy radiated from her like heat off a stove.

Finally, realizing she had prolonged the handshake into the what's-the-matter-with-this-freaky-person realm, she let go. "It's great to meet you too, Ms. Malloy," Mary said. Her family life had been far from happy, and she had never pressed her father too hard on other relatives—her father being the kind of man you didn't want to talk to unless you absolutely had to. "You're really my great-aunt?"

"That's what Delinda determined," Taylor said. "And from what she's told me I see no reason to doubt her. May we join you two?"

Will Streeter slid over on his bench. "Have a seat, ma'am. Please."

Delinda squeezed next to Mary on the opposite bench. "I did a little research online," she said. "With Mitch's help. We checked with the printer who manufactured the calendar for the oil company, went through rodeo records for the years before and after, called some old rodeo announcers we tracked down, and finally came across someone who remembered Taylor appearing in that calendar. I finally found her, living over in Searchlight, of all places. She has her own ranch there."

"This is so great," Mary said. "Living so close, you must have seen my parents sometimes. Which side are you—"

"A ranch?" Will interrupted. "You look like the cowgirl type in that painting. Did you rodeo yourself, ma'am?"

"Yes, I did," Taylor said. "A little, anyway."

"She's way too modest," Delinda put in. "Taylor broke all kinds of women's rodeo records in her day. You should see her trophy case, with all her ribbons and statues and belt buckles in it. It's amazing. She even won—what was that one trophy called that didn't fit in your case?"

Taylor's fine, pale skin turned bright pink. "It's a Golden Calf Award," she said. "They used to give it for best all-around cowgirl." She laughed. "It's silly, really—a statue of a golden calf. The thing must be almost life-size."

"I wonder why my folks never took me to see you rodeo," Mary said. "Did my father know—"

"I've never met a real Golden Calf winner," Will said. He looked at her as if she had sprouted wings and a tiara. "They stopped giving those away decades ago. I've seen a couple of the statues, though, at the Hall of Fame."

"You've met one now, Will, for whatever that's worth. That and about five dollars will buy you a cup of coffee, I suppose," Taylor said. "Delinda tells me you still have one of those old calendars. I'm surprised that any of them still exist. Honestly, I can hardly remember posing for that picture, it was so long ago, and I think the last one I saw was on a gas station wall in the seventies. A man tried to cheat me on an alternator replacement, and then asked me to sign it when he recognized me. You must have been holding on to that thing for a long time."

"Quite a while, yes, ma'am."

"And Delinda says you know your way around rodeo stock too."

"That's right, ma'am. Rodeoed as long as I could without breaking something couldn't be set right again."

"You look plenty big and strong," she said. "Kind of like Dale Ritter. Do you know Dale?"

"I know of him," Will said. Mary didn't recognize the name, but it was clear from Will's face that he did and appreciated the comparison.

"Taylor, do you know if—" she began.

She wasn't even surprised when Will interrupted. It was like she had turned invisible and silent, and only Taylor could catch Will's attention. "Could be I've spent a few too many hours looking at those Pro Rodeo Hall of Fame exhibits. Do you really think I look like Dale Ritter?"

"A little, physically," Taylor replied, regarding him closely. "But more in the way you carry yourself, your stature. I never saw a man who could handle himself on the back of two thousand pounds of beef like he did, and then when he was thrown, he could get up so fast and give the crowd a nice, friendly wave. Like their applause was all he had come for, not the prize money. He was a true champion, that man."

"That's what I've heard. Who else do you know?"

Taylor laughed. "Oh, I know them all. Some better than others, of course." She blushed again, cast her gaze toward the ground. "A few real well, but you know, a lady doesn't talk about that."

"Well, you're a beautiful lady, so I'm not surprised one bit," Will said. "Can you tell me about Shorty Hotchkiss? I always wanted to know how he set so many records."

"Oh, Shorty, well, he rode bareback like he was part of the horse," Taylor began. "Like his butt and the horse's back had joined together, and a saddle was just something that got in the way. I went to a party with Shorty and Larry Mahan once, in Tulsa. Let me tell you . . ."

Delinda nudged Mary, who glanced at her friend, made eye contact, and nodded. Meeting Taylor Malloy had been a treat, but it didn't take long to see that Will Streeter planned to dominate the conversation, and Mary had begun to feel distinctly like a fifth wheel. Or a seventeenth. Taylor had been Will's dream girl for so long, it didn't matter that she was old enough to be his grandmother. He didn't want to date her, he wanted to worship her. Especially now that it turned out she was not just a model but also a rodeo queen.

Mary and Delinda gathered up the paper plates from the burgers and beans Mary had shared with Will, and the two of them left the table together. Will and Taylor, utterly engrossed in their conversation, didn't seem to notice when Mary and Delinda walked away.

Delinda leaned over so her head was close to Mary's. "I told you he'd like you."

"It's not me he likes," Mary corrected her. "It's Taylor. She happens to look like me—or she did once upon a time. But I think it's great that you found her, Delinda. Incredible, really, since Will tried for so long and never got anywhere."

"Never underestimate a Deline."

"I never do. The point is, he isn't interested in me at all." She ticked her head back toward the two of them, still sitting together on the picnic bench, rapt. They might not notice she had left until the sun came up, if then. "And that's okay. He's a nice guy, but there are plenty of nice guys around. Even if we were perfect for each other, I could never compete with her. I'm not sure even Taylor can compete with herself—she's a real woman, not a figment."

"I know," Delinda said. "When I did find her, I was so torn. Should I really bring her over, or just let him keep imagining her the age she was when the calendar picture was painted? It wasn't until I found out she was related to you that I decided to go for it."

"Well, I appreciate it," Mary said, giving Delinda's arm a friendly squeeze. "Since she doesn't live too far away, maybe I'll be able to visit her once in a while. Only without Will." She really did intend to pursue that—Taylor Malloy might be a source for all kinds of information about her family, things she had never wanted to ask her father about. The whole family couldn't be as bad as him. Maybe somewhere out there, the clan she belonged to, the people she had always sort of thought must exist somewhere, really waited for her.

But she'd never find out while Will was around and monopolizing Taylor's time.

"I know she'd like that," Delinda answered. "She really was more excited about meeting you than Will, once I told her about both of you. I'll give you her number."

The two young women emerged from the park-like grounds and headed toward the casino entrance. The lights and buzz and clatter and clang of modern Las Vegas erupted like Steve Wynn's volcano at the Mirage, embracing them both in arms that welcomed winners and soothed losers every day and night of the year. Mary didn't mind that romance had not blossomed between her and Will. She'd had romance and passion with Danny McCoy and with Jake Porter, and she would have more shots at it down the line. Delinda too had been with Danny, and other men as well. Both were, for the moment, without any particular romantic interest. But both were young and vibrant, attractive, and interesting. Meeting Taylor Malloy had been a gift, reminding Mary that life was long, full of surprises, packed with adventure. Romance came and went; over the horizon or around the corner another man waited. But friends—the kind who would make the

effort to find a long-lost relative—were worth keeping close.

As they passed through the doors into that special
wonderland called the Montecito, Mary let out a delighted laugh.

"What?" Delinda asked. "Something funny?"

"Nothing," Mary said, knowing she could never
explain, and it would only embarrass Delinda if she
tried. "Never mind."

"Okay, whatever," Delinda said. "Sometimes I just
don't get you, Mary."

Mary laughed again, smiling so hard her cheeks
hurt. "And then sometimes you really, really do."

Danny had seen Ed serious, grim, upset, pissed off,
enraged, and furious enough to bite off someone's
head. He had seen him cheerful too—even down-
right jovial at times. Ed's emotions could be mercu-
rial, changing as circumstances did. He kept them to
himself much of the time, but when he felt them
strongly, everyone in earshot knew about it. When it
came to the safety and security of his guests, he was
very serious indeed.

But when Danny walked into Ed's office to tell
him what he'd learned about Glen Tidwell, the Ed
Deline he saw looked positively solemn, almost as if
someone had already died. Furrows ridged his high
forehead. He had run fingers through his curly hair,
leaving it in atypical disarray. As Danny came
through the door, Ed plucked nervously at his goatee.
Danny didn't like it—he had never known anyone as
self-confident as Ed, never worked for someone so

collected under pressure. Especially under pressure. Faced with a challenge, Ed thrived. Faced with a disaster, Ed triumphed. Danny had almost, he realized, come to think of Ed as a man who could not be fazed, who could not lose, no matter what life threw at him.

The Ed sitting at his desk did not look invulnerable at all.

"What's up, Ed?" he asked, dreading the answer.

"Sit."

Danny sat. Ed started to say something, leaning forward slightly, hands spread above the surface of his desk, mouth opening just a little. Then he stopped, closing his mouth, tipping back in his chair. He brought his hands together, palms flat, fingers pressed against each other. He held the pose for a long minute. Danny waited.

"We've been played," Ed finally said.

"What? By who?"

"Look at these," Ed said. White sheets of paper lay on top of his desk, upside down. He lifted them, handed them over to Danny, who realized they were photographs. He started to ask about them, then decided to wait until he saw what they showed.

They showed Garrick Flynn, in ranger uniform, in Iraq. Danny recognized the scenery, the mud buildings, the scraggly palms in the background. Telephone and electrical wires were strung between poles that cocked to one side or another like sticks a child had jammed into a mud puddle. And Danny recognized the uniforms, desert camo, the helmets, the guns. It all took him back, to someplace he hoped he would never have to return to again. Life was tenuous there; any minute a rocket or an IED or a rifle in the hands of an insurgent, a villager, a woman, or a small boy could steal it away. He had never slept well there, waking every twenty or thirty minutes, checking to make sure he and his comrades still breathed. That hadn't changed upon his return home, not for a long time. Not until he had filled his head with life, real life, and pushed the bad thoughts to someplace in the back of his mind where he could ignore them.

Not forget them, he knew. He would never forget any of it, but he could set it aside, move on from it. These photographs, though, brought it all crashing back. He shook his head, trying to clear it of the past, stay in the now. "Flynn. Where'd you get these?"

"I made some calls," Ed said. "Got these e-mailed to me and printed them here."

"Who are these other guys?" Danny asked.

"That's the thing. I figured Flynn's weird ideas didn't come from nowhere. Guy doesn't live in a vacuum, right? So I dug around, found out who his real buddies were over there. The ones who were with him when he started to change. That's these guys."

Danny studied the pictures again. The light was bad, bright and direct, creating deep shadows under helmets and behind walls. And he had only seen one picture of Tidwell at Natalie Benz's house, an old one. But one of the guys could have been Tidwell. "I think I know who this one is," he said.

"Who?"

"A guy named Glen Tidwell. Flynn made a call from a pay phone here at the Montecito. I mean, he might have made more, but one that I know of. I tracked it to a house in Henderson, and the woman who lives there says Tidwell was her common-law husband and a friend of Flynn's. She also says he's been missing for most of the last year, but he was there this morning when Flynn called. Now he's gone again. And he's like Flynn in some ways—he's turned really straight and intolerant of everything he sees as sinful."

"Sounds about right," Ed said. "Judging from what little I could get on the rest of these yahoos."

"What are they, religious nuts?"

"I don't know if they're nuts, Danny. I don't even know if they're religious. I just know some of their ideas are on the extreme side, and if they had their way, there wouldn't be a Las Vegas. These guys would get rid of every bar, strip club, porn shop, casino, liquor store, and Internet connection in the country. Flynn might have had some offbeat ideas of his own, but when he hooked up with these guys, he became more and more judgmental. Turned against his own buddies, the guys in his unit who he had to work with. You know what happened after that."

"I know he came home, got hired by Coleman, went back, got into a fight, and got canned."

"That's right," Ed said. "But when he went back, with Coleman, some of these guys were still there. Even more hard-core, from what I hear. Flynn hooked up with them again, and he went over the edge."

"Over the edge how?" Danny asked. "You mean the fight?"

"The fight, and everything else that led up to it. It

didn't come out of nowhere—there were signs, but you know how it is in combat. Hard to spend a lot of time trying to psychoanalyze one guy. A security team over there is just like a military one—you've got to be able to depend on the guys around you. You watch their backs and they watch yours, and if you don't get that down, you're not going to make it through. Flynn, according to what I found out, got to the point where he wanted to pick and choose whose back he would have and whose he wouldn't. Sinners weren't worth saving. If you wanted Flynn on your side, you had to be on his."

"Guy like that's lucky to last a week over there."

"That's right. Flynn lasted, but only because the guys he worked with were too decent to let him cowboy it on his own, no matter how big a pain in the ass he was. But when he stopped covering them, things went to hell in a hurry. That's when the fight happened."

Danny refocused on the photos. He couldn't see anything unusual about Flynn's friends, even Glen Tidwell. They just looked like grunts, like regular soldiers sent far from home to kill the enemy and not get killed themselves. That was the theory, anyway, even though it didn't always work out that way. He pointed to Tidwell in one of the pictures. "That one's Tidwell," he said. "Do you know who these other guys are?"

Ed smiled, but it was a bitter smile, without humor or enjoyment. "That's the thing," he said. "I ran facial recognition on them and got some matches." He nodded toward the built-in flat screens on his wall, clicked a button. Split-screen images winked into view, with faces from the photos with Garrick Flynn on the left, and frames from Montecito surveillance cameras on the right. MATCH showed beneath the faces, spread across both sides of the screen.

Four soldiers on the left. Four cowboys on the right.

"Those are the guys who started that stampede," Danny said when he recognized them. "The ones who took off instead of coming inside."

"Yeah," Ed agreed. "That's them."

"So Flynn was in on it from the beginning."

"Like I said, Danny, we've been played." Ed punched another button and the screens went blank. "And I hate being played."

27

"Sam, it's Burl."

"Where are you, Burl?" Sam asked.

"I'm at the arena," he said. "If you ever want to see me with all my parts intact again, you'd better get out here."

"Oh my God, they went for it?"

"I've been training all afternoon," Burl answered. "I'm about to go for my first ride."

She had almost forgotten the deal she had tried to put together with some rodeo cowboys, on behalf of her whale, Burl Bradenton, who desperately wanted to try his hand at bull riding.

Obviously, the cowboys had not forgotten.

"Don't get on yet!" she almost shouted into the phone. "I want to be there!"

"I'll wait a few minutes, but I think the steer's about ready to go," Burl said.

Sam had been sitting in the Sports Book with Byron Hammer, watching the results from an out-of-state ball game. He hadn't even made it to the door of the Elton John show before deciding he didn't want to go. Marcella, he said, had given his ticket to a young woman standing outside the doors.

She squeezed Byron's shoulder. "I have to run,

Byron. I'll be back in a little while, or else I'll catch up with you somewhere else."

"Okay, Sam. I'll probably stick around for the rest of the game and then move on."

She didn't expect him to make it another fifteen minutes, but one never knew. People, she had learned, could surprise you.

Take Burl, for instance. She had not expected him to even be interested in rodeo—he was as urban as they came, a lifelong city dweller. But it turned out he watched rodeo on TV all the time and had intentionally timed this trip to coincide with the Stampede, hoping for just such an opportunity.

She rushed through the casino. The crowd changed as night descended. Especially with the big speech tonight, the mix of players had shifted to include fewer cowboys and cowgirls and more people dressed in elegant evening wear. Sure, there were still tourists in shorts and souvenir baseball caps, young hotties in miniskirts and halter tops, and every kind of clothing option in between. But at night you also saw the ones who still treated a night at a casino the way they did in the old days, as an excuse for a sophisticated evening on the town. Dinner, a show, and a little gambling. Sam liked seeing these people come in, preferred watching those who enjoyed themselves at the casino to those who looked desperate to make the mortgage payment or those who went through the motions robotically, because gambling was, they believed, the only thing to do here.

Sam knew better. You could do almost anything in Las Vegas.

Including, it seemed, learn to ride a bull.

Near the outside door, she spotted Delinda. "Hey," she said, still walking. "Want to come watch a hunka-hunka burnin' whale get thrown by a bull?"

"I've been thrown some lines of bull," Delinda said. "Is that the same thing?"

"Not even close." Sam grabbed Delinda's upper arm. "Come on, let's watch the fun."

Outside, they hurried to the arena that had been set up on the Montecito grounds. Bright stadium lights burned down toward it, although the grandstand was empty. As they drew nearer, though, Sam spotted some cowboys perched on the fences surrounding it. One of them looked down at her, and she recognized the short guy from the day before.

"Hey, Sam," the cowboy said. "Come to see Burl take his ride?"

"Wouldn't miss it," she said. "This is Delinda, another interested spectator."

He touched his hat brim for Delinda's sake, then dropped down off the fence and opened a gate for them. They stepped inside, the odors of dirt and manure, chewing tobacco, and sweat instantly enveloping them. It smelled warm, musky, and yet somehow more pleasant than Sam would have expected.

"Over here, ladies," the cowboy said. He guided them up a wooden ramp, inside the fence. At the top Sam could see Burl Bradenton, sitting on a rail beside one of the cattle chutes. He wore a protective helmet, almost like a motorcycle helmet, instead of a cowboy hat. Otherwise he was in his street clothes—a long-sleeved cotton shirt, khakis—with leather gloves on his hands. Sam couldn't see his feet, but hoped he at least had boots on instead of the loafers she had last seen him in.

Inside the chute she could hear the bull stamping and snorting. A bell hung around his neck clanged with every motion.

"Hi, Sam!" he shouted.

"Are you nervous?"

"Nervous as all hell," he answered. "But I think I'm ready." He raised his foot toward her, and she saw that he had indeed been given some boots, complete with dull spurs.

"He's going to survive this, right, guys?" Sam asked.

"I'd give him a fifty-fifty chance," one of the other cowboys replied. He leaned down into the chute, and although she couldn't see his hands, she knew he moved them briskly. "We've done what we can, though. Plenty of rosin on the rope, and I'm rubbing it in, to make it stickier. Got some bullfighters ready in case he gets thrown." All the cowboys laughed at that.

"In case," another one echoed.

"You ready, Burl?" the one beside him on the fence said.

Burl stared down at the bull, then back at Sam and Delinda. "I guess."

"You don't have to do this, Burl," Sam told him. "It's okay to back out."

"No problem here," the cowboy on the fence said.

"Entirely up to you. Old Terminator there might be disappointed, but I reckon he'd get over it."

"The bull's name is Terminator?" Sam asked.

"That's right," the cowboy said.

"Burl . . ."

"Sam, I want to do this," he said. "Really truly."

If she'd been given a choice, she would have vetoed the idea. But it was his life, his Vegas fantasy. People came to Las Vegas to reinvent themselves, or to live for the duration of their trip as somebody else, the person they could only be in their dreams. This was Burl's chance, and she didn't intend to take it away from him.

Even if she could. At this point, things had gone beyond her control.

"Have fun," she said, meaning it. "I almost said 'Break a leg,' " Sam whispered to Delinda, "but decided that would be a bad idea."

"Good catch."

"Just slide down on him like you was showed," the cowboy on the fence instructed. He took hold of Burl's arm to help him ease onto the bull's back.

Burl swallowed anxiously, but he moved off the fence rail. Sam couldn't quite see what happened next but guessed that he went down onto the bull's back and was handed the rope. Through the slats, she caught a glimpse of his helmeted head rising and falling as the bull shifted.

"Go!" the cowboy on the fence shouted. The gate banged open and the bull charged from the chute. As far as Sam could tell, Burl's form was good, his legs pressed against the bull's flanks, free hand in the air, right hand gripping the rope like it was the only thing tethering him to Earth. Terminator's hide was concrete-gray dappled with black, like shadows of trees over a sidewalk on a sunny day. His horns curved out like scimitars and Sam guessed they could be every bit as deadly.

"One, two," the short cowboy said. Sam realized he was counting down seconds because there was no clock operating in the arena. Terminator spun and bucked. His hind hooves kicked high into the air and Burl shot forward off his back as if he'd been catapulted.

"Three," the short cowboy said at the same time Burl hit the dirt of the arena floor.

Terminator snorted, ducked his head, and charged at Burl as the man tried to rise to his hands and knees. Two cowboys intercepted, distracting the bull and leading him back toward the chute. Two more ran out into the arena and helped Burl to his feet, hustling him out of the arena in case Terminator broke free and came back for more.

"How do we get down there?" Sam asked the short cowboy. "I want to see Burl."

"Just follow me." He slid gracefully off the fence and led Sam and Delinda through what seemed to be a maze of bars and rails. Finally, they emerged into an open area where Burl sat on a folding chair in front of a white-coated doctor, who examined his wrist.

"Burl!" Sam cried, running across the open space to him. "Are you okay?"

She had seen Burl win a quarter million dollars in one night, but she had never seen him grin like he was doing now. The helmet had smashed his hair into new shapes, his shirt was torn, and his arm didn't look right. "I must have died and gone to heaven," he said, still smiling. "I'm seeing angels."

"No angels here," Delinda replied. "Better check for a concussion, doctor."

"This is Delinda Deline," Sam said, gesturing toward Delinda.

"That was quite a ride," Delinda said.

"Thanks," Burl said. "I've had quite a good time at the Montecito. Is Ed your dad?"

"Don't tell anyone," Delinda joked.

"He runs a first-class operation, start to finish. And you can feel free to tell him that."

The doctor examining Burl changed the subject abruptly. "This wrist is broken," he said. "I'll set it, and then I'd like you to see your own doctor as soon as you can."

"You broke your wrist?" Sam asked.

"Looks that way," Burl said.

The doctor put a splint against Burl's arm and started wrapping tape around it. "This might hurt," he warned.

"Doctor," Burl said, "I'm already starting to feel the wrist. You really think splinting it will hurt more than breaking it?"

"I'll give you something for the pain in a couple of minutes," the doctor told him. "It's going to get a lot worse before it's better. Are you staying at the Montecito?"

"I don't know," Burl said. "Sam, are you going to

take away my suite if I can't play for a few days?"

"Of course not," she assured him. She squatted beside his chair, unwilling to let her Gilbert Gilmore pants touch the dirt. "It's yours for as long as you need it, Burl. It's the least we can do."

"Then I guess you can make it as strong as it needs to be, Doctor," Burl said. "But it'll be a while before my regular doctor can see it."

"We can run him over to Sunrise Hospital," Delinda offered. "Daddy says they're the best. They can see him there."

"That'll work," the doctor said. "He needs to be X-rayed for sure. I think the splint will do the job, but there could be more severe damage than I can tell from a manual examination."

"Not a problem, Doctor," Sam assured him. Burl looked like a kid who had just ridden his first bicycle. The pain showed in his eyes, but he beamed, radiating contentment.

"That was a pretty good ride," the short cowboy said, walking up behind Sam and Delinda. "Two seconds better'n my first. You sure you haven't done that before?"

"Not in this lifetime," Burl said. "But thanks. Thanks for making it happen too." He reached over with his left hand. Sam took it in both of hers. "And thank you, Sam."

"Not a problem," she said again. "I like to see my clients happy." She inclined her head toward his broken wrist. "I prefer to see them in one piece too, but happy is good."

"I am happy," Burl said. He winced as the doctor twisted the tape around him. "Definitely happy. You know what, Sam?"

"What?"

Burl pumped the air with the one fist he could move. "I love Las Vegas!"

28

Mike didn't know Greg very well, but he knew the guy was solid—could have played ball in school, and maybe even gone pro—and reliable. If he said he'd do something, he did it. If he said he'd be somewhere, he showed up. When Mike stepped off the elevator on the thirty-seventh floor, with a barely restrained Leroy Snead, anxious as a hound dog on the trail of a juicy rabbit, Greg was already there, waiting.

"What's up, Mike?" he asked.

"Got to go to 3729," Mike said. "And keep Mr. Snead here from killing the room's occupant, Eustace Barnes, or Mrs. Snead, who we're pretty sure is in there with the aforementioned Barnes, and probably not playing bridge, if you catch my drift."

"Love triangle? Sorry to hear it, Mr. Snead," Greg said.

"Save it," Snead said. "When I'm through with them, there won't be enough left to make a triangle."

"Please, Mr. Snead," Mike said. "Let's handle this like adults."

"I am an adult," Snead said. "Don't worry, Mike, I promise I won't kill anyone."

"Glad to hear it," Mike said. "Come on, Greg."

Greg led the way to the door. Mike had watched Linda Lou Snead walk toward it so many times on the surveillance footage that he got a weird sense of déjà vu when he did it himself. He glanced at the ceiling-mounted camera as they passed beneath it, knowing that he was now digitally recorded in the same spot through which Linda Lou had sashayed in her horrible leopard pants. Outside the door, Greg paused, waiting for Mike.

"Knock and announce," Mike instructed him.

Greg did that. He gave two sharp raps, then called out, "Hotel security!"

Apparently, discretion was not high on the list of virtues held by Linda Lou Snead or Eustace Barnes. Mike heard a muffled screech, then banging and rustling from inside. He couldn't tell quite what they were doing—possibly trying to cage a wild wolverine, from the sound of things.

"They're in there, all right," Snead said. His face had turned violet and his fists were clenched. Mike thought he might start to growl and snap in a minute, and he wished he had a literal leash to fasten around the man's neck, just in case.

"Of course they are," Mike said. He pressed past Greg and pounded on the door. "Hotel security!" he shouted. "We're coming in." He pushed a passkey card into the slot and when the door beeped, he twisted the knob. "Mr. Barnes, Mrs. Snead, please excuse the interruption, but we're engaged in a criminal investigation."

When they got inside, Linda Lou was shoving the tails of her western-style shirt into her unbuckled jeans and trying to fasten its snaps over her expansive bosom. Her hair—the real, blond stuff, not the red wig, which had been abandoned on the floor next to the rumpled bed—was tousled, hanging down in her face and looking, to Mike, far more attractive than the usual sprayed tuft that floated around her head like a separate entity. A flush colored her cheeks and her red lipstick had been smeared. She looked as if she'd been having a good time, and Mike felt momentarily sorry that he had interrupted them.

That feeling vanished when he realized that Eustace Barnes was making a dash for the open sliding glass door that led out onto the balcony. His shirt was off completely, leaving him clad in a white sleeveless undershirt, jeans, and white socks. In his right hand he clutched a glass vial that could only be what remained of Cavanaugh's Virtue's jerky juice.

"Freeze, Barnes!" Mike commanded. Barnes remained unfrozen, his right hand clawing at the edge of the glass door.

Greg hurled himself toward the man, but Barnes, impressively agile, twisted away from Greg's grasping hands and gained the balcony, stopping at the rail and leaning out.

"If you're going to jump, Mr. Barnes," Mike said, "you might want to reconsider, since I can see you're not packing a parachute—"

"Or much of anything else," Leroy Snead interrupted.

"—and that's a thirty-seven-story drop," Mike finished, ignoring Snead.

"I'd be happy to help you over the side, you son of a bitch," Snead offered.

"I'm not going over the side," Barnes said. Instead,

he stuck the hand holding the vial over the railing. "But if you folks don't back out of my room, this here will. Then nobody gets it. Don't bother me a bit. That way we have a level playing field, which is all I ever wanted in the first place."

"Level except that you'll be right down there with it," Snead warned. His face had gone dark purple, his hands curled into claws as if he wanted to rip Barnes apart. His every muscle was tense, coiled, and ready to strike. "You may even beat it down."

Linda Lou, her clothing largely restored, tucked a stray lock of hair behind her ear. "Now, don't let's get all worked up, Leroy," she pleaded. She stayed deftly out of Snead's reach, did a pirouette, and headed out the glass doors onto the balcony. There she snuggled in next to Eustace Barnes. "I'm sure this can all be worked out, can't it, Eustace, honey?"

Eustace draped his free hand protectively over her shoulders. "That's right, Linda Lou. Now that Leroy knows what the score is, we can all come to some kind of agreement."

"That's stolen property, Mr. Barnes," Mike cautioned him. "You don't want to make things worse."

"You know something worse than being financially ruined and sent to prison?" Barnes asked. "Because I can't actually think of nothing offhand."

Linda Lou stroked his hand gingerly. "Don't you worry about a thing, Eustace," she said. She turned in his arm, pressing her breasts against his ribs, standing on tiptoe to give him a kiss on the cheek. The way he smiled, Mike thought maybe he really did love her.

But then Linda Lou reached across Barnes and

snatched the vial from his hand. He grabbed for her. She performed another swift pirouette, surprisingly light-footed, dodged him, and jumped back into the room.

Greg moved faster than Snead or Barnes. He lunged, throwing both arms around her, and tackled her like the ballplayer Mike believed he had been. They both hit the floor together, although Greg's landing was padded by Linda Lou. She gave an outraged squeal and Mike cringed, expecting to hear breaking glass.

Greg hoisted himself to his feet, however, holding up the intact vial in his left hand. "Got it, Mike," he said. "I gather this is something important?"

"It's important, all right," Snead said, stalking forward.

"Let him have the vial, Greg," Mike said. "It's his. You knew what it was, you probably wouldn't want to hang on to it anyway."

Greg handed it over. Leroy Snead took the vial, holding it up and inspecting it from every angle, as if worried that it might have been replaced with an exact duplicate. Mike was afraid he'd open it up and sniff, but apparently a visual inspection satisfied him.

"I guess now I know what's important and what isn't around here," Snead said. He stared daggers at his wife as he spoke.

"Baby, I—" she began.

He cut her off. "Save it, Linda Lou. I don't care what you have to say and I don't want to listen to you right now." He shot an angry look at Barnes. "I'll deal with you later," he said. "I'm not going to kill you, Eustace—I'm going to crush you, destroy your business, and make you wish you *had* jumped."

Barnes, standing in the balcony doorway now, swallowed nervously but didn't answer. He had held all the cards for a minute, but now his hand was empty and he knew it. Mike decided to play on his anxiety. "Don't leave this room, Mr. Barnes," he said, taking a forceful tone and punctuating his command with a jabbing finger. "The police will be up here in a few minutes, and they're going to want to talk to you." Barnes gave a defeated nod. Mike wanted to get out of there before the man started crying. He took Leroy Snead by the arm, guiding him toward the room door. "Let's go, Mr. Snead."

Linda Lou went out the door first. She looked chastened, but not especially sorrowful—and still, in her disarray, sexier than she had before. Mike could understand what had drawn Leroy Snead to her in the first place, at least physically. He just wasn't sure it would be enough to bring them back together now, or if they had something else, beyond the physical, which could overcome all that had happened between them.

He didn't know them, really. Maybe there hadn't been anything but the business tying them together. Maybe Barnes had just been the latest in a long line of playmates, and the only difference this time was that they had stolen from Snead as well. With the show ending and the auction tonight, it didn't seem likely that Mike would ever find out.

Just as well, he thought. *Life's too short to take everyone's problems onto the Cannon shoulders, broad and sturdy as they are.*

Linda Lou walked down the hall toward the elevators, hips swaying as if to a steady drumbeat. By the time Leroy, Mike, and Greg reached the elevators, she had already hopped on board one and disappeared. "Leave me be, Mike," Snead said, gesturing with the vial. "I got to get this under lock and key again, and then I reckon I need to have me a talk with Linda Lou before the auction."

"I think that's a good idea," Mike said. "We'll just wait up here for the Vegas cops, to make sure Barnes doesn't get any crazy ideas."

When Snead's elevator had gone, Mike dialed Las Vegas Metro and told the story to Detective Sarnat. Folding his phone, he saw Greg looking at him, perplexed. "What the hell happened in there, Mike?" he asked.

Mike gave him the rundown—the theft, his investigation, Linda Lou's constant demand for updates on his progress. In the telling, it all became crystal clear to him—she had wanted to know if she was a suspect, or if Barnes was. If he had let on that he was closing in on them, she and Barnes might well have left town. As long as she thought they were in the clear, though, she had felt safe sticking around, keeping tabs on things and deflecting suspicion away from herself.

"But at the end, taking the vial away from Barnes?" Greg interrupted. "What was that about?"

"She would have given it back to Snead if you hadn't jumped her," Mike speculated. "All Barnes wanted was to level the playing field, like he said. If nobody had the stuff, it was almost as good as him having it, because then he and Snead would both be starting over from scratch. But level didn't do Linda Lou any good. If Barnes had gotten away with the soul sauce, he'd have been in for some big paydays down the line, and she would have shared—probably at a more than equal share, since she was already equal partners with Leroy, and Barnes wouldn't have had his big break without her. But since he'd been nabbed, she had to get it back into Snead's hands. Destroyed, it would have been totally worthless to her. If Snead can auction it for a million bucks, she has a chance at a piece of that, even if they get divorced. Community property."

"Even if she goes to jail for stealing it?"

"Leroy Snead will never press charges against her," Mike assured him, feeling pretty confident in his judgment of the man. "He'll be happy to see Barnes rot in prison. But even if he divorces Linda Lou, even if his lawyers can fix it so she never sees a dime, he won't want her to do the time. The man loves her, that's his biggest problem. Almost as much as he loves horses."

"Different strokes," Greg said, nodding his understanding. "But, Mike . . . ?"

"Yeah?"

"Soul sauce? Did you really say that?"

Mike dropped his head, temples landing in the palms of his hands. "I give up," he said. "A brother tries to be sensitive to people's feelings, and what does he get? Nothing but grief, that's what. Nothing but grief."

29

Still sitting in Ed's luxurious office, Danny ran Garrick Flynn through the Montecito's state-of-the-art video IQ system, enabling him and Ed to track Flynn's movements any time he was within range of the casino's cameras. Most of the time, Flynn had behaved as the intelligence professional he was. He had walked every path that Klaus Aickmann might be expected to take while on the premises, studying every angle, looking for every possible opening an attacker might use. He double- and triple-checked the Montecito's own security measures, testing, for example, to see how far he could walk, unchallenged, into an employees-only corridor. He scoured the various routes to make sure no weapons or explosives had been planted along the way. He spent hours studying the crowd, presumably watching for any known terrorists or criminals, and reading through records of registered hotel guests for the same reason.

When appropriate, he worked with other members of his team and the Secret Service as well as with Danny's people. At other times, he worked alone. He seemed single-minded in his devotion to the task at hand. When some of his colleagues were off duty, they gambled on the floor, attended shows, or went out shopping. When Flynn's shifts ended, he ate, slept, and then devoted his personal time to more of the same things he had done during working hours.

"Guy's a workaholic," Danny observed. To a scary degree. If he was this intense about everything in his life, it was no wonder he didn't get along in the military. Even under fire a guy had to be able to relax sometimes.

"It's Las Vegas and he's horrified by everything that happens here," Ed pointed out. "I guess he could spend all his free time in church, but that'd take him pretty far away from the property."

"That's true," Danny agreed. "He could watch TV, maybe. We get some cartoon channels, right?"

"We get everything," Ed said. "But he might have to pass by some of those, what do you call 'em, adult entertainment channels. Probably make his head explode."

Danny went back to watching Flynn, scanning through the footage in reverse, speeding it up so that everybody moved like people did in those early silent slapstick comedies, completing their actions before they began. He knew Flynn had been on the floor during the stampede—the ex-ranger had helped him clear a path for the marauding cattle. But he was surprised to learn that Flynn had only hit the floor moments before the ruckus started.

"I'm slowing it down here," he told Ed. "This is where we know he was last in the same general vicinity as his old wartime buddies."

"That's right," Ed said. "I'm getting full rundowns on who those other guys are, by the way. If that one guy, Tidwell, is from here, maybe the rest are too.

And if they're not, then they must have been staying at one of the hotels. If they're still in town, I want to know about it."

"Of course." Danny watched the footage, cutting from camera to camera. Flynn walked, backward, off the casino floor. Then the image switched to one in a restricted-access corridor—which Flynn, while wearing his ID badge, had every right to be in. He emerged from a service elevator into the corridor.

"What the hell's he doing in there?" Ed asked.

"No idea." Danny kept studying the footage. It didn't show which floor the elevator had come from, but the next segment showed Flynn inside the service elevator, carrying a briefcase and pushing the button for Subbasement 2.

Danny paused the image. "He didn't have that briefcase when he came out."

"So he must have left it in the subbasement," Ed said. "We've got to find out why."

"But we don't have very many cameras down there," Danny said, starting the footage rolling again. The images backtracked to Flynn getting on the elevator in the same service corridor, then to him crossing the casino to that corridor from the guest elevators, and finally to him bringing the briefcase down on a guest elevator from his own room.

"Hartung's whole team has keys to the service elevators, and access to every floor," Danny said. "They insisted on it."

"I know," Ed said. "I didn't argue about that because I figured it was a legitimate request. But if Flynn is using his position with Hartung's group for some other purpose—or if their whole team is up to something—we need to put a lid on it, and now."

"Do you think that whole stampede thing was just meant to distract our attention from him carrying the briefcase downstairs?"

Ed raised his eyebrows, furrowing his brow. "It worked, didn't it? Nobody spotted him going down there because we were all obsessed with watching the stampede video over and over. Even if someone in surveillance had noticed him getting on the elevator or coming off, by the time the stampede was under control they would have forgotten, because it seemed relatively innocent at the time. They never would have remembered the briefcase."

"Maybe it still is innocent," Danny said. "We don't know that he's trying to pull anything."

"But we can't take the chance that he's not. Let's get down to that subbasement, and fast. Aickmann goes onstage in fifteen minutes. I wanted to be in that ballroom when he goes in."

"Me too," Danny said. "I arranged the staffing so that you and I would be redundant, but still . . ."

"Yeah. Still." Ed rose and hurried toward his office door, stopping only to grab a couple of flashlights from inside his closet. Danny dropped the remote control onto Ed's desk and followed. As they passed through the door, Ed tossed one of the flashlights. Taken off guard, Danny almost fumbled the catch. He managed to hang on to it, though, and clicked it on briefly to make sure it worked.

They were almost out the door when Mike Cannon breezed in, all smiles and loose limbs. "Another case cracked," he said. "What's up with you guys? And the flashlights?"

"We've got to check on something, Mike," Danny said. "No time to bring you up to speed on it. Why don't you get to surveillance and bring up whatever you can get on Subbasement Two?"

"Nobody goes down there," Mike said.

"We are," Ed said impatiently. "Please, Mike."

"Sure, Mr. D. Anything you say." Mike turned around, headed for the surveillance room, and Danny rushed to catch up with Ed.

Everything he had learned about Flynn warred with his initial reaction to the man. As an army ranger, Flynn had been a warrior, a hero. Only the best made it into that elite group. What could have turned Flynn away from the patriotism and sense of duty that must have spurred him in the first place?

"Ed, you think he could be pulling something because he believes it's his duty somehow? Religious, patriotic, moral, something like that?" Danny asked as they boarded a service elevator of their own. Ed jabbed at the Subbasement 2 button.

"If he is, then he's doubly dangerous," Ed said. "There's nothing like a fanatic to screw up your day." His words carried the weight of experience, and Danny had learned not to doubt that Ed's experience was usually hard-won. "You know what? I don't even think Aickmann is his target."

"You don't?" Danny couldn't figure out where that had come from. "Why not?"

"I think Flynn's been playing us the whole time. He's like a stage magician, using misdirection to keep us from catching what he's really up to. I mean, that whole business with the CD? I know our guys are good, but finding that was just a little too pat. Why would the bad guys put their plans down on something like that and then leave it someplace where anyone else might find it?"

"That always bothered me too."

"If Flynn wanted to take out Aickmann, he wouldn't need some kind of complicated plot. He wouldn't need to plant a bomb in the basement or try to bring in seven guys with guns. He's one of the few people allowed to carry a gun into the ballroom during the speech. All he'd have to do is be willing to sacrifice himself—and if he's a fanatic, that shouldn't be a problem—and he could take the shot."

"What do you think he's after, then?"

"That's what I don't know. Something more important, in his twisted mind, than taking out Aickmann. Which means it has to be something big, something that would really make a splash."

The elevator doors slid open onto the subbasement. A wide, concrete block corridor, painted white with green trim, stretched out before them. Wheel marks from dollies and carts tattooed the floor. A tangle of wire, conduit, and pipes obscured much of the ceiling. This basement, Danny knew, housed key control panels for electrical and communications systems, as well as the main furnaces and boilers for heat and hot water. The hallway provided access for maintenance crews who needed to work on those or on certain other plumbing and ventilation issues. The air was dry, with odors of grease and the ozone stink of electricity flavoring it. A low background drone from all the equipment grated on Danny's nerves. Spending any significant time down here would surely result in a massive headache.

"Well, from down here someone could definitely cause trouble," he said.

"No kidding," Ed agreed. "Electrical, phones and Internet, ventilation, plumbing . . . we gotta find that briefcase."

Ed and Danny switched on their flashlights, playing the beams over the network of pipes and wires on the ceiling and the nooks and crannies at ground level. From the hallway, various doors led into different rooms, and beyond that other side halls created a veritable warren. Danny knew they'd never cover the whole thing in the ten minutes or so remaining before Aickmann's speech. "Should we bring in more bodies?" he asked.

"We need all hands upstairs," Ed said. "Besides, by the time they got down here and we told them what to look for, we'd probably have found it."

"If we *can* find it," Danny said. He pushed open a door. Inside this room was yet another room, glass-walled, containing a network of linked servers. The outer room served only as insulation, and he knew the temperature inside the server room was closely regulated. All of the resort's computer systems ran out of here. A single man worked inside the inner room, wearing a white shirt and striped tie, checking one of the machines with a clipboard in his hands. Danny let himself into the inner room, looking at the guy's ID badge. The picture on it matched the man's face.

"Danny McCoy, head of surveillance," he said.

The guy nodded in recognition. "Sure thing, Mr. McCoy. Something up?"

"You see anybody strange down here earlier today? Guy in a suit, carrying a briefcase?"

"Not during my shift," the man said. He indicated a surveillance camera mounted on the ceiling. "You can check the tapes, though."

If Flynn had entered this room, he would have shown up on the footage selected by video IQ. Danny thanked the man and backed from the room, beaming the flashlight around the perimeter of the outer, insulating room, just in case. Taking out these computers would wreak havoc on all of the Montecito's systems.

He went back into the hallway just in time to see Ed emerging from a room on the opposite side. "Nothing in there," Danny reported.

"Ditto," Ed said. He checked his Polanti wristwatch. "Eight minutes and counting."

"Ed, we're never going to cover this whole basement in eight minutes."

"That's just how long until Aickmann goes on," Ed pointed out. "If he's not Flynn's target, then whatever Flynn is up to might be on an entirely different schedule. We could have hours."

"Or he could be planning to pull something *before* Aickmann's speech," Danny said. "For all we know, it started when he first came down yesterday, and whatever it is, it's been going all this time."

"Then we should spend less time talking and more time looking."

Danny and Ed continued their search, using the flashlights, even in areas with adequate overhead lighting, to focus their gazes. Without that technique, Danny knew, eyes tended to dart this way and that instead of covering the space in an organized fashion. Ed took the left-hand side of the corridor, and Danny the right. They opened every door and quickly scoured the rooms those doors closed off.

"Four minutes, Danny," Ed told him.

Danny, not a person ever willing to admit defeat, looked at how much territory still needed to be covered with despair tugging at his heart. If Flynn's timetable coincided with the beginning of Aickmann's speech, they'd never make it.

He pushed on the handle of the next door, but it didn't give. "Locked," he said. Few of the doors they had encountered before had been, since no one came to this level who didn't have business here.

"What's in there?" Ed asked.

"I don't know." All the doors had started to look the same to Danny, and although he prided himself on knowing the Montecito as well as anyone alive, he hadn't spent much time on this floor. He swiped his master key card through the lock and pushed again.

This time, the door swung open. On the other side was a massive room, taking up not only this subbasement but the one above it and maybe a third story above that. A huge ventilation unit bulked into the darkness overhead, with ducts reaching like tendrils in every direction.

Beside it were three men, all wearing ID badges. One of them was Garrick Flynn. He knelt on one knee beside his briefcase, working its combination locks.

The other two men pointed guns squarely at Danny.

30

Heinrich Hartung met Klaus Aickmann at his suite, to accompany his employer to the ballroom where his speech was to be given. Hartung found his own room perfectly comfortable, but he couldn't help being impressed by the size and luxury of Aickmann's suite.

He was, of course, long since accustomed to seeing the wealthy Aickmann enjoy the best of everything. Hartung had no complaints about his own pay. He drove a perfectly satisfactory Mercedes and lived in a large house outside Hamburg. But Herr Aickmann lived in a genuine palace—which was just one of his several homes—and he tended to prefer Bentleys and Jaguars, although part of his trucking fleet consisted of Mercedes trucks.

As Hartung waited in the suite's living room, he considered the fact that Aickmann would not have to pay for this luxury. He rarely saw his employer actually part with cash, wasn't sure if the man even carried any. Although the man could have bought the Montecito without thinking twice, he seemed to be given most everything he had for free. Hartung remembered a day in Beverly Hills when they had both gone to a Rodeo Drive jeweler to look at wristwatches. He had spent seven thousand dollars on a

Patek Philippe, while Aickmann had been handed one, with the shop owner's compliments. Maybe the man thought that Aickmann would return again, or would invest in his business—no telling, really, but neither had, in fact, happened. Aickmann still wore his from time to time, but Hartung found that any pleasure he might have taken from his had been eliminated by the man's pointless gesture toward his boss.

So perhaps I am a little envious, he thought, enjoying the way the soft leather sofa cushioned his body. *It is to be expected, no? If we did not long for the things we could not afford, why would we make any effort to improve our situations?*

When Aickmann emerged from the bedroom, in a dark blue suit that Hartung knew had been tailored for him in Hong Kong—and wearing the Patek Philippe, which made Hartung glad he had left his at home—he beamed broadly at Hartung. "Well, Heinz, it seems to be time, doesn't it?"

Hartung resisted the impulse to check the watch he was wearing, a low-end Rolex. "Yes, it does, Klaus."

"We have been through many of these occasions, you and I," Aickmann went on, "But somehow, this one feels different to me. Perhaps it's because I am usually invited to speak due to my wealth, my business acumen, or what have you. This time, my address is not on behalf of myself but of Germany, of all Europe. Yes, I think that's why I . . . I confess, Heinrich, to a small bit of nervousness. Can you imagine that?"

Hartung hoped that Aickmann's anxiety didn't stem from some premonition of trouble. He and the others had covered every possible angle, he believed. Whether or not the CD plot had been real, he thought they could defend against any scenario that arose.

Still, he had a superstitious streak, and that bad omen of a dream had raised its ugly specter. Aickmann's words poked at him unpleasantly, like a thorn in his sock.

"Yes, Klaus," he said at length, using the sofa's padded arm to push himself to his feet. "I can certainly understand some nerves on such an occasion. But I know that you will, as always, meet this challenge and emerge victorious."

Aickmann clapped him on the back, a little harder than was absolutely necessary. His throat caught as he spoke and Hartung realized he was genuinely anxious, not just saying so, which only increased Hartung's tension. "Thank you, old friend. You are always such a treasure to have on my side."

Outside the door, a crew waited to escort them downstairs. Agents of the Secret Service, members of the Montecito staff, and Dieter Klasse from his own operation filled the hallway. Each carried a weapon of some kind, and each was, Hartung believed, ready to sacrifice his or her own life for Aickmann's if the need should arise.

A glance at Aickmann, who indicated his readiness with a raised eyebrow and a tick of his head, and Hartung opened the door, blocking it with his body until he could determine that the way was clear.

Outside, he saw the people he had expected, and nobody else. Five men, plus himself. Good. He tugged the door farther and stood to one side, letting Aickmann pass him. He would bring up the rear. He felt the Steyr GB in his hip holster and unbuttoned his jacket so he could reach it quickly if he needed to. It shouldn't be necessary—the floor had been sealed off, an elevator held for them, and on the ground floor a protected passageway would have been cleared by the time they arrived.

One couldn't base one's protective measures on what should be necessary, though, or the person being protected would probably have a very short life indeed.

They covered the distance to the elevator in silence, feet shuffling across the carpeted floor like short, swift strokes of sandpaper.

On the way down, no one spoke. He had been in similarly silent elevators many times, usually in big office buildings where no one knew anyone else, but this time a mood of unsettled anxiety filled the small space. Aickmann cleared his throat loudly a couple of times and shot Hartung a wry smile, as if he found his lapse in manners embarrassing.

Hartung tensed again as the doors parted. He put his hand on the stock of his weapon, comforted by its solidity. As promised, guards had parted the crowd like Moses at the Red Sea. Tourists, curious locals, and Montecito employees jockeyed for glimpses of the great man. Hartung felt pride well up in him as cameras flashed and an excited buzz ran through the onlookers. For all his grousing, at moments like these he was pleased by his association with Klaus Aick-mann.

Aickmann worked the rope line like a practiced politician, tossing out waves, clasping some of the offered hands. His smile was like a floodlight, washing over everyone, but his eyes were lasers, picking out individuals and making them feel, for those few instants, that they were the focus of his undivided attention. With his escorts grouped in front and behind, he moved briskly between the ranks, not allowing the onlookers to slow him down, and in a few moments they passed into the hallway that ran behind the ballroom.

Here Charles Hooper of the Secret Service met them. All business, he nodded at Hartung without smiling. He directed them toward the door that opened behind the dais, through which Aickmann would walk when his introduction was finished. Guards at the casino doorway secured that door. Another guard, holding the ballroom door open a crack so he could watch, waited to give them the signal.

Aickmann took a few deep breaths. He looked more tired now, as if the energy of the crowd through which he'd passed had fed him a rich meal that wore off quickly. Hartung knew that when he stepped through the door, the applause would lift him again, and the crowd's enthusiasm would carry him through the speech. They would never notice the little things that Hartung did, the lines around Aickmann's eyes and upper lip, the droop of his eyelids.

As it should be. Aickmann was his own man, but sometimes he became, for brief periods, the public's man as well. At those times he presented the image the public wanted to see. He could have been a politician, if he had wanted to make less money or reduce the influence he wielded. Instead, he preferred to push his agenda from behind the scenes—with rare exceptions like this one.

Through the slightly opened door, Hartung heard Aickmann's name, followed by a rush of applause. The agent at the door tugged it open and Aickmann strode through, brisk and full of purpose, moving into the ovation like a swimmer into gentle surf. Hartung, Hooper, and the other security personnel filed in behind him, heading off to the right side of the dais, where chairs waited for them.

Scanning the room, Hartung noted with satisfaction that all of his people had taken their posts, securing the room.

Or had they?

No—on a second sweep he realized that one was missing, after all.

Garrick Flynn, the American.

Hartung's stomach sank.

Where could he be?

Danny whipped back around the corner, out of the doorway, putting eight inches of concrete wall between himself and the gunmen. "Ed, the ventilation system! They're in here!"

"Then why are you standing around out here?" Ed asked.

"They have guns!"

Ed frowned, reached beneath his suit coat and drew out a fistful of dark, shiny metal. Danny recognized it as a Glock 9 mm Parabellum semiautomatic pistol. Ed tossed it to Danny, who caught it in the hand not holding the flashlight. "So do you."

He knew Ed would have gone through the door with him in a heartbeat if they had both been armed. But with only one weapon between them, Danny's chances were better with Ed out of the way. Shooting might start as soon as he went back in, and he didn't want to have to worry about the unarmed Ed's position.

The steel felt familiar in Danny's hand, comfortable in a way that made him uncomfortable to think about. Flynn may have been a warrior, but so was Danny McCoy. Sometimes it seemed a lifetime ago, sometimes as close as a whisper, like only the thinnest of veils separated him from the marine who had fought and bled and wept and survived deadly combat in a faraway place. The fighting had been just like this, at times—kick through a door into an unfamiliar house, knowing people had gone inside who meant to kill you, but not knowing if they remained inside, if they had guns leveled at the doorway, or if they had gone out the back and left innocent, unsuspecting civilians behind in their wake. Danny never knew, when passing through one of those doorways, if he would come out under his own steam or be carried away in a body bag.

He tried to reason through the options here. Flynn and his companions wouldn't have been inside this particular room unless they were trying to sabotage the ventilation system in some way. If Danny charged in and a firefight started, then the ventilation system might be damaged by flying bullets. So might whatever they were planning to use on it or release into it. The idea filled him with dread—poison gas? Ebola? A dirty bomb? Something else equally horrible?

He didn't want to be responsible for releasing their material by puncturing the briefcase with a stray bullet.

"Ed, get the power shut off down here!" he whispered.

Ed didn't ask why. He opened his phone, dialed a number, spoke a few quiet words. Within seconds, the entire floor went black. The steady hum of equipment that had been drilling into Danny's brain ceased, followed by the most oppressive silence Danny had ever experienced in Las Vegas. He and Ed clicked off their flashlights, plunging themselves into the darkness.

"You're too late, McCoy!" Flynn shouted, breaking the silence. "There's no way to stop us now!"

You just keep thinking that, Danny thought. He had seen Flynn messing with the briefcase. If he'd been too late, the briefcase would have been open already.

He hoped.

Then again, if the briefcase was key, why would Flynn have brought it down and left it here hours earlier?

The answer came to him almost as soon as the question. Because he had been able to take advantage of the stampede to do so. This close to Aickmann's speech, the casino was on high alert. No way could one of Hartung's security people have carried a briefcase into a restricted-access area now without raising a red flag. It must have been hard enough for Flynn to slip away from his post, much less to meet up with his accomplices and get them down to this level unnoticed.

But then, Flynn had spent days studying the casino, learning the placement of all the cameras, planning out routes. Not to keep Aickmann safe, but to pull off his own operation.

Whatever it might be.

Sucking in a deep breath, Danny spun around the doorjamb, back into the ventilation room. The men inside had just fished out their own flashlights, and they beamed them toward the doorway. Danny had already cleared the door and struck out along the near wall, at a crouch, moving soundlessly. If the men tried to find him, they would, with no difficulty. Danny had no cover here, nothing to hide behind.

From out in the hallway, he heard Ed's voice again, louder this time than before. The men trained their lights through the door, as if searching for Ed, and Danny took advantage of the sound of his voice to cover his own light footfalls. "That's right, the entire ventilation system, Mike," Ed said. "Shut it all down. I don't care. And isolate all the ducts coming from the ventilation room in the subbasement."

"That's clever, Deline," Garrick Flynn said. "It might even work. Then again, it might not. The toxins I've just released into the ventilation system—you wouldn't even recognize the name—are pernicious bastards. Stubborn as all get-out."

Danny focused on the sound of Flynn's voice, homing in on it. He stepped through the blackness, drawing closer. If Flynn had already released the toxins, as he claimed, then maybe Danny could risk a shot, aiming at the source of the voice.

Only as a last resort, he decided. Every possibility still existed that Flynn was lying, trying to buy himself a few seconds more. The briefcase had still been closed when the lights went out. Probably whatever toxic brew Flynn had inside it remained there, and shooting would only increase the risk of releasing it.

Danny barely allowed himself to breathe. He drew in shallow breaths, letting them out without sound. Moved forward on the concrete floor, one step, another step, then another.

"Why would you do that, Flynn?" Ed asked from out in the hall. *Good old Big Ed*, Danny thought. He understood that Ed used his voice to cover any sounds Danny might make, knowing Danny had made it into the room and was likely closing in on Flynn. "Have we done something to piss you off?"

"Don't take it personally, Deline," Flynn answered. "It's nothing to do with you—not just you, anyway. It's this city. It's full of sin and degradation. Sodom and Gomorrah would have looked like kindergarten playgrounds next to Las Vegas." Danny could hear another sound now, one he thought was Flynn still monkeying with the briefcase locks, trying to open it by feel. "And the thing is, the really disgusting part, is that it's all about making money. None of you care what you're putting people through, how all those lives are being wasted, destroyed. You encourage deviant behavior and terrible, mortal sin because there's a buck to be made. That makes you and those like you the worst sinners of all."

"Coming from you, I take that as a compliment," Ed said, a trace of humor in his voice. "You're a whack job, Flynn. You need to get some professional help."

A couple more steps. Danny thought he could smell Flynn, sweat and cologne mixed with an undertone of fear. He hoped the toxins were safely confined, because this close he would be exposed, even though the ventilation system was down. That went in his favor, though—Flynn hadn't been wearing any kind of protective mask, and as long as Ed kept him talking, he could tell by the man's unmuffled voice that he hadn't put one on.

"Come on, Flynn, let's get it done and get out of here," one of Flynn's compatriots said. His voice startled Danny, who had almost run right into the guy in the dark. He figured they kept their lights off for the same reason he and Ed did: so they didn't give away their positions. They could guess from his voice that Ed hadn't entered the room, but they'd have to assume that Danny had, and they couldn't know how many others were outside the room, maybe working their way in. To click on a light would invite a bullet.

Is that guy between me and Flynn? Danny wondered. He didn't think so, but he needed to be sure before he acted. Flynn had the briefcase. He had to be the first one to go down.

Danny might only have time to take one shot. If he miscalculated, one of the others might put a bullet in him. That would probably give Ed time to finish off the other two, even without a weapon, but if Danny didn't drop the guy with the briefcase first, then the toxins might still be released, and who knew what kind of catastrophe that might unleash?

A single step to the right, he decided, should be enough to ensure a clear lunge at Flynn. Danny shifted his weight onto his left foot, reached out with his right, brought that foot into contact with the hard floor with the same care that he'd taken ever since he'd entered the room. Finally, he shifted his weight again, centering himself, tensing the muscles in his calves and thighs, ready to spring—

And something slammed into the side of his head like a club. Fireworks burst in his eyes. Sprawling to the concrete, he tried to parse out what the weapon had been. In his memory he felt fabric, a button, against his temple. *Guy decked me with his forearm*, he thought. *Lucky shot.*

The instant he hit the floor he started scrambling, trying to regain his balance. His flashlight skittered across the concrete but he held on to the gun. His left hand touched down, pushed off, restoring his equilibrium in the dark space.

But he couldn't move fast enough. The guy landed on him, smashing Danny against the ground, his left fist slamming into Danny's solar plexus. He had a gun in his right hand too, but instead of firing he tried to bludgeon Danny with it. The barrel scraped Danny's cheek, bit into the tender flesh at the corner of his eye.

Danny fought back, using his own pistol in the same fashion. With his empty left hand he grabbed his attacker's arm, ensuring that he had a sense of the man's position in the dark. He swung his right, the hand holding the gun, in a wide arc. At the peak of the swing it collided with what must have been the man's chin; hard, unyielding flesh. The man groaned and hot blood sprayed into Danny's face. The man slipped back off Danny, who performed a power sit-up, bringing himself to a seated position. He kept moving, trying to get his legs under him, and lashed out with the gun again. This time he hit the other guy in the chest, but with the gun adding weight to his fist, the blow was enough to drive the man off balance.

The guy hit the ground at the same time Danny lurched to his feet. "Drop the case, Flynn," Danny ordered. He pointed the gun toward where Flynn had been, but in the pitch-black Flynn and the other man could have gone anywhere.

The guy Danny had put down, however, was not out of the fight. He scissor-kicked Danny, sweeping Danny's feet out from under him. *Guy was probably a ranger too,* Danny thought as he dropped to the floor, on his stomach this time. He managed to keep his face from hitting, but only by throwing out both hands. The one with the gun in it hit hard, the steel cutting his flesh.

Danny scrambled to turn over, but the guy had already been in motion. He hurled himself onto Danny's back, and a strong arm, of a smoker—Danny recognized the smell of the sleeve from when it had hit his head, starting the brawl—wrapped around his throat.

Unable to catch his breath, a knee on his back forcing air from his lungs and the arm choking him, preventing him from sucking any more in, Danny thought he was blacking out, but in the impenetrable darkness of the basement, he couldn't see anything anyway. He felt light-headed, unable to focus. His hands swung uselessly at the man on top of him.

Then a muzzle flash lit the dark, and the boom of a pistol shot rattled off the ductwork. The shot went wild, out into the hallway, ricocheting off the concrete. One of the other two men had shot at Ed in the doorway.

Danny had not wanted the fight to degenerate into a gun battle, but if that's how it was going to be, he would play their game. He still had the gun in his right fist, its steel surface slick now with his blood. He knew where the man behind him was—the positions of his knee on Danny's lungs and his arm on Danny's throat made that fairly evident. Hoping he wouldn't actually nail his own shoulder, Danny managed to tilt his wrist enough to aim the gun over his own back. Had to make it fast, though. His hands shook, and he couldn't keep a clear thought in his head.

He pulled the trigger.

So close, the muzzle flash exploded in his eyes like a miniature sun going nova. The report blocked out all sound, deafening him for a moment. He didn't hear the man react, only felt his weight shift as he fell away from Danny's back, and the damp spray of the man's blood on his back and neck.

"Danny!" Ed called through the darkness.

"Fine!" Danny tried to reply, but his voice didn't

work right and what came out was more of a retch than a word. "I'm fine!" he tried again.

Another shot went off in the hallway, someone shooting toward Ed's voice. If only Ed had kept the gun, this might all be over already. As it was, one guy had gone down, Danny was about half in, and Flynn and his other man seemed to be on the move.

Danny started toward the door—where he believed the door was, anyway, given that he had lost his flashlight. Before he reached it, he heard sounds of a struggle, the blows and sharp exhalations of men locked in combat. Aiming for those sounds, hands out ahead of him in case of unseen obstacles, Danny made his way. When he reached the doorway—a fact confirmed by touch, feeling the jamb on one side, the hinges of the open door on the other—he heard another sound: a voice, unmistakably Ed's, shouting a martial-arts cry, then the rapid rustle of motion, a couple of sharp impacts, and the heavy thud of a body falling to the floor.

"You okay, Ed?" he asked.

In response, Ed clicked on his light, training its beam at the guy he had taken out. The man, like Flynn, had been a ranger—Danny recognized his face from the photos in Ed's office, as well as from the pre-stampede surveillance footage he had screened so many times—and was twenty years younger than Ed.

Ed had dropped him like the proverbial sack of potatoes.

"I'm great," Ed said. His breaths came fast and heavy but he seemed unhurt. "You?"

"Fine," Danny said. He'd lost a little blood but had

his breath back after the choking incident. "Is Mike catching this?"

"Not enough cameras down here," Ed said. "I didn't give him the full rundown, just told him what needed doing."

Which left only one question, and Ed asked it. "Where the hell's Flynn?"

31

Charles Hooper darted his gaze about the room. Montecito employees stood guard, along with his own agents and Hartung's crew, at the seven doorways. More sat interspersed among the audience members. If there were any others in the room, he didn't know them.

But he still believed that if someone was going to try to take Aickmann out, it would be a Montecito employee. Only someone on the inside could hope to bypass the tight security and sneak a weapon into the ballroom. He tried to read the intentions of each of the Montecito staffers in the way they stood or sat, the sweat dripping down their temples, the flicker of their eyes.

And where the hell were Deline and McCoy? Their seats remained empty. Hooper had whispered the question into his radio, but no one volunteered an answer. Hartung too had been making hushed queries—apparently one of his guys had vanished as well.

Aickmann had been talking for ten minutes or so without departing from the expected script. Europe had changed, unified into something like a United States of Europe. The various nations would never be as cohesive as the United States, because nationalism still ran strong and each country held on to its own internal government. But they cooperated in new ways, and they could step in for the United States, offering the world a new alternative when international muscle was needed.

Hooper had expected nothing less, but that didn't mean he liked listening to it. Sure, acting as international cop and enforcer could be expensive, but with that came influence and power. The idea of Europe usurping some of that power rubbed him the wrong way. He liked Europe weak, chaotic, and easy to push around.

He had a hard time listening to the speech, though, because the empty seats near him consumed his thoughts. Were Deline and McCoy in on the plot all along? Maybe they weren't here because they knew bullets would fly, and they wanted to survive to profit in some way from Aickmann's murder.

Looking at Ed's empty chair, a new and sudden thought raised goose bumps on Hooper's arms. Maybe it wasn't about Aickmann at all. Maybe it had always been about him.

He knew Ed had never trusted him. Back in Honduras, he had followed orders that came from high above Ed's pay grade and his own. Ramirez had turned out to be the wrong guy for the job. He'd had to be sacrificed, martyred to the cause. If he could have told Ed, to save him the trouble and risk of showing up at the cottage that night, he would have—but once again, the decision had come down from on high. The thing had left a bad taste, but what could a man do about that?

Not long after that he had made the switch, from military intelligence to the Treasury Department. In a war, he knew, people died. In the Secret Service, he had hoped, his job would be more about protecting lives than ending them.

For the most part, it had been. He'd done his job well and been rewarded accordingly. But life's decisions left fallout sometimes. Ed Deline still had contacts high up in official Washington; he could have pulled some strings, had Hooper assigned to this case in order to get his revenge, served very cold.

If he turned out to be the target, would his crew react differently than if the attack had been on Aickmann, as expected? Would he? He had to hope not. Habits long ingrained should be consistent no matter what.

Aickmann talked on, his movements animated. The crowd responded with laughter and applause at what seemed to be the right spots. The people assigned to protect him stood their ground. But Hooper's head swam, as if someone had stuck the whole ballroom on a turntable and started it spinning.

The more he dwelled on it, the more convinced he became that Ed Deline had planned this whole thing.

When he saw the guy again—if he survived the speech—he was going to kill him.

"Get the lights back on, Ed," Danny suggested. "But keep the elevators shut off. He's got to be down here somewhere."

"Right," Ed said, and he made the call. Danny,

Glock in hand, listened for any sound that might indicate Flynn's presence, hoping he didn't zero in on
Ed's voice in the dark.

A few moments later, the overhead lights flared
on. Danny blew out a held breath. There had been
Montecito employees working on this level; in the
dark, he'd been afraid to shoot at what he thought
was Flynn for fear of hitting one of them. Now that
fear had vanished. They were all still in danger—
Flynn might decide to take a hostage, or simply to
shoot any who crossed his path. But at least Danny
and Ed would be able to see him too.

Ed scooped up the automatic pistol dropped by the
man he'd taken out. "Let's get this bastard," he
growled. "Not that I mind missing Aickmann's
speech—nothing's more boring than political
speeches—but Flynn has really pissed me off now."

"Right there with you," Danny said. He hadn't
heard Flynn make a sound since his escape. Then
again, he hadn't really expected to. The guy was a
pro, no question about that.

Was he pro enough to take on Danny McCoy and
Ed Deline? That was the significant question, and it
needed to be answered.

Danny decided to try a little psyops warfare on
him. "Flynn! You're trapped down here!" he shouted.
"You might as well give it up now!"

"Is he?" Ed asked.

"Is he what?"

"Trapped down here."

"I think so," Danny replied, not really sure what
Ed was driving at. "Even if there is another way off

this floor, he's not getting out of the building alive."

"That's exactly what I was thinking about," Ed said. "Out of the building."

None of what Ed said made sense to Danny, but as he and Ed made their way down the hall, his attention remained riveted on listening for Flynn. Ed dialed his phone again. "Call the other hotels on the Strip," he said. "Biggest to smallest. Tell 'em to send well-armed squads to check their ventilation systems, and to do it right now. Not ten minutes from now, not soon. Right freaking now."

"Other casinos?" Danny asked when Ed had disconnected.

"What you said about him getting out of the building made me think," Ed said. "Why would he run from us? If he's a fanatic trying to make some kind of moral statement, why not go down with the ship? He took off with his briefcase when he could have just shot a hole in it and let out whatever's inside. I think he wants to save it to use somewhere else, since he knows he's busted here."

"You really think?"

"And we know he's not working this alone. You didn't see that guy Tidwell, did you? For all we know, there might be other groups at the other hotels trying to pull the same stunt simultaneously. Wrecking our business by releasing toxins into the ventilation system would be bad for us, but if he really wants to shut down Las Vegas, the way to do it would be to hit several at once. Tourism would stop dead, and with it all the other industries that depend on it."

"That's true," Danny said. Just like Ed, always

thinking two or three steps beyond everyone around him. If he hadn't turned to espionage and then the casino business, he'd have been a hell of a chess player. Danny would have to hone that skill, he knew—he had worked his way into a great position at the Montecito, but if he ever hoped to truly fill Ed's shoes, he'd have to shore up his abilities and acquire new ones. And chess had never been his game.

They approached another intersection, where smaller hallways converged with the main corridor from both sides. If Flynn wanted to ambush them, this would be an ideal spot for it. Without verbal communication, both men slowed, spread to the walls, and went around the corners at the same moment, their weapons preceding them.

Danny's side looked clear. Behind him, Ed gave a low *hssst*. Danny whirled to find Ed pointing his weapon at a door left ajar, a black strip revealing the darkness inside.

Danny nodded his agreement. None of the doors they had seen in this subbasement had been left open. No reason for this one to be different, unless Garrick Flynn had passed through it in a hurry, or had been worried about making noise by shutting it.

Or, Danny thought, *he's waiting inside to blow us away when we go through.*

With hand gestures, Ed indicated that he would go in low and Danny should go high. Ed still held a flashlight in his left hand. Just before he gave the nod, he clicked it on. Then his foot slammed into the door, shoving it open the rest of the way. Danny moved in time with Ed, going in over his boss and covering the back half of the room. Ed went in low, as he had indicated, and swept his light and gun in unison across the big, mostly empty space.

Empty except for a few wooden packing crates, barely big enough for Flynn to hide behind, and a steel staircase spiraling up into the darkness above. The staircase was enclosed in a cage, and the door was shut. From overhead, Danny could barely make out running footsteps. "Damn it, I forgot about this," he said. "There's a staircase connecting both subbasements. It gives access to some of the ductwork and electrical that runs between them." He realized Ed probably knew all this already, and clamped his mouth shut.

"Flynn's gone up there," Ed said. "If he can get out on the next level, he can make it into the casino. Releasing the toxins there won't be as effective as getting them in the ventilation system, but it'll still shut us down. Maybe for good." He yanked on the door of the cage surrounding the stairs. "Locked," he said. "You don't have a key?"

"Me? No."

"Maintenance would, but getting someone here would take too long." Ed shone the light on the lock, walked around behind the cage, and illuminated it from that side as well. "No, it's not just locked, he broke something off in the lock. It's jammed. It'll take a blowtorch to get through that door."

Danny looked into the darkness above. "I'll go up through the ductwork," he said. As he spoke, he didn't know precisely how he could do that but figured there must be a way. "If Flynn really didn't release anything from the case, then it should be safe, right?"

"*If,*" Ed echoed.

"We think he didn't," Danny amended. "But he still has the case, so if the threat is real, then it's still out there."

"I'm not saying you shouldn't go," Ed said. "I just want you to be careful. And if you're going, don't stand around here talking about it."

Danny started to reply, then thought better of it. He turned and ran from the room, back toward the main ventilation system where they had interrupted Flynn in the first place.

As he sprinted down the main corridor, his footfalls echoing around him, he felt very alone indeed.

Ed knew he was in good shape for a guy his age. Some colleagues he had known quit working out when they left the life behind, choosing to spend their retirement years indulging in TV and junk food and all the rest of the things they had deprived themselves of during their spy days. The good life, some of them thought. The reason they had done their jobs in the first place, preserving the right of everyone to get lazy and fat.

Not him, though. He hadn't retired, had just shifted his energies toward a different application. One that demanded many of the same skills, and, often enough, the physical strength and coordination of his spy days as well. He could still do most of what he'd been able to at his physical peak.

Crawling up a damn ventilation shaft might not have been beyond his abilities. But because he had Danny, he didn't have to find out. *Fine with me.*

He started in the same direction Danny had just run,

but at a walk. He took his phone out again, punched up the surveillance room. Mike answered. "I want eyes on every camera on Subbasement One," Ed said.

"I'll get on it, but everyone else is on the Aick-mann thing," Mike reminded him.

"Aickmann's not the target," Ed said. "Don't take everybody off that, but we need a fix on Garrick Flynn, one of Hartung's ops. He'll be somewhere on Subbasement One, probably trying to work from there up to the basement and then the ground floor. We need to stop him before he does. Send a security squad down too, with a picture of him. And guns. He's armed and very, very dangerous."

"Got it, Ed," Mike said.

Ed suppressed the desire to ask how the Aickmann event was going. If there had been a problem, he would have been alerted. And keeping Mike on the phone talking about it would slow his response to Ed's demands. Ed broke the connection, tucked the phone away.

Then a banging sound, like distant thunder, broke the silence. Danny, forcing his way up through the ducts, Ed guessed. For a second, he wished he had been the one to volunteer after all. Not that he didn't think Danny could handle himself; he knew better than that. But Danny would get the fun of taking Flynn out, and most of the credit.

Ed didn't give a rat's ass about the credit.

He hated missing out on the fun.

This would, Danny thought, *be a lot easier with a map.*

The insides of the ducts, narrow and claustrophobic, all looked the same. He had found his flashlight on the floor of the ventilation room and brought it along, so he had light. But it didn't do him much good, illuminating one stretch of gray steel rectangle after another. There were joints, rivets, and corners. Nothing beyond that to indicate where he was or how much progress he had made.

Danny had worked construction for his father, during his youth, and then again when he briefly ran the company after his father's death. He had installed ductwork and repaired it—astonishing what one could do with a roll of duct tape—and both, sometimes, required shimmying up inside it.

But this time he was engaged in a race, with the highest stakes imaginable. He had to get Flynn before Flynn made it to the casino. That meant taking the most direct route to the next subbasement. Which was where the map would have come in handy.

The one thing he knew for sure was that he needed to go up. He had opened an access panel at floor level and climbed in, choosing the nearest duct that led toward the floor above. The ventilation system remained off, which he considered a blessing, since it might have been uncomfortable, not to mention distracting, to have cold air blowing past him as he climbed. Dust coated the insides of the ducts, and he sneezed a couple of times, but moving air would probably have made that worse too. He only hoped that whatever he breathed in didn't include Flynn's toxins.

He pressed his hands and feet against the sides of the narrow shaft and forced himself up, up.

At the first corner, he was sure he'd made a horrible mistake.

He managed to get his head and shoulders through. But then his head and back jammed against the wall, the corner pinned his arms, and he couldn't get enough purchase with his feet to force himself any farther.

On the bright side, he thought, *if I die here, once all the flesh has rotted off my bones, my skeleton will fall back down to the opening.*

He didn't intend to die, though. If this had been his day to die, it would have been down below, in the dark, when he had run into a room where three men waited with guns. Using the muscles in his shoulders, back, and stomach, he wriggled and twisted until he had pushed through enough to unjam his back and free his hands. Then he carefully brought his hands up past his head, turned them outward, pressed them against the duct walls, and hauled himself another few inches.

He had made the turn. Now he traveled through a flat section, which did him no good in the long run. He knew he hadn't climbed high enough to reach the next level. After a few minutes on the flat stretch, another duct intersected from above.

This corner—from a prone position, on his stomach, to a standing one—proved even harder than the last. He had to raise his head and shoulders from the gut, like a caterpillar scenting the breeze, his hands feeling blindly in the darkness overhead. He had tucked the flashlight and gun into the waistband of his pants, so they'd be handy when he needed them, but the truth was that half the time in the ducts he couldn't even get to his waistband. Every inch he traveled made a terrible racket too, certainly alerting Flynn as to his whereabouts.

Why did I think this was a good idea? he wondered as his feet finally left the flat part of the duct. He headed up again, inching his way along, muscles straining, quaking as if they might forsake him at any moment.

With any luck, Ed's already caught him.

Then another stray thought flitted through his mind—him, emerging from the ductwork, filthy and disheveled, over Aickmann's head as the billionaire wrapped up his speech. Members of three separate security teams pointing guns at his head as he dangled upside down from the ceiling. He bit back a laugh. He hadn't gone far enough yet to make it to the next sub-basement up, much less two more floors above that.

He moved higher, pressing his shoe against the slight ridge of a joining between two sections of ductwork for support. The joint gave way under Danny's weight, popping rivets. At other points Danny had heard rivets pinging away into the darkness—when this was over a team would have to come through here and repair the whole thing.

Inching higher, wishing there were some other way, wishing he didn't make such a racket, Danny climbed.

Finally he reached a spot where a rivet had fallen away some time before, and through the minute hole it left, he saw light. He pressed his eye to the hole, trying to figure out where he was.

He couldn't gather enough information from the narrow view, however. He thought he saw a wall, concrete block like the ones on the level below. But he couldn't tell for sure if he had really reached Sub-basement 1, or if this wall looked like the others because he was still on the lower floor. For that matter, the dark and narrow spaces had disoriented him, and he might be looking at a floor or a ceiling.

He didn't know definitively that he had reached the right place until a bullet ripped through the steel duct wall.

32

The gunshot echoed through the ducts, bouncing around, amplified by Danny's proximity to the steel walls, so that it felt like it ricocheted inside his skull. Metal tore like paper as the bullet sliced through the duct, less than six inches over his head, and out the other side. He smelled the bitter tang of gunpowder and hot steel. More light blazed in through the new holes.

Danny folded his hands and feet in, allowing himself to drop several feet before catching himself against the sides. He guessed that Flynn had put the shot where he'd wanted it—where he believed Danny had been. The guy was just too good a marksman to have missed by that much. His failure had been one of estimation, not of aim.

Another difficulty presented itself. Danny had been so concerned with reaching the right level, he hadn't really given a whole lot of thought to how he would get out of the ductwork when he got there. He had kind of pictured himself swinging his feet against one of the joints and breaking through, but pressed into the duct, holding on with palms and feet, he couldn't swing both feet at once, and he could only swing one or the other a few inches—not enough to power himself free.

Maybe I should order Flynn to surrender, he thought.

Of course, opening my mouth would guarantee a bullet in it.

As if on cue, another shot gashed the steel duct, more than a foot above his head. Flynn still didn't know precisely where in the duct Danny was. Danny hoped he could keep it that way.

Danny reached into his waistband, drew out Ed's Glock. With the weapon in his hand, he barely had room to aim it—and he didn't know for sure what he was aiming at. He knew from the trajectory of the shots approximately where Flynn was, but his guess would be even worse than Flynn's had been. Flynn was off by only inches, his target confined in a space less than two feet across. Danny would be shooting blind into a much bigger space, in which Flynn might well have taken cover. And his shot would give away his own vertical location.

But if he didn't take it, Flynn would find him with another shot, two at the most. His only other alternative would be to drop back down into the ducts and lose any hope of catching Flynn before he carried his briefcase of death into the casino.

Las Vegas had been built on the idea that sometimes long odds paid off, he decided. Without the willingness to gamble, after all, no one would have located a city in the middle of a sweltering desert, in Indian country, with only a small perennial spring to support it. And even if, by some miracle, it had been built, people wouldn't have continued flocking to it— to stay, to build new lives in the desert, as well as just to visit in hopes of winning a jackpot—if not for the unfailing human urge to take a chance.

Danny took a chance. Guessing where Flynn should

be, based on where the two bullets had entered the duct, he aimed and fired.

The shot tore through the duct and into the room, the explosion reverberating in Danny's head as if he'd climbed inside a church bell and let it ring. The gun's kick in the small space slammed Danny's elbow against the back wall so hard that the weapon dropped from his hand. It clattered down the duct, leaving Danny unarmed.

Unarmed and exposed. If Flynn had survived the shot—almost a foregone conclusion—now he knew Danny's precise location. Danny waited for the bullet that would slice through him as it did through the thin steel walls around him.

It didn't come.

Had he hit Flynn? Or had Flynn already left, his greater scheme more important to him than finishing Danny off?

Only one way to find out. Danny located the nearest weld and scooted his waist slightly above it. Pressing his back and shoulders against the rear wall, he managed to squeeze his knees up against his chest. Exhaling to empty his lungs, glad he hadn't had dessert after dinner last night, he worked them up another couple of inches, getting his feet against the weld. Then he willed himself to expand, sucking in air, forcing his feet against the steel with every muscle he could put into play at such an awkward angle.

Ears still ringing from the gunshot, he didn't hear the first rivet pop, or the second. When the third went, the weld itself started to give way too. That, he heard. Light streamed in around his feet, illuminating what was left of four-hundred-dollar leather Salvatore Ferragamo shoes. Danny took a couple more deep breaths, tried not to think about childbirth, and kicked at the weld.

The fourth time he kicked, the weld split and the section of ductwork below him drooped, leaning into the room. He lowered himself from the section above, tense, waiting for the bullet that would tear through his flesh, smash bone, rend muscle, until his head cleared the duct wall and he could see again.

The room was empty. Flynn had taken off again.

Then he saw the gun abandoned on the floor, blood spatters around it.

He hadn't missed, then, not altogether. His guesswork had been better than he had dared hope, and he had hit Flynn's hand or his weapon. The ex-ranger had dropped it and fled, and Danny, deafened by the echo and the sound of his own weapon falling away, hadn't heard.

He smiled, unkinking himself and heading for Flynn's gun.

He had lowered himself into a stiff-legged crouch when Flynn returned, charging through the doorway with a four-foot length of steel pipe in his hands. He let out a scream and swung the pipe at Danny.

Danny threw his left arm up to block it. The pipe glanced off his forearm instead of shattering the bone, but it still delivered a jolt of pain that Danny felt all the way down his spine. He winced and yanked his arm away even as Flynn jabbed at him with the pipe like a long, heavy sword. Danny, muscles aching and slow to respond from his time in the ductwork, tried to sidestep the attack, but the pipe caught him in the ribs. Air expelled from his lungs, and Danny fell to his knees.

Flynn came in for the kill, swinging the pipe in an arc that would have taken off Danny's head. Danny chose not to leave his head there. Instead, he hurled himself flat against the floor. As the pipe whistled over him, he clawed Flynn's gun off the ground. His bullet had hit the weapon's barrel, he realized, and he didn't dare fire it. Opting for second best, he threw it at Flynn, who lifted the pipe over his head to bring it down in a killing stroke.

The weapon hit Flynn square in the face, opening a cut between his eyes and stunning him. Danny used the split second it bought him to drive between Flynn's legs, catching one in each hand. The other man went over like a felled tree, pipe clanging to the concrete floor behind him. Scrambling to his feet, Danny kicked the pipe away and stood a couple of feet back from Flynn, so the man couldn't do the same to him that he had done.

"It's over," he said between panting breaths. "You don't even have the briefcase anymore."

"It's never over, McCoy," Flynn shot back. "As long as your kind festers like a boil in the world, it won't be over."

"Ed's right, you do need help. If you don't like the things people do, why not just ignore them? Why do you expect everyone to live by your narrow version of morality?"

Instead of answering, Flynn drew a knife from somewhere beneath his clothes and began lurching to his feet. Danny tried to kick the knife from his hand, but Flynn yanked his arm back, dodging the kick. He lashed out with the knife, slicing through Danny's pants as his leg swooshed by. Danny backed away a step. Flynn made it to his knees before Danny closed again. Desperate to get him before Flynn gained his feet, Danny loosed another snap kick. This one, Flynn took on his right shoulder. He staggered back but held on to the knife.

Blood flowed down Flynn's face, lining both sides of his nose, running into his mouth, and dripping from his chin. The knife in his fist had a sharp, double-edged blade that glinted wickedly in the overhead light. His blue eyes glittered with rage and madness. Danny knew that he had to take Flynn down fast and hard, once and for all. Surrender didn't seem to exist in Flynn's vocabulary. If he didn't kill the guy, or at least render him unconscious, Flynn would keep fighting until he had killed Danny.

Danny had never liked the idea of killing. He avoided it when he could, and those he had killed in combat haunted his dreams. In this case, though, it wasn't just a matter of him or the other man. If Flynn won the battle, he might well win the war, releasing his poison into the casino. Hundreds could die, if not thousands.

Danny braced himself for anything.

Flynn got his feet beneath him, but instead of standing upright, he launched himself like a missile from that position, uncoiling his legs with furious energy. Danny caught Flynn's right wrist with his left hand, holding the knife away from his throat, but Flynn's powerful surge forced Danny back. He swayed unsteadily on his feet. At the last moment, he decided to go with that motion, to use Flynn's momentum against him in classic judo fashion. Still holding Flynn—his right hand grasping Flynn's shirt collar—he let himself tumble backward, landing flat on the hard floor. But he pulled Flynn down with him, and the force of the man's own attack carried him over Danny. Danny helped him along with one knee.

Purely from his own momentum, Flynn would have sailed harmlessly past Danny. But with the extra thrust from Danny's upraised leg, Flynn soared across the room, mouth open in a wordless scream. He kept his grip on the knife, but he hit the floor hard, face-down, and skidded into the ductwork Danny had already destroyed.

Amazingly, he wasn't out of it yet. He grabbed on to the broken duct with his left hand, hauling himself back up to his knees. He turned his ruined face toward Danny, shooting him a look of pure hatred, and tried to stabilize himself against the ductwork.

And the entire thing dropped out from beneath him.

Flynn plunged into the hole. Danny saw him disappear down it as if he had taken a swan dive, his feet kicking until they too had fallen out of sight. Danny heard a rumbling crash, then a louder one, and the sound of Flynn's screams over it all. Danny was sure Flynn would stop when he hit the section of flat ducting below.

But then, with an even greater crash, the impact of his descent broke through that level, and the ceiling beneath it as well.

Guy would have to be Superman to walk away from

that, Danny thought. Flynn was a lot of things, but he was no Superman.

Or so Danny hoped.

Flynn got up.

Ed could hardly believe it.

This guy was bleeding from the face and head. He had just plummeted from the ceiling, punching through it with steel ductwork that shredded his flesh as he dropped. His clothes were torn and filthy, one eye bruised and swollen half shut. As he rose, he spat teeth and blood onto the floor. Straightening up made him wince, agonized.

"You gotta give up," Ed pleaded. "I'd feel better about beating up a Girl Scout."

Flynn fixed him with a glare of pure hatred. He might have shaken his head, or maybe he just couldn't hold it still. Ed couldn't tell for sure.

What he didn't do was give up.

Instead, he lowered his right shoulder and ran at Ed like a quarterback trying to muscle through to the goal line. Ed braced himself for the charge, spreading his feet for stability. At the last moment he swiveled away from Flynn's attack, reaching out to grab on to Flynn's clothing, and he twisted Flynn over his hip, sending the man flying into a wall.

The ex-ranger got up again, faster than Ed had anticipated, shaking off evident pain. He closed his bruised hands into fists and threw a left jab at Ed's jaw—a feint, which he followed with two rights to Ed's gut. Ed took them both without difficulty, as

Flynn's strength seemed mostly devoted to keeping himself upright. He caught Flynn's left wrist and drew him close, then aimed a solid right hook at the other man's chin. It connected, snapping Flynn's head back. Flynn's legs buckled.

He clawed at the floor, trying to rise again. "You're done," Ed said. "I want you able to talk, so I'm not going to finish knocking your head off. But don't think I'm not tempted."

33

Later, in Ed's office, Danny reclined on a cushy leather couch with his feet up on the coffee table. Under ordinary circumstances, Ed would have objected to his taking such liberties—maybe to the point of slapping his feet down physically—but tonight had been no ordinary night, even by the Montecito's standards.

Charles Hooper sat in one of the nearby guest chairs, visibly relieved that Klaus Aickmann's speech had gone off without a hitch, if one didn't include the audience becoming uncomfortably warm and Aickmann, who had taken off his jacket midway through, sweating dark patches through his shirt. Hooper seemed smaller than he had before, as if, his objective accomplished, he had lost physical presence. He scratched nervously at his neck while he and Danny waited for Ed to finish a phone call. Midnight had come and gone, but of course the Strip lights outside Ed's window burned as bright as ever.

Finally Ed hung up and looked at the waiting men with a broad smile on his face. "Flynn's buddies tried the same trick at three different casinos on the Strip," he reported. "But they got the word in time, and all three managed to round the bums up before any damage was done." He fixed his gaze on Danny. "That guy Tidwell was one of them."

"I'm just glad they got 'em," Danny said. "If they had pulled it off—"

"If they had pulled it off, a year from now Las Vegas would be nothing but a watering hole in the desert again," Ed said. "One with a lot of concrete around it."

"Homegrown terrorists can be the worst kind," Hooper commented. "They know your strengths and weaknesses, know how to get around security."

"There's no good kind of terrorist, far as I'm concerned," Ed said. The words were innocent enough, but Ed snapped them off, giving Danny the impression that some tension had developed between him and Hooper. "But I get your point. By insinuating himself into a security gig, Flynn got into a position where he could do a lot of damage. Fortunately, his friends didn't have the same kind of access at those other casinos as he did here. They had to rely on being able to outsmart those security teams, and in this city that's almost always a losing bet."

"And all the toxins were successfully contained?" Danny asked. A hazmat team had taken away Flynn's briefcase, promising a full report on its contents within the next couple of days.

"Yeah," Ed said. "Flynn wasn't as careful about that as he might have been, and the stuff in his briefcase wasn't entirely airtight. But our ventilation system worked just like it's supposed to, isolating the area where we know he had the case, and it's been thoroughly scrubbed. You'll want to go to the doctor, Danny, and be checked out, but there's no reason to think you were exposed to harmful levels of anything nasty."

"Don't worry, I will," Danny said. He had put his life on the line for the Montecito many times. Part of the gig, he knew. But he didn't like the idea of succumbing to an enemy he couldn't even see, much less fight.

"Hartung's going to have to answer some hard questions about his screening parameters," Hooper said. "He should have been able to identify Flynn as a troublemaker long before things reached this stage."

"He was probably just glad to get an American, and a veteran, on the squad," Ed said.

"Plenty of vets looking for work," Danny said. "And most of them aren't freakin' nuts like—"

A knock on the office door interrupted him, and Mike Cannon stuck his head in. "This a private gathering?" he asked.

"Come on in, Mike," Ed said, gesturing him inside. "And thanks for your help with the Flynn thing. We're just shooting the bull in here."

"As long as it's bull and not horse, I'm down with it," Mike said, grinning. He took another visitor chair and fell into it, all his joints seemingly as loose as if they weren't really connected at all. Danny envied Mike's ability to relax almost anywhere and anytime, no matter what chaos reigned around him.

"You get that situation taken care of?" Ed asked.

"The horse thing? Yeah, it's done. Two suspects are in custody, the owner got his love lotion back, and it fetched 1.7 million bucks at the auction. He's using some of it to bail out his lady after her arraignment, and then he's probably getting a painful and expensive divorce."

"Who hasn't?" Hooper asked glumly.

"Not me." Danny wagged a ringless left hand. "I've never been married."

"Neither have I," Mike said.

Ed touched a framed photo of himself with his wife, Jillian. "Thirty-two years," he said.

Hooper looked at the floor, his ears turning red, seemingly diminished even more by the response he had earned. Danny got the idea that he was not a happy man, and it made him glad the ex-spy he worked for was Ed and not Charles Hooper.

An awkward silence followed, which Mike broke after a while by saying, "What a long day, though, man."

"I hear that," Danny said, realizing just how little sleep he'd had. "Long couple of days."

More footsteps sounded in the hall, and Delinda came into the doorway, trailed by Mary. A cloud of fresh, floral scent seemed to accompany Delinda, whereas Danny caught a vague whiff of wood smoke when Mary sat down next to him on the couch. She smacked his feet off the coffee table. "Okay if we come in, Daddy?" Delinda asked, having already helped herself to a chair.

"Ahh, sure," Ed said, with the tone of a man who realizes he never really had a say in the question. "Help yourselves."

"Good," Mary said, "because we're beat."

"Oh, right," Danny said. "The chuck wagon thing? How'd that go?"

"Late is how it went," Mary said. "I couldn't tell if people kept getting back in line because they liked the food or the entertainment."

"That cowboy band?" Mike asked. "I heard a little bit of them. Pretty cool."

"They were good too," Delinda said. "But she's talking about the Ezra and Gunther show."

"Gunther and who?" Ed asked. "I didn't realize Gunther was a performer."

"He can be when he wants to," Mary explained. "Ezra's my chuck wagon cook. He and Ezra kept each other happy telling cooking stories and bad jokes and insulting the diners."

"And each other," Delinda added.

"And they liked that, these people?" Ed asked, incredulous.

"They ate it up," Mary said. "No pun intended."

"Oh, come on, Mary," Delinda said. "You've been using that line all night."

"Busted," Mary said with a shrug and a laugh. Her smile, and Delinda's, brought a whole new vibe to the office, a sense of joy that it hadn't had when Hooper's miserable nature had been bringing it down. Danny noticed that Hooper hadn't said a word since the ladies had come in, just sat in his chair with his arms folded over his chest, as if he had suddenly found himself somewhere very uncomfortable. Danny couldn't be certain, but he thought maybe the man had fallen asleep with his eyes open.

"Did I hear Mary talking about her bust again?" Sam asked, suddenly standing in the doorway. Danny hadn't heard her approach.

"No," Mary said quickly. "You didn't. And what do you mean again? You bring it up more than I do."

"You don't have to bring it up," Sam shot back, "because it's always right there." Of everyone in the room, Sam looked the most alert, even bordering on perky.

"You're in a good mood," Danny observed. "Everything go okay for you today?"

"Once I solved the case of the missing bunny rabbit," Sam replied. "Rest of the day was a piece of cake."

"Mmm, cake," Mike said. "Suppose I could still get some dessert at Mystique?"

"That could be arranged," Delinda offered. "If you know anyone who can pull a few strings for you."

"I believe I do."

"Then I believe you could get some cake."

"Sounds good to me," Danny said. "Anyone else? Mr. Hooper?"

Hooper rose from his chair, shaking his head. "I think I'm gonna hit the rack," he said, making for the door. "Early flight in the morning."

Mike, Mary, Danny, and Delinda all stood, ready to top off the long day with rich, sinful desserts. Sam had never left the doorway, where she leaned casually against the jamb, arms crossed. "You do all work in the morning, right?" Ed asked.

Danny glanced around at the others, as if taking a head count. "Yeah," he answered. "What, you're worried we'll sleep in?"

"It's just that you look like a pretty sorry bunch right now," Ed said.

"We'll be here," Danny promised.

"Good to know," Ed said. He paused for a moment, as if waiting for some additional response. When none came, he waved them toward the door. "Anyway, get out of here. I got some paperwork to finish up."

"Don't work too late, Daddy," Delinda said. "You know Mom's waiting up for you."

Danny saw Ed's gaze flit to the picture of Jillian on his desk. "You're right," Ed said. "The hell with it. There's nothing going on here that can't wait until morning."

They all filed from the office, Sam first, then Mike, Delinda, Mary, Danny, and finally Ed. Ed flicked the lights off on his way out. "And by the way, everyone?"

The others stopped, waiting, in the hall outside his office.

"You did good work today. All of you. Stay out as late as you want tonight, and get here when you can tomorrow. You've earned it, and Las Vegas . . . well, Las Vegas doesn't ever sleep. It'll be here."

ABOUT THE AUTHOR

Jeff Mariotte has written more than thirty novels, including the supernatural thriller *Missing White Girl*, the original horror epic *The Slab*, and the Stoker Award–nominated teen horror series *Witch Season*, as well as books set in the universes of *Buffy the Vampire Slayer*, *Angel*, *Conan*, *30 Days of Night*, *Charmed*, *Star Trek*, and *Andromeda*. He is also the author of many comic books, including the original Western/horror series *Desperadoes*, some of which have been nominated for Stoker and International Horror Guild awards. With his wife, Maryelizabeth Hart, and partner Terry Gilman, he co-owns Mysterious Galaxy, a bookstore specializing in science fiction, fantasy, mystery, and horror. He lives with his family and pets on the Flying M Ranch in the American Southwest, a place filled with books, music, toys, and other products of American pop culture. More information than you would ever want to know about him is at www.jeffmariotte.com.

Printed in the United States
By Bookmasters